Leigh Russell

SILENT TIES

NO EXIT PRESS

First published in the UK in 2026 by No Exit Press,
an imprint of Bedford Square Publishers Ltd,
London, UK

noexit.co.uk
@noexitpress

© Leigh Russell, 2026

The right of Leigh Russell to be identified as the author of this work has been asserted in accordance with the Copyright, Designs and Patents Act 1988. All rights reserved. No part of this book may be reproduced, stored in or introduced into a retrieval system, or transmitted, in any form or by any means (electronic, mechanical, photocopying, recording or otherwise) without the written permission of the publishers.

Any person who does any unauthorised act in relation to this publication may be liable to criminal prosecution and civil claims for damages.
A CIP catalogue record for this book is available from the British Library.
This is a work of fiction. Names, characters, places, and incidents either are the product of the author's imagination or are used fictitiously, and any resemblance to actual persons, living or dead, businesses, companies, events or locales is entirely coincidental.

ISBN
978-1-83501-282-6 (Paperback)
978-1-83501-283-3 (eBook)

2 4 6 8 10 9 7 5 3 1

Typeset in 11 on 13.9pt Times New Roman
by Avocet Typeset, Bideford, Devon, EX39 2BP
Printed and bound in Great Britain by
CPI Group (UK) Ltd, Croydon CR0 4YY

The manufacturer's authorised representative in the EU for product safety is Easy Access System Europe, Mustamäe tee 50, 10621 Tallinn, Estonia
gpsr.requests@easproject.com

CRITICAL ACCLAIM FOR LEIGH RUSSELL

'A million readers can't be wrong! Clear some time in your day, sit back and enjoy a bloody good read' **Howard Linskey**

'Taut and compelling' **Peter James**

'Leigh Russell is one to watch' **Lee Child**

'Leigh Russell has become one of the most impressively dependable purveyors of the English police procedural' ***Times***

'DI Geraldine Steel is one of the most authoritative female coppers in a crowded field' ***Financial Times***

'A brilliant talent in the thriller field' **Jeffery Deaver**

'Brilliant and chilling, Leigh Russell delivers a cracker of a read!' **Martina Cole**

'A great plot that keeps you guessing right until the very end, some subtle subplots, brilliant characters both old and new and as ever a completely gripping read' ***Life of Crime***

'The latest police procedural from prolific novelist Leigh Russell is as good and gripping as anything she has published'
Times & Sunday Times Crime Club

'A fascinating, gripping read. The many twists kept me on my toes and second guessing myself'
Over The Rainbow Book Blog

'Well paced with marvellously well-rounded characters and a clever plot that make this another thriller of a read from Leigh Russell' **Orlando Books**

'A well-written, fast-paced and very enjoyable thriller' **The Book Lover's Boudoir**

'An edge-of-your-seat thriller that will keep you guessing' **Honest Mam Reader**

'Well paced, has red herrings and twists galore, keeps your attention and sucks you right into its pages' **Books by Bindu**

'5 stars! Another super addition to one of my favourite series, which remains as engrossing and fresh as ever!' **The Word is Out**

'A nerve-twisting tour de force that will leave readers on the edge of their seats, Leigh Russell's latest Detective Geraldine Steel thriller is a terrifying page-turner by this superb crime writer' **Bookish Jottings**

'An absolute delight' **The Literary Shed**

'I simply couldn't put it down' **Shell Baker, *Chelle's Book Reviews***

'If you love a good action-packed crime novel, full of complex characters and unexpected twists, this is one for you' **Rachel Emms, *Chillers, Killers and Thrillers***

'All the things a mystery should be: intriguing, enthralling, tense and utterly absorbing' **Best Crime Books**

'A series that can rival other major crime writers out there...'
Best Books to Read

'Sharp, intelligent and well plotted' **Crime Fiction Lover**

'Another corker of a book from Leigh Russell... Russell's talent for writing top-quality crime fiction just keeps on growing' **Euro Crime**

'A definite must read for crime thriller fans everywhere' **Newbooks Magazine**

'Russell's strength as a writer is her ability to portray believable characters' **Crime Squad**

'A well-written, well-plotted crime novel with fantastic pace and lots of intrigue' **Bookersatz**

'An encounter that will take readers into the darkest recesses of the human psyche' **Crime Time**

'Well written and chock full of surprises, this hard-hitting, edge-of-the-seat instalment is yet another treat... Geraldine Steel looks set to become a household name. Highly recommended' **Euro Crime**

'Good, old-fashioned, heart-hammering police thriller... a no-frills delivery of pure excitement' **SAGA Magazine**

'A gritty and totally addictive novel'
New York Journal of Books

Also by Leigh Russell

Geraldine Steel Mysteries

Cut Short
Road Closed
Dead End
Death Bed
Stop Dead
Fatal Act
Killer Plan
Murder Ring
Deadly Alibi
Class Murder
Death Rope
Rogue Killer

Deathly Affair
Deadly Revenge
Evil Impulse
Deep Cover
Guilt Edged
Fake Alibi
Final Term
Without Trace
Revenge Killing
Deadly Will
Cold Justice

Ian Peterson Murder Investigations
Cold Sacrifice
Race to Death
Blood Axe

Poppy Mystery Tales
Barking Up the Right Tree
Barking Mad
Poppy Plays Fair

Lucy Hall Mysteries
Journey to Death
Girl in Danger
The Wrong Suspect

To Michael, Joanna, Phillipa, Phil, Kezia and Leon.

Prologue

THE AUTUMN MIST COOLED his face as his feet pounded on the damp pavement. The sun had only just risen when he had gone out, leaving his wife asleep in bed. He had been careful not to disturb her as she did not like to be woken so early. He inhaled deeply, enjoying a rare sense of freedom before the working week began. He didn't relish the prospect of another busy week, stuck behind his desk. Life hemmed him in. With the approach of winter, this was a depressing time of year and, whichever way he turned, he was trapped: his job bored him and at home his wife was constantly nagging him.

Until quite recently, his only consolation had been his daughter, yet even she seemed to be pulling away from him. Once a cheerful child, always eager to spend time with him, lately she had begun treating him with barely concealed resentment. He told himself that it was just part of growing up. Adolescent girls were notoriously challenging and her animosity towards him was nothing personal. To be fair, she seemed to regard her mother with open hostility, even though they had always been close until recently.

His legs were beginning to ache but he ran on, musing wretchedly on the change in his daughter. The deterioration in his relationship with his wife had happened so gradually they had both had time to grow accustomed to the unacknowledged rift between them, but the change in his daughter seemed to have occurred almost overnight. Reaching the river that ran through the centre of the city of York, he slipped on to a path that ran beside trees, half obscured in mist rising from the water. Here he was forced to slow down because it was muddy; he had to be careful not to lose his footing. Focused on where he was stepping, at first he didn't notice someone coming up behind him on the path. Once he was aware that his were not the only footsteps squelching in the soft mud, he moved aside and stopped. No one passed him. Turning to look back over his shoulder, he was just in time to see a hooded figure whirl around and scurry away, slithering frantically on the wet ground.

A shaft of sunlight penetrated the haze and he thought he glimpsed a knife in a flailing hand before the figure vanished in the mist. With a jolt, Peter stumbled, almost tripping over a tree root. Reaching out, he grabbed an overhanging branch and steadied himself. His legs were trembling and he was conscious that his heart was racing. He glanced over his shoulder but there was no one in sight. The hooded figure had disappeared. Telling himself he was overreacting, he nevertheless turned and retraced his steps, peering cautiously around in case the shadowy figure was waiting for him. It would curtail his run, but he was afraid to continue along the deserted path. He tried to laugh off his irrational fear, but terror gripped him and he could no longer control his thoughts. By the time he reached his own street, his panic had subsided, but he told himself he would never run by the river again so early in the morning. A route that had once appealed to him for its isolation now seemed threatening.

'I was almost mugged on my morning run,' he told his wife later, as they were having breakfast together.

His wife barely paused in the act of pouring milk into her tea. She had never had a very expressive face, but he was surprised when she appeared indifferent to what he was telling her. Disconcerted by her blank response, he started to question whether he had imagined the incident.

'At least, I think that's what happened.' He backtracked, feeling awkward. 'It was down by the river, early. You need to watch yourself if you go walking along there on your own,' he concluded lamely.

'I won't go walking along there at some ungodly hour in the morning when anyone in their right mind is fast asleep,' she replied, adding another dash of milk to her tea. 'Did you report it?'

'What?'

'Did you call the police?'

'What for?'

'To report it.'

He shrugged. 'There's nothing to report. Nothing happened.'

'You just told me you were mugged and now you're saying nothing happened,' she said, adding under her breath that he should make his mind up.

'I said I was *nearly* mugged. That is, I think I was.'

'You think you were nearly mugged? What does that mean?'

He shook his head. 'I don't know. It was just some oddball with a knife. He probably wasn't intending to mug me at all.'

Christine gave an involuntary gasp and looked at him for the first time since they had sat down together that morning. 'Are you telling me someone threatened you with a knife?'

'Not exactly. As soon as I turned round, he ran off.' He gave her a reassuring smile. 'I think he was more frightened than I was.'

'That doesn't sound very dangerous,' she said, reaching for the butter and grumbling as she scraped it with her knife. 'You know how upset she gets when there are crumbs in the butter.'

He grunted, irked that she seemed more concerned about a few crumbs in the butter than about the danger he had possibly faced. 'I never said I was in danger, only that I thought I might have come across a mugger, but I was probably mistaken. It was misty down by the river and it was difficult to see much.'

Before he could say any more about his encounter, they heard

Daisy clomping down the stairs. At fourteen, she sometimes looked quite grown up and at other times she still seemed like a child. She had been suffering with existential angst for about three months which, according to her form teacher, was common at her age and nothing to worry about. Christine and Peter were not so sanguine. It was easy for the teacher to tell them their daughter was 'just going through a phase'. She didn't have to live with Daisy.

In an uneasy discussion, Christine and Peter had agreed to ignore Daisy's surliness and her garish experiments with her hair and make-up. She was such a pretty girl – Peter was baffled by the way she chose to ruin her appearance by smearing greasy muck all over her face. She had transformed her glossy brown hair into yellow straw. Christine claimed to be unperturbed by their daughter's experiments. One thing they did agree on was that their teenage daughter's growing rebellious streak wasn't helping their own relationship.

'Do you think I haven't tried?' Christine had replied, when Peter had suggested his wife talk to Daisy. 'Do you really think I haven't done everything I can think of to get her to talk to me?'

'And?' Peter prompted her.

'And nothing. She tells me she hasn't got anything to say to me. When she speaks to me at all, that is.'

Daisy had spent the summer holiday in her bedroom. Peter had hoped she would be more communicative once she was back at school, but she remained surly and withdrawn.

'It's not just what she says.' Peter had sighed, struggling to comprehend what was happening to his family. 'She looks as though she's been – I don't know, living on the street.'

'Don't be ridiculous,' Christine had snapped.

'You have to admit, she looks neglected.'

'Well, what do you expect me to do about it? She's not a child. I can't dress her.'

'I thought she confided in you.'

'She used to. I don't know what's happened. She's changed so much. It's all part of growing up, I suppose. I guess we'll have to let it run its course. In the meantime, just be careful not to do anything that might set her off.'

'That's rich, coming from you.'

'What's that supposed to mean?'

'I'm not the one who keeps upsetting her.'

Their exchanges frequently led to bitter spats, where they blamed each other for their daughter's rancour, even though they both knew neither of them was really at fault. Daisy was the main cause of the friction between them, but they were careful not to quarrel in front of her. Wary of saying anything that might send her spiralling into one of her foul moods, they dropped the subject of Peter's early morning encounter and fell into an uneasy silence as Daisy entered the kitchen.

'Here,' Christine urged, pushing the box of cereal towards her. 'Or I can make you some toast, if you like. There's peanut butter,' she added hopefully. 'You ought to eat breakfast.'

Muttering that she wasn't hungry, Daisy gulped down half a cup of tea before stomping off to collect her school bag.

'She hardly eats,' Christine complained quietly.

'I heard that,' Daisy shouted from the hall. 'If you're going to talk about me behind my back, you could at least wait until I've left the house.'

Christine put her spoon down and Peter sighed. He felt out of his depth in his own family. An only child, his few playmates had all been boys before he went to senior school. His mother had been a distant figure and his father had warned him that she was 'fragile' and not to be bothered. The girls he socialised with as a teenager had struck him as boring and unpredictable, to be approached with caution. He had been interested in them as girlfriends, but he had never really felt close to a woman until he had met Christine – and even she remained a mystery to him most of the time.

'Is it always like this?' he murmured to his wife. 'Puberty, I mean, with girls.'

Christine glared at him. 'I don't know what you want me to say,' she replied. 'We put up with her moods; her school has the reputation for being one of the best in York and I don't see what more we can do.'

Peter hesitated. He wanted to reassure Christine that she wasn't responsible for their daughter's waywardness, but if Christine was blameless, where did that leave him?

With a shrug, he stood up. 'I'm off.'

After all his years of hard graft for his family, no one could even be bothered to say goodbye when he left the house in the morning.

'And you have a nice day too,' he muttered angrily.

It scarcely seemed worth calling out before he left and no one responded when he yelled, 'Goodbye.' Recently he had been coming home from work late. From now on, he decided, he might as well go out early and grab breakfast on his way to the office. Sitting at the table at home first thing in the morning was miserable and he was no longer prepared to start his day risking a temper tantrum from his daughter or griping from his wife. Something needed to change, he just wasn't sure what.

1

GERALDINE DROPPED HER TODDLER off and exchanged a few words of greeting with the childminder, before driving to York police station. Her colleague and friend, Ariadne, looked up and smiled a greeting when Geraldine entered. They were about the same age and both had dark eyes and black hair. Occasionally they were mistaken for sisters. Ariadne had recently had her glossy locks cut short, like Geraldine's, but where the latter's hair was straight, Ariadne's was curly.

'I really like my hair like this. It's so much easier and it dries so quickly.' Ariadne grinned, running her fingers through her hair. 'I should have done this years ago. I thought Nico would want me to grow it again, but he likes it like this. At least, he says he does. I can never quite tell with him whether he's just trying to be nice.'

'Don't complain.' Geraldine smiled. 'There's nothing wrong with being nice. Although if everyone was nice it might put us out of a job,' she added and grinned.

Her own partner, Ian, had never commented on her hair which she had always worn short. They had known each other for years, since he had been an eager young detective sergeant and she had been his inspector. Not everyone managed to sustain a long-term relationship while holding down a stressful career, but Geraldine and Ian were both now detective inspectors working in serious crime, living together happily.

Geraldine was absorbed in her work when she and Ariadne were called to the major incident room. Dropping what they were doing, they hurried along the corridor and entered the room to see a team of detectives gathering. No one knew why they had been summoned, but clearly something was up. They waited in an atmosphere of subdued excitement until Detective Chief Inspector Binita Hewitt strode in, her open jacket swinging around her narrow hips and her heels tapping sharply on the floor. Turning to face the assembled officers she tossed her head to flick her hair back off her forehead, her expression grim.

'A suspicious death has been reported,' she announced, her shrill voice taut. 'The body was discovered at eight fifteen this morning by a local resident on her way to work. There was no ID on the body but an empty wallet was found in the gutter nearby, so for now we're working on the assumption that this was a robbery that turned violent.'

Geraldine and Ariadne were sent to Blossom Street, where the body had been discovered just past the junction with Holgate Road. Geraldine was gratified to be put in charge of the investigation and they set off without delay, aware that the sooner they viewed the crime scene the better. With every moment that passed, traces left behind by the killer would be deteriorating. Fortunately it wasn't raining, but there was a brisk wind and with the corpse exposed to the elements, crucial evidence might already have been lost. Geraldine in particular was impatient to get there as quickly as possible. It wasn't that she didn't trust the scene of crime officers to conduct a thorough search of the site, but she liked to see the scene for herself, preferably before anything was disturbed.

'I like to get a feel of the place,' she told Ariadne. 'You can't get that once the body's been moved. It's not the same.'

'I don't see what you expect to find that the SOCO team haven't already observed and recorded,' her friend replied. 'We always learn a lot more from their reports than we can possibly hope to spot for ourselves. It's their job to be thorough and notice everything. It's not as if we're the first eyes on the scene.'

They were repeating a conversation they had gone through many times.

'I know, I know,' Geraldine replied. 'It's just that written reports can't capture the atmosphere. I can't explain it. I don't even understand it myself, but sometimes just being there seems to throw up a few ideas about what might have happened.'

'Ah, the famous DI Steel intuition,' Ariadne said with a grin. 'Picking up clues from the air like a modern Sherlock Holmes. Your nose is positively twitching. But you know perfectly well it's not helpful to speculate before we have all the evidence, as you're always so keen to remind us.'

'At least it's not raining yet,' Geraldine said, ignoring Ariadne's good-humoured joshing and glancing up at the overcast sky. Gusts of wind seemed to be blowing at them from every direction, sending yellow and brown leaves skittering wildly across the pavement. 'It looks as though it might start pouring soon, so come on, let's get over there and take a look around, while the crime scene is still fairly intact.'

A forensic tent had been erected in Blossom Street before Geraldine and her sergeant arrived. Driving past, they saw a couple of uniformed police officers standing guard, preventing passers-by from approaching, to ensure no one could contaminate the scene. As Geraldine and Ariadne drew up outside a house further along the street, they heard shouting. Spectral from a distance, the tent appeared to solidify as they approached. Drawing near, they saw a large woman in a red coat haranguing a young constable. Their colleague's expression remained doggedly resolute, but they both suspected he must be feeling intimidated in spite of his uniform.

'I have every right to walk along this pavement,' the woman was insisting stridently. 'I pay my council taxes, same as you. Just because you're in a uniform doesn't mean you can tell me what I can and can't do. I'll report you for this, don't think I won't.'

The constable's response was too quiet for Geraldine and Ariadne to hear, but if he was trying to pacify the woman, he was clearly failing.

'I don't care what you think. If one of my neighbours has been killed, I have a right to know all about it,' she screeched in response to his comment. 'And don't think you can stop me from walking along the street. It's a public right of way. Anyone can walk here and that's the law. If you think you can stop me, you need to think again. I know my rights.'

Leaving the constable to deal with the irate local resident, Geraldine passed through the cordon and pulled on a protective suit and shoes. Aware that Ariadne was hesitating to accompany her, and hearing the woman still shouting at the constable on duty on the pavement, Geraldine suggested her colleague go and offer him some support. They would need to speak to the constable, who had been the first officer on the scene, and Ariadne could talk to him once they had sent the angry woman packing.

'Take her name and address, and you might ask her why she's so eager to contaminate a crime scene,' Geraldine advised her friend. 'If she thinks we suspect there's a reason she's desperate to plant her footsteps near a body, she'll soon be quiet. Threaten to take her in for questioning if you have to.'

Ariadne threw her a grateful glance before she scurried off to talk to the constable. Ariadne didn't like viewing murder victims before they had been cleaned up. Geraldine suspected discomfort around cadavers had held her friend back in her career, but she had never challenged Ariadne about it. Far from judging her friend for being squeamish, Geraldine sometimes wondered whether she herself was lacking some common human trait as she had never been disturbed by the sight of a corpse, even one that was badly mutilated. On the contrary, she regarded the bodies of victims of violent death as a kind of intellectual exercise, an opportunity to gather vital information about what had killed them. She couldn't help questioning whether there was something ghoulish in her fascination. Much as she tried to identify with her colleague's response, she was too eager to discover the truth to allow anything to deter her from visiting a crime scene as soon as possible. Drawing in a deep breath and focusing her thoughts on the job at hand, she made her way to the forensic tent which loomed ahead of her like a gigantic spectre.

2

THE FIRST THING GERALDINE noticed as she entered the forensic tent was the stillness of the air. Sheltered from the capricious autumn breeze, all she could hear above the muffled drone of distant traffic was a faint shuffling and scuffling, as scene of crime officers moved around. Assiduously examining the ground, they searched for possible evidence, communicating little. Only an occasional grunt or muttered exclamation indicated their engagement with their task. Giving a quick nod to the nearest officer, whom she thought she recognised behind her mask, Geraldine turned her attention to the reason they had gathered in the tent.

The victim was lying on his back, forming a dark mound on the ground. From the far side of the tent Geraldine could see only that he was a large man in a black coat. Taking care to follow the common approach path, she drew close enough to gain a clear view of the body. His coat was unbuttoned and had fallen open, exposing a dark stain on his chest around the location of his heart. The dark patch showed up clearly against his grey jumper. It was easy to see he had not died from natural causes. Either a tragic accident or else a violent assault had killed him. His age was difficult to gauge because his face was bruised and stained with blood from a gash on his forehead. His features were further obscured by a smattering of leaves and earth that had stuck to his bloody face, presumably when he had fallen to the ground. If the head injury itself had not proved fatal, the chest wound almost certainly would have done.

Geraldine knew she ought to hold back from conjecture at this early stage, but it was difficult to refrain from speculating about the sequence of events leading to this death and one obvious theory immediately struck her. She guessed he had been stabbed in the chest and that injury had caused him to collapse and pitch forward, sustaining a head injury when he fell. He might have rolled on to his back as he lay dying, or perhaps his assailant had turned him over to check he was dead. She shook her head, making a conscious effort to dispel her hypothesis. Watertight evidence was needed in a murder investigation, not supposition. They would know more after the post mortem. For now, she had seen enough to confirm what the initial assessment team had concluded, that this man had most probably been violently assaulted. It was for others to confirm exactly what had happened, but there was only a very remote chance that she was looking at the victim of an accident. Before very long, she suspected she would be working with a team to track down and apprehend a murderer.

'There was nothing in his pockets,' the nearest SOCO said, seeing Geraldine staring at the corpse, lost in thought.

'I don't suppose we know his name or why he was killed,' Geraldine replied. It wasn't really a question, but the SOCO responded anyway.

'That's your job to find out who he was.' He turned away from Geraldine to resume his examination of the ground around the body. 'There are no tracks,' he added over his shoulder. 'That is, no recent footsteps that we can see. That's not to say no one else was here. The ground's quite dry, in spite of all the damp weather we've been having. And these pesky leaves have been blowing around everywhere, so any disturbance might have been covered up by the time we arrived. The medic placed the time of death some time between five and eight, when he was found.'

'Eight fifteen,' Geraldine corrected her colleague automatically. 'He was found at eight fifteen, so any time between five and eight fifteen.'

'Eight, eight fifteen. He might have cared about punctuality once, but it makes no difference to him now.' He jerked his head towards the body.

Geraldine stifled a sigh. Recording the exact time the body was discovered might be important to the investigating team, but her colleague was right to say that nothing would ever matter to the victim again.

'You're not the only one who's wondering who he was,' the SOCO continued. 'And why he was killed. I suppose you're working on the assumption that it was a mugging that went wrong, because we found an empty wallet nearby.'

'That's certainly a possibility,' Geraldine agreed.

'Then again,' the SOCO continued thoughtfully, warming to his train of thought, 'the killer might have wanted to hide the victim's identity, if they were associated with him in any way.'

'True,' Geraldine agreed. 'Although if that was the case, why didn't they just take his wallet away and dispose of it somewhere that wouldn't be immediately associated with the body?'

'I hadn't thought of that. But that's why you're a detective and I'm just a SOCO,' he replied with a rueful laugh. 'And now, I'd better get on. I shouldn't have stopped to chat. They'll be wanting to move him soon and I need to finish up here before they do. Not that we're ever really finished,' he added. 'We leave that to you and your team.'

Geraldine stepped back carefully. She took another long look around the scene, doing her best to memorise every detail of the pavement. The grey of the stone slabs wasn't uniform. Some were almost chalky white while others were quite dark. The pavement was further discoloured in one place by a pool of dark blood that had oozed into the gutter and down a drain, making it impossible to tell how much blood the victim had lost while he lay dying, although it did seem to confirm that the victim had been attacked in the street where he had been found. The stain on his front suggested the chest wound had caused significant bleeding. Additionally, there was the head injury, but she couldn't tell much from that. It could be superficial, but she would have to wait for the post mortem to learn whether it had caused any serious damage.

On reflection, she realised her initial hypothesis might have put the injuries the wrong way round. The victim could have been knocked out with a blow to the head before he was stabbed. She sighed, realising she was pointlessly going round in circles with her theories. There was nothing more she could learn at the crime scene. It was time to move on and leave the SOCO team to gather evidence. Right now, she needed to focus her efforts on identifying the dead man. As she was dropping her protective gear in the bin outside the tent, a van arrived to transport the body to the mortuary. If she had arrived ten minutes later, she would have missed seeing the body at the crime scene. She wondered if the SOCO she had spoken to had finished and whether he regretted having paused in his work to talk to her.

Zipping up her jacket against a chill breeze, she caught sight of Ariadne seemingly engrossed in conversation with one of the uniformed constables who was on duty at the cordon and called her. Ariadne looked round with an anxious frown. As they walked away, Geraldine glanced over her shoulder and took a last look at the scene on the street. The roadway was closed off, but a small crowd of onlookers had gathered beyond the cordon. She gazed at the row of people waiting with varying expressions of anticipation and apprehension. Thinking that any one of them could be a violent killer, she suppressed a shudder.

'Did you manage to find out anything from that constable?' Geraldine asked.

'Only that the public have a ghoulish interest in dead bodies,' Ariadne replied. 'He was being pestered to let people go in and have a quick peek. Someone asked if they could take a photo. Honestly, can you believe it? Some people seem to treat a murder victim like a kind of fairground attraction.'

Geraldine shook her head. 'I wonder if there are any journalists there. I wouldn't put anything past them.'

'No doubt someone would have taken a photo of the body, given half a chance, journalist or no journalist. I wonder what a news channel would pay for a picture of a murder victim at the scene of the crime?'

They were silent for a moment.

'So, where do we go from here?' Ariadne enquired as they drove off.

Geraldine sighed. 'They might think they've got away with it,' she muttered to Ariadne, between clenched teeth, 'but we'll find them. Wherever they are, we're not going to let them get away with it.'

'I never for one moment thought that we would.'

Neither of them added that they had no idea how they were going to set about looking for the killer, when they didn't even know the identity of the victim.

3

CHRISTINE FORCED A SMILE. Daisy had enough to contend with, without having to worry about her father going AWOL. Christine did her best to defend him, but it was proving increasingly difficult. This wasn't the first time he had gone off without telling her where he was going. Sometimes she wasn't able to contact him all day, and more than once he had gone out and forgotten to tell her that he would be away overnight. This time, she had no option but to tell Daisy that he had been called away suddenly for work. It was obvious straight away that Daisy didn't believe her. She might be a surly teenager, but she wasn't stupid. After some provocative jibes, she challenged her mother outright.

'Why didn't he say goodbye before he went?' she demanded.

'He did. You just didn't hear him, with your music on so loud.'

'You're lying to me, I can tell. I didn't hear him go out. He didn't come home again last night, did he? Did he? This is all your fault and you don't even care.' She sounded almost hysterical.

'Of course he came home.' Christine hated lying to her daughter, but there was no alternative. She was afraid the truth would upset Daisy even more. Unless she admitted that she had no idea where Peter was, there was nothing else she could say.

'Well, even if he did come home last night, you don't know where he is *now*, do you? Has he left you? Because I wouldn't blame him. He's probably had enough of you. You think we'll be better off without him, don't you? I know it's true, so there's no point denying it. I heard you having a go at each other yesterday. It's not as if it was the first time. You're always arguing.'

Christine did her best to calm Daisy down, but it was difficult, not least because she was finding it hard to control her own feelings. Her initial bewilderment was soon ousted by an almost overpowering rage at Peter, but she forced herself not to react to her daughter's accusations. She knew Daisy didn't mean to be malicious, she was just unhappy. Puberty was a difficult time for many young people.

'You've got this all wrong,' Christine said in a tone of forced calm that sounded really fake. 'It's just work. He'll be back soon.'

'You're lying,' Daisy repeated. She glared at her, as though Christine was the one who was letting her down, not Peter. 'You're always lying to me. You must think I'm an idiot.'

'This isn't my fault,' Christine muttered, biting her lip.

'Well, actually it is, because you're the one who's lying,' Daisy replied sourly. 'You're supposed to support me, not make my life even more difficult than it already is. Why won't you just admit that you don't know where he is?'

'I know he's at work and I know he'll be home soon,' Christine repeated doggedly, still hoping to convince Daisy.

Far from seeming satisfied, Daisy snorted. 'Well, I hope he has gone for good and I wish you would go off and leave me alone too. I'd be better off on my own. I'm going to school. At least when I'm out of the house I can get away from you and dad yelling at each other all the time. I've told them about it at school, you know, about how you're always fighting.'

Christine wanted to beg her daughter to be kind to her, but she didn't dare in case her pleading prompted another outburst. Reminding herself of what the teacher had said about Daisy going through a phase, she took a deep breath and lowered her eyes.

'Your father's going to be home soon,' she bleated. She wasn't even sure she wanted that to be true any more. It was hard to believe that their marriage had gone downhill so rapidly. 'Everything's going to be all right, you'll see,' she went on, doing her best to sound confident. 'There's no need for you to worry. Your dad's fine. He'll be home soon. He never stays away long. And you know our quarrels are never about anything serious, just normal squabbles, like all families have.'

She was babbling anxiously, fearful of saying the wrong thing and sending Daisy off into one of her tantrums. According to Christine's friend, such behaviour was not unusual in teenagers but that assurance gave Christine little comfort when Daisy flew into a rage.

'I don't remember flying off the handle like that when I was her age,' she had complained to Peter.

He had ignored her, but then he rarely paid attention to anything she said. Her repeated complaint that he never listened to her was one of the things they argued about.

Daisy refused her offer of a lift to school, insisting she preferred to take the bus.

'You make me feel as though you're ashamed to be seen with me,' Christine said, trying to sound as though she was joking.

Daisy glared at her before turning away and flouncing out of the house. With a faint shudder, Christine let out an involuntary sob and realised she was crying. This was all Peter's fault. He knew how vulnerable Daisy was at the moment. But this was nothing new. Even though Daisy was his daughter too, he had never really supported Christine in bringing her up. Now Daisy was upset that he had gone out without saying goodbye and was venting her anger on Christine. The injustice of it burned. None of this was Christine's fault, yet she was being punished, while Peter had sauntered off without a thought for the family he had devastated. With a sudden burst of rage, she ran upstairs and flung his wardrobe open: shirts hanging up, ironed and all facing the same way; jeans folded on a shelf; gardening clothes left in a neat pile on the floor of the wardrobe; everything in its rightful place for him to find. She had done all that.

Even when they had both been working full-time, she had done his laundry and kept the house clean and all without once complaining or receiving a single word of thanks. When she thought of everything she did for him, it made her furious. He didn't deserve her. If she was honest, he had never really appreciated her. Once the initial glow of their romance had faded, she had come to resent the supercilious way he treated her. Christine had put up with her marriage for her daughter's sake, but she was beginning to realise that might have been a terrible mistake because, despite all her efforts, her parents' antagonism was upsetting Daisy. Christine had sacrificed her own peace of mind for nothing because by staying with Peter she hadn't made Daisy happy. In fact, it was quite the opposite. She regretted not having left Peter years ago. But the thought of facing life alone had always frightened her. She wasn't sure how she would manage to deal with household bills and maintenance on her own even though she told herself that, with enough money, nothing would be a problem. If they were to divorce now, he would have to support her for at least as long as Daisy was at school. But what would she do after that, all on her own with no income?

Turning away from the wardrobe, her eyes fell on the small pine desk in the corner of the bedroom. She felt drawn to it, almost against her will. Her hands shook as she opened the bottom drawer and took out the black ring binder containing their important documents: bank statements, household bills and the life insurance policy Peter had taken out when Daisy was born. As she was about to open it, she noticed the album of photos from their wedding which had been stored under the black file. Putting the financial documents to one side, she opened the white album. Looking through it reminded her of how pleased they had once been with one another and she wept for her lost happiness.

There was another album with family photos. The record of Daisy as a young child stopped abruptly, succeeded only by obligatory school photos. Christine sighed. It was a pity that electronic photos had replaced the old-fashioned printed ones. She studied a picture of a smiling little girl with glossy brown hair, dressed in a party frock and laughing at a birthday parties, sitting on a swing in the park, and playing with favourite toys. Turning her attention from the child, she looked at older images of holidays before Daisy was born, searching Peter's face for signs of his lost devotion. Surely all that love between them couldn't have vanished forever.

The shrill tone of her mobile shook her from her reverie. With a start she hurriedly replaced the photo albums and the file of financial documents. She had looked at the contents before, trying to work out the figures. The details confused her, but if they were to split up she might get half of the house and a share of her husband's pension. Perhaps she would be able manage without him after all. She might even be quite well off. She sighed as she closed the drawer on mementos of past happiness. If she was angry with Peter, then at least she still felt something towards him. People said the opposite of love was not hate but indifference, so perhaps their love could be revived, but she was no longer sure she even wanted to try and resolve their issues. Everything had gone horribly wrong and she had no idea what to do to make things better. While she was replacing all the paperwork in the desk she missed the call, but a few minutes later her phone rang again. With a sigh, she answered.

'Christine, how are you?' her friend asked.

Tempted to blurt out the truth, Christine gave a noncommittal response. Given the situation, it was essential to be discreet.

4

THE BODY, WHICH SO far remained unidentified, had been reported by a young woman who had discovered it on her way to work. She had already been questioned at the scene by a female constable. Nevertheless, Geraldine was keen to have a word with the witness. Earlier in her career, she had been criticised for always wanting to do everything herself. Some of her colleagues had taken exception to this, feeling that she didn't trust them to carry out tasks independent of her supervision. It had taken some effort and soul-searching on Geraldine's part for her to restrain herself from constantly wanting to micromanage her colleagues. Even now, in important instances, she preferred to rely on her own instincts about witnesses than to depend solely on other officers' written reports. She had learned to be discreet in her enquiries so that she didn't appear to be checking up on other members of the team. Despite her efforts, she was aware that a few of her colleagues still resented her compulsion to corroborate their findings, which they felt undermined them as professionals. But most of them were content to accept what a few still interpreted as interference, because they had learned to respect her intuition and fierce intelligence which, so far, had not let them down.

The woman who had found the body had been questioned by a relatively inexperienced young constable; privately, Geraldine felt justified in speaking to the witness again. Without telling anyone exactly where she was going, she went to York Explore Library. Situated beside Museum Gardens, it was an impressive listed building, about a hundred years old. A broad red-brick frontage boasted elegantly designed high arched windows, and white stone columns supported a raised portico above the entrance. Climbing stone steps to the entrance, Geraldine went straight over to a plump middle-aged woman seated behind the desk and asked for the witness by name.

'Oh, this'll be about that body she reported,' the woman said, nodding.

Geraldine wasn't surprised to learn that the news had spread. Even for a detective working in serious crime, viewing a corpse wasn't a common occurrence. A librarian who had stumbled on a dead body was bound to talk about her experience.

'Did she tell you what happened?' Geraldine enquired.

The librarian shook her head. 'Not really. Only that she found a dead body on her way into work. She's fine now, but she was quite shocked yesterday, and we sent her home early. You won't be getting her all upset again, will you? She had nothing to do with it; she was just unlucky enough to be the first one on the scene.'

'So she's back now?' Geraldine confirmed.

'Oh yes,' the librarian answered, seeming faintly indignant at the question. She didn't add that it would take more than a dead body to put a librarian off her work for long, but she might as well have done.

Miranda was a young blonde with a striking spiky hairstyle crowning a plain but pleasant face. From the notes taken by the constable, Geraldine knew that Miranda's route from her home in Mount Parade would take her along The Mount to Blossom Street before crossing the river and reaching the library.

'I'm just thankful I found him,' she told Geraldine with a slight grimace, as though she had picked up a half-eaten burger someone had dropped on the floor of the library. 'It could have been a child that came across him, or rats!' she added, with a shudder.

Having confirmed the time of the discovery, Geraldine enquired gently whether Miranda had ever seen the dead man before. Miranda hesitated before shaking her head, causing her spiky hair to jiggle alarmingly.

'You don't seem very sure,' Geraldine hazarded and waited.

In her experience, it was generally best not to press witnesses for answers once they had begun to talk. They were understandably often unsure of the most appropriate language to use when speaking of the dead.

'It's just that I didn't get much of a look at his face, not so that I'd be able to recognise him, even if I knew him, because it was covered in leaves and mud,' Miranda finally admitted. 'And blood. I think he'd fallen over and maybe rolled on the ground or something. I thought he looked quite old,' she added, as though she felt something more was expected of her. 'Not young, anyway. And he was a bit fat. It was horrible. His eyes were open as if he was looking up at me. I wanted to close them but I couldn't go near him, let alone touch him.' She shuddered. 'It was horrible. I saw the blood...' She broke off with a helpless shrug. 'I thought I was going to be sick.'

Geraldine nodded and waited, but Miranda didn't say anything else.

'Before you saw him,' Geraldine prompted her at last, 'did you notice anyone else nearby? Did anyone walk past you as you were approaching the scene?'

Just over twenty-four hours had passed since Miranda had called the police, but it was still possible she might have registered some detail that she had forgotten to mention at the scene in her agitation at finding a body.

Miranda shook her head and once again her hair quivered. 'I don't remember seeing anyone else,' she replied, 'but I wasn't really looking around. Once I saw him lying on the ground, I just stood there, staring at him. I think I was waiting to see if he would move. I wasn't aware of anything or anyone else. Who was he?'

'I'm afraid I can't share any details yet,' Geraldine replied.

'Oh, of course. You'll need to notify the family before you tell anyone else.' Miranda sighed.

'Do you always walk that way to work?' Geraldine asked.

Miranda nodded. 'I didn't do anything different,' she said, looking anxious. 'I didn't know, I mean, I couldn't have known—'

Geraldine hastened to reassure her that the police had no reason to suspect her of any involvement in the incident and the girl heaved a shuddering sigh. Geraldine was satisfied that the witness had nothing further to tell the police about her discovery. There was no point in wasting any more time in questioning someone who had already told them all she could. Thanking Miranda for notifying the police and for being so helpful in answering their questions, she stood up and glanced at a message on her phone.

Miranda shrugged and gave Geraldine a guarded smile. 'What else could I do in the circumstances?' she asked. 'Anyone else would have done the same.'

Unless they had just killed him, Geraldine thought. It crossed her mind that Miranda might have done that herself and reported the body to explain any trace of her own DNA at the scene, but the first response team had been ahead of her on that and Miranda had apparently raised no objection to having a sample of her DNA taken in order to eliminate her from the enquiry. She claimed not to have touched the body and the evidence bore that out.

Until they could identify the body, there was little they could do beyond check security cameras near the scene of the murder and carry out door-to-door questioning. The victim had most likely lived in the vicinity. It probably meant nothing that he hadn't been wearing a wedding ring, but it was possible he had lived by himself and no one had missed him yet. In any event, it was going to be a time-consuming and painstaking task to find out if anyone had been missed from one of the houses in the neighbourhood. And in the meantime, the chances of tracking down the killer were growing more remote with every hour that passed.

'It's frightening to think whoever killed that poor man could still be right here, in York, living among us. It could be someone who comes to the library. You will find him, won't you?' Miranda asked.

'We'll find him,' Geraldine assured her.

She didn't add that she was nowhere near as confident of success as her words suggested. Nor did she confide that Miranda was right. It was disturbing to think a killer might be living in York, mingling with customers in shops, waiting at bus stops, eating in restaurants alongside other diners – a dangerous man at liberty in the community she was pledged to protect.

5

GERALDINE RETURNED TO THE police station to log her report. While they were busy collecting information, speculation was rife among her colleagues. They were divided between those who thought the victim had been accidentally killed by a mugger and those who believed the equally plausible theory that he had been murdered in a deliberately targeted assault.

When the pathologist communicated that he had completed the post mortem on the unknown man, Geraldine asked a constable to drive her to the hospital. For the first time she allowed herself to feel positive about the investigation. At last they were going to receive some definite information. Detective Constable Sam Cullen was excited to be attending the post mortem with Geraldine. She had taken the young constable under her wing and liked to invite him to accompany her whenever she thought he would learn something useful from the experience. He was always thrilled to leave his paperwork for what he called 'real police work'. Geraldine repeatedly pointed out that studying reports logged by others so he could keep up to date with all aspects of the investigation was at least as important as going out looking for evidence, but Sam insisted that he wanted to be away from his desk and she liked his enthusiasm. Another reason she warmed to him was that he reminded her of her partner, Ian, whom she had met when he had been an eager young officer, not much older than Sam was now. Ian had developed into a relatively staid detective inspector, but he had worked on risky projects in the past, sometimes endangering his life in the process. Now that he and Geraldine had a child to consider, she had made him promise to stop pursuing perilous undercover missions and he had agreed with her that Tom changed everything in their lives. They were both happy to make the compromises they felt were appropriate, as responsible parents, but the choices forced on them weren't always easy.

With Sam beside her, Geraldine could forget about her responsibilities outside work and revel in his enthusiasm for the job.

'You make me feel young again,' she had told him once, and he had laughed.

Vaguely miffed that he hadn't responded that she *was* young, she was taken aback to realise that she was old enough to be his mother. He was only twenty-four. It was sobering to acknowledge that he considered her old.

'It had to be a mugging,' Sam piped up as he drove Geraldine to the hospital.

'How do you come by that conclusion?' she asked.

'Well, it's obvious. I mean, how else do you explain the fact that someone nicked his wallet, emptied it and chucked it away?'

'I can think of several possible reasons for that,' Geraldine replied. 'The most likely one is that whoever killed him didn't want to leave any clue as to his identity. So credit cards, driving licence, any other personal effects he might have been carrying would have to be removed from the scene, along with his phone of course.'

'Then why take his money? That couldn't identify him.'

'If we're exploring the idea that this man was deliberately murdered, wouldn't it make sense for the killer to take his money hoping to mislead us into thinking the victim had been mugged? That way we might be distracted from shining a spotlight on the people who knew him. If one of them killed him, throwing us off the scent in that way would seem like a very reasonable thing to do. In any case, why not take his money,' she added. 'Wouldn't you, if you were in the killer's shoes? There's surely no downside to pocketing some extra cash. Anyone could be tempted to keep money that came their way, regardless of whether they had set out intending to steal it in the first place. Our killer might have seen it as a little bonus, a tip for a successful job.' She smiled at Sam's crestfallen expression. 'Of course, you're quite right, the likelihood is that this was a mugging that went wrong, but until we know for certain, we need to keep an open mind.'

'But how are we ever going to know for certain? The victim can't tell us.'

'Well, that's not necessarily true either. We're about to meet a man who may be able to tell us a lot more about how our John Doe died, and hopefully he'll be able to give us some indication of whether the death was caused deliberately or not.'

Geraldine hurried Sam past the garrulous anatomical technology assistant. Avril had finally stopped prattling about her wedding, but she was always keen to regale Geraldine with accounts of her most recent holiday or the holiday she was planning.

'We should go out together some time,' she had suggested wistfully on Geraldine's last visit to the mortuary. 'Leave the little one with his father and have a night off. We could go clubbing, if you like.'

'It's not really my kind of thing,' Geraldine had replied, feeling awkward.

Avril seemed keen to spend time with Geraldine, who didn't point out that she and Avril weren't actually friends, but colleagues who only met occasionally in the course of Geraldine's investigations. Her trips to the mortuary were not social visits. It hadn't escaped her notice that Avril's friendly overtures had intensified since the technology assistant's wedding, but she didn't comment on that. Efficient at her job, Avril nevertheless struck Geraldine as young and rather silly. Sam wasn't the only one who made Geraldine feel old.

'She seems nice,' Sam said as they left Avril in the office and made their way to the examination room.

Geraldine nodded without commenting.

The pathologist greeted them with an effusiveness more in keeping with an office Christmas party than a post mortem. Sam looked slightly surprised, but Geraldine understood that Jonah relied on joviality to make the gruesome details of his grisly job bearable. Aware that behind his comedic persona he was meticulous and professional in his approach to his work, she appreciated his lighthearted approach which tended to make her visits less depressing than they might otherwise have been. Only occasionally did the pathologist appear distressed by his task, usually when the victim was very young or in some way particularly pitiful.

'What can you tell us?' she asked, once the usual lighthearted pleasantries had been exchanged and she had introduced Sam and tolerated Jonah teasing her about trading Ian in for a younger model.

'Looks like I've missed my chance,' Jonah remarked, twisting his unattractive features into so droll an expression that she couldn't help laughing.

'Now,' she said firmly, 'what about him?' She pointed to the mound of white flesh lying between them on a cold metal slab.

Jonah heaved a loud sigh. 'Oh, very well, let's get to work. You know,' he added, addressing Sam, 'every time this goddess walks through the door, I think finally it's my lucky day, but she's more interested in the dead than in me. I sometimes think I'm going to have to commit hara-kiri before she will look kindly on me.' He laughed and Geraldine scolded him for being flippant about the dead.

'You do understand, don't you, that this is his way of coping,' she said, turning to Sam, who nodded uncertainly.

'Coping with you constantly breaking my heart,' Jonah murmured theatrically.

SILENT TIES

'You wouldn't think it, but he's a happily married family man,' she added, still speaking to Sam. 'Now, enough of this silliness, Jonah. Let's talk about our victim here. Was he definitely murdered or are we wasting our time launching a full-scale investigation?'

Jonah glanced down at the corpse. 'You're not wasting your time.' He looked up, all trace of his previous good humour vanished. 'There's no doubt about it. This poor fellow was murdered.'

6

WITH JONAH'S SOLEMN PRONOUNCEMENT, the mood in the room became serious. The pathologist drew in a deep breath before launching into a detailed account of the dead man's injuries, starting with the gash on his temple. His face had been cleaned and Geraldine could see his features clearly for the first time. With a large fleshy nose, thin lips and a square chin, while not exactly good-looking, he was nevertheless imposing. Even in death he exuded an air of authority. His eyes were closed, giving his face a mask-like quality. It was impossible to gauge what his complexion had been like when he was alive. Geraldine imagined him with ruddy cheeks and a loud, bluff voice that no one would ever hear again. In death, his face was a ghastly white, contrasting with his cropped black hair shot through with grey. Minor abrasions on his cheek were no more than pale irregularities on the surface of his skin, unsightly in the glare of the examination room but probably barely noticeable in less powerful lighting. There was a hideous livid laceration on his right temple which Jonah assured them was just a superficial wound.

'The head wound might have bled quite a lot,' he added, 'but there was no serious damage. I doubt it would even have knocked him out. He might have been stunned temporarily, especially if he was caught off guard, but by the time he hit his head he had already suffered a fatal injury. Do you have any questions or shall I continue?'

'Please, go on.'

Looking at the body as Jonah was speaking, Geraldine thought the victim appeared to have shrunk since she had first seen him in the forensic tent. Without clothes, he was in some respects still a large figure with a portly white belly, but his limbs were slender relative to his body, making him look almost childlike. Probably he had cut an impressive figure when fully clothed. Naked, he just looked vulnerable and weak. She wondered idly if that was what lay behind the expression 'clothes maketh the man'.

After talking about the dead man's muscle tone turning to fat, his generous diet and his liver that showed signs of coping with a significant amount of alcohol, Jonah directed their attention to the wound on the dead man's chest. He didn't need to tell them it had been caused by a knife.

'The blade entered to the left of the sternum, passing between the ribs to penetrate the left ventricle of the heart.'

'Did that kill him instantly?' Sam enquired in a hushed voice.

'No, not instantly,' the pathologist replied.

'He bled from his head injury when he fell, which means he was still alive after he was stabbed in the chest, even if only briefly,' Geraldine said.

Jonah nodded. 'Exactly.'

'But he was killed by being stabbed in the chest?' Sam asked.

The detective constable was staring at the wound with a horrified expression and Geraldine reminded herself that he was still quite young and relatively inexperienced. She resolved to keep a closer eye on him than she had been doing. But for now, she turned her attention to what the pathologist was saying.

'The cause of death was heart failure, brought about by a combination of blood loss, shock and exposure,' Jonah said. 'If he'd received urgent medical attention after he was stabbed in the chest, it's possible his life could have been saved. But alas, that was not to be. He lay in the street bleeding and by the time he was discovered,' he waved his hand with a flourish, 'he was dead.' He heaved a sigh and then looked up with a weary smile. 'It's unlucky for him that he was found too late. Unless he stabbed himself and then somehow disposed of the murder weapon while lying on the ground unconscious, someone else wielded the knife and made off with the weapon, leaving him to die. So I'd say you're definitely looking for a murderer.' He nodded his head sombrely.

'How soon after he was attacked did he die?' Sam asked. 'I mean, was he definitely dead when his killer left him? Is it possible his attacker might have thought he was just injured and run off in a panic expecting him to recover?'

'If he'd been resuscitated, he might have been able to tell us who had attacked him,' Geraldine pointed out. 'It's possible the killer panicked, as you say, or more likely they thought he was dead. But either way, this was murder.'

Jonah nodded. 'Both of those scenarios are possible, but our friend here would have needed immediate and expert medical care for survival to be even a possibility. I'd say the killer could have been fairly confident the victim wouldn't be attended to in time to save his life. He would have been as good as dead after that attack. If it were me wielding the knife, I wouldn't have hung around to check whether he was dead or dying.' He shrugged.

Geraldine nodded. 'Anyone could have come along at any moment and seen what was happening. I'd say the killer was bound to run off at once. They'd already taken a huge risk killing him in the street.' She paused. 'He was found on a relatively busy road, so this wasn't a particularly well-thought-out attack.'

'It looks like it was a spur-of-the-moment impulse,' Sam suggested.

'By someone carrying a weapon,' Geraldine added.

They agreed the nature of the attack, together with the empty wallet, suggested this could have been a violent mugging.

'Did he resist his attacker?' Geraldine asked.

'No, which is a bit odd,' Jonah replied. 'That is to say, it struck me as odd because there's no evidence he attempted to fight back, although you might not think that's anything unusual.'

'Odd in what way?' Geraldine asked, pouncing on the word which hinted that Jonah had something more to say.

'He was a hefty man, in his prime and fit for his age. I'd say he must have been strong. Although he was beginning to run to fat, he was still quite muscular and you'd think he would have put up a fight when someone pulled a knife on him. Yet there are no defence wounds.'

'Perhaps he was taken by surprise,' Sam said. 'His assailant could have stabbed him suddenly, without any warning.'

'So there's nothing that could help us identify his assailant?' Geraldine asked, although she knew that Jonah would have told them by now if there had been any trace of the killer's identity on the body.

Jonah shook his head.

'Maybe he knew his killer and wasn't expecting them to attack him,' Geraldine suggested before turning to address Jonah again. 'What can you tell us about him before he died? Is there anything else you can tell us about his lifestyle and general health?'

'Like I said, he had good muscle tone. I'd say he looked after himself, exercised regularly and didn't smoke. He'd eaten well the previous night and clearly enjoyed his food. He wasn't wearing a wedding ring, but of course that doesn't mean anything.'

'Is there anything to suggest any specific line of work, or any particular sport or pastime? Anything that might help us trace his identity?'

Jonah looked up, clearly troubled by the question. 'Do you mean to say you still don't know who he was?'

'No, not yet.'

Jonah shook his head. 'He probably had a sedentary job, but that's more of a guess than anything definite. I can't say I've noticed any distinguishing features that suggest any particular activity,' Jonah said. 'I wish I could give you more to go on. If I notice anything I'll let you know straight away.'

'How old would you say he was?'

He shrugged. 'That's hard to say. I'd put him anywhere between early fifties and late sixties. It's difficult to be more precise than that.'

Geraldine thanked him.

'I'm sorry I can't be more helpful. It looks like you've got your work cut out with this one,' Jonah said grimly. 'Good luck with finding his killer!'

Thanking Jonah again for the information he had shared with them and urging him to contact them immediately if he discovered anything that might help the investigation, the two detectives took their leave.

'He really tries to be helpful, doesn't he?' Sam said when they were driving away.

'Shame he couldn't find any identifying features,' Geraldine agreed. 'That would have been helpful.'

'So we're on our own with this one.'

'You, me and the rest of the team,' Geraldine replied. 'Don't worry, we'll find who did this.'

'How are we supposed to do that?' Sam replied. 'We don't even know the first thing about the victim.'

'Patience,' Geraldine replied. 'The hard work begins here. And we don't stop until we're done. Because there's one thing I do know. We've never yet caught a killer by giving up at the first hurdle. So come on,' she went on brightly. 'No time to waste. Let's get back to the police station and start digging in earnest. If no one's missed him yet, someone must notice his absence soon. He can't stay unidentified forever. And it's still possible something might have been caught on one of the security cameras on the street.'

Sam grinned, his good humour restored. Geraldine returned

his smile confidently, but inwardly she was desperately hoping her optimism wasn't misplaced. Right now, it was all that stood between her and a growing sense of helplessness.

7

CHRISTINE WAS IN THE kitchen, trying to decide what to make for supper. Lately, Daisy had turned her nose up at whatever was put on the table, if she even deigned to eat at home.

Christine had tried all kinds of meals to tempt her daughter, but Daisy refused to do more than toy with the food on her plate. When Christine attempted to challenge her, Daisy became irritable and refused to discuss her eating habits, claiming what she ate was her personal choice and no one else's business. She denied having lost any weight but her school uniform was hanging loosely on her and when she was in her own clothes, she chose baggy outfits that concealed her figure.

'You can try and hide it, but I can see you're losing weight.'

'What's it to you?' Daisy retorted, turning her back on Christine.

'I'm your mother and of course it matters to me when you're not eating properly. You're pale and you don't look well. Seriously, Daisy, you need to listen to me. I'm your mother.'

'You may be my mother, but you don't know everything. And you don't know the first thing about me.'

More often than not Daisy would storm out of the room after such an acrimonious exchange. With a sigh, Christine slid some spaghetti out of a packet into a pan and lit the gas. Daisy used to love spaghetti. As Christine was waiting for the water in the pan to boil, Daisy shouted out suddenly from the living room.

'Mum! Come and look at this!'

Christine hadn't heard her sounding so enthusiastic for months, almost like her old self again.

'Come here quick!' Daisy called out.

The urgency in her voice galvanised Christine who abandoned the pasta and ran to join her daughter. No longer slouching on the sofa in front of the television, Daisy was sitting bolt upright, staring at the screen.

'What is it?' Christine asked. 'Is something the matter?' When Daisy didn't answer straight away, she added, 'I'm making spaghetti bolognaise. Your favourite. How does that grab you?'

'Never mind about that, someone was mugged yesterday,' Daisy cried out in a curiously triumphant tone. 'And he died!'

'Oh, turn that off,' Christine replied. 'I don't know why you're watching the news. For goodness sake, Daisy. Turn it off and go and do your homework. There's no point getting worked up about a random news item. You need to focus on your school work and forget about problems that have nothing to do with us. There's nothing to be afraid of,' she added more kindly. 'No one's going to mug you. You're quite safe.'

'But don't you see?' Daisy replied, scowling impatiently. 'Dad said something about a mugger before he went away, didn't he? It might have been the same one.'

'I really have no idea what you're talking about. Someone being mugged has got nothing to do with your father. Now, do you want to go and do your homework or shall I make supper first?'

'Don't you see?' Daisy went on, ignoring her mother's question. 'I heard you and Dad talking about how he was nearly mugged. What if he knows who it was that attacked him and they decided to return to silence him. Because now they've gone and killed him and he can't possibly go to the police and tell them what happened!' While she had been speaking, her expression had grown curiously intense. 'I know he didn't come home again last night. He's gone for good, hasn't he? We need to go to the police and tell them. Once we tell them Dad's disappeared, they'll know it's him.'

'They'll know what was who? I don't know what you're talking about.'

Frowning, Christine sat down, gazing anxiously at her daughter as, with a show of exaggerated patience, Daisy repeated that a man had been killed in an attack on the street.

'And now Dad's gone missing, hasn't he? They said it was a middle-aged man who was killed. Stabbed to death!' Her eyes were bright with anguish… or possibly exhilaration. 'It was dad. It must have been. He knew who had attacked him and now they've gone and killed him.'

Christine shook her head. She wasn't sure whether to laugh at Daisy's absurd logic or feel worried about her daughter's state of heightened animation. She wondered if Daisy was high on drugs.

'There are any number of middle-aged men in York. There's no reason to suppose anything's happened to your dad,' she began, in as steady at tone as she could muster. She didn't add that she had been trying to call Peter but he didn't seem to have a signal. Either that or he had turned his phone off.

Daisy interrupted her. 'If the police don't know who this man is, then that means no one's reported him missing. It could be Dad.'

'You can't assume they don't know who he is – or was – and you certainly can't assume this has anything to do with your father,' Christine insisted firmly, but she was beginning to feel confused.

Telling Daisy to forget her ghoulish speculation, she promised she would go to the police to report Peter missing if he still hadn't come home after a further day's absence.

'But I'm sure he'll be back tomorrow,' she added with fake brightness. 'I told you, it's just a work thing. It happens sometimes. I expect he told me about it and I've forgotten, and that's all it is. Let's not make a drama out of nothing.'

'You're such a bad liar,' Daisy said, her straw-like hair jiggling as she shook her head reproachfully.

With a scowl, Daisy turned back to the television and began flicking through the channels. Christine nearly said that she had been trying Peter's mobile phone without success, but she thought better of it. In defending herself against the accusation that she didn't care where Peter was, she would only fuel Daisy's anxiety.

'Daisy, turn the TV off and do your homework, please.'

Daisy took no notice and with a sigh of resignation Christine went back to the kitchen to find the spaghetti had boiled over, drenching the gas ring with scummy water. Swearing under her breath, she removed the pan and cleared up the hot sticky liquid. The saturated gas ring wouldn't light, so after wiping the bottom of the pan she plonked it on another one. Lately, it was just one problem after another. She knew Daisy would have to grow out of this horrible teenage phase eventually, but her moods were hard to deal with.

Not for the first time, Christine wondered if the school were right to dismiss Daisy's disturbed state so readily or whether something ought to be done to help her. The mother of one of Daisy's friends had confided that her daughter had seen the school counsellor, but Christine wasn't sure whether that would be a good idea or not. Sometimes it was better not to go poking wasps' nests. There was no knowing what Daisy might blurt out about her parents and if the police starting looking into her home life, it was never going to end well. Daisy might even be taken into care. As it was, there was no knowing if Daisy had really said anything to her teachers. She claimed to have told them about Christine and Peter's arguments, but somehow Christine couldn't see Daisy confiding in her form teacher. She finished making the dinner, but there was no answer when she called out. A moment later, she heard loud music thumping upstairs. She sat down at the table by herself, but she had no appetite. It was frightening how quickly her carefully nurtured family had disintegrated in front of her eyes and she felt helpless to do anything about it.

8

EARLY ON WEDNESDAY AFTERNOON, Geraldine learned that a woman called Jeannie Hodgson had been to the police station that morning claiming that her husband was missing. Disappointed that the report hadn't reached her straight away, Geraldine scanned it quickly. The missing man, John Hodgson, was a sixty-one-year-old bank manager, who worked in a branch near the city. He had been married for twenty-five years and his wife said she had never been unable to account for his absence before. He had left home on Monday morning as usual and had failed to return home. After waiting for forty-eight hours and having called every hospital in York, she had reported him missing. Attached to the document was a copy of the photo the woman had handed in. Geraldine studied it and forwarded it to the pathologist before going to talk to the desk sergeant who had spoken to the woman.

Ray was a cheerful officer whose mood seemed to improve each day he drew nearer to retirement. He greeted her with a grin that made his bright eyes almost disappear in the folds of his eyelids. After they had exchanged brief greetings, he told her Jeannie Hodgson had seen on the news that a body had been found and she was dreadfully afraid that her husband was the victim. Ray had reassured her that the police would look into the matter and contact her if they discovered anything about the dead man. Returning to her desk, Geraldine called the pathologist who agreed that John Hodgson looked very like the unidentified dead man. It was impossible to be absolutely certain; a person's appearance could change when they died, sometimes almost beyond recognition. If the resemblance was close enough for them to be fairly sure the cadaver was John Hodgson who had been missing for a couple of days, a DNA test would give immediate and conclusive proof.

With heavy steps, Geraldine made her way to the car. This was probably the worst part of her job, having to share the news of a violent death with the family of the deceased. A natural death from sickness or accident was traumatic enough, but to lose someone whose life had been deliberately snatched away by some evil nemesis or heedless psychopath must be almost unbearably painful. She wasn't sure if it was cruel to raise the spectre of death to the family when there remained an element of uncertainty over the identification of the deceased, but they had to follow up any lead that might help in determining who had been killed.

John Hodgson lived – or possibly had lived – in a side turning off the A1036, about a mile from where the body had been found. It was a neat little house with a colourful display of late-blooming autumn dahlias in the small front garden. Geraldine rang the bell and the door was opened almost at once by a small, thin woman who looked out expectantly. Her dark brown hair was tightly curled and everything about her appeared unnaturally rigid. She looked younger than the dead man, probably in her forties, and Geraldine hesitated, wondering whether she might actually be his widow. She could almost have been his daughter, but the Hodgsons had no children. Seeing Geraldine on the doorstep, the woman looked dismayed. Her head seemed to sink into her shoulders. Geraldine wondered if she was always so tense or if worry about her husband was affecting her posture.

She peered nervously up at Geraldine. 'Yes? Yes?' she stuttered, as though she was too stressed to remember more than that one word.

'Are you Mrs Jeannie Hodgson?'

'Yes.'

Geraldine introduced herself and the little woman drew in a sharp breath that hissed between her teeth, while her shoulders rose still higher. She grasped the edge of the front door so tightly her knuckles turned white.

'I'm Jeannie Hodgson,' she whispered. Her eyes grew round with apprehension, but she didn't pose the question that must have been tormenting her.

Jeannie and John, Geraldine thought with a sudden stab of sympathy. Perhaps they had laughed about their names and thought they were made for each other. She sighed and suggested they go inside and sit down.

'What do you want?' Jeannie replied without moving. She looked as though she might collapse if she let go of the door. 'Is it about John?'

'We think we may have found your husband,' Geraldine replied gently. 'I'd like to ask you a few questions. Shall we go inside?'

After a moment's hesitation, Jeannie inclined her head and led the way into a neat, old-fashioned living room comfortably furnished with leather armchairs and matching sofa. A collection of photographs were displayed above the fireplace and on several shelves. Almost all were of Jeannie and her husband, although a few were of scenic or iconic locations. At a glance, the Hodgsons appeared to have no close relations. Geraldine hoped there would be friends available to comfort Jeannie if it was indeed her husband currently lying in the mortuary.

'You said you may have found him which means he's dead, doesn't it?' Jeannie asked once they were both seated. Geraldine on an armchair, her reluctant hostess perched stiffly on the sofa. 'Dead or unable to talk,' she added in a whisper, her eyes round with apprehension.

The cushion next to Jeannie was worn and misshapen as though it was accustomed to bearing the weight of a heavy body. Perhaps she and her husband used to sit together on the sofa.

'Is he dead?' Jeannie repeated. She appeared to have regained control of herself, and stared dully at Geraldine.

'A body was discovered and we cannot discount the possibility that it is your husband's.'

Jeannie's expression didn't alter. Geraldine had the impression that she was holding herself very still for fear of breaking down.

'We are going to need a sample of your husband's DNA before we can be sure.'

On hearing this, Jeannie let out an involuntary wail and her head fell forward. With a visible effort she straightened up, her expression stony again. Only her eyes seemed to burn with grief. 'You want a sample of his DNA?' she murmured. 'That means he's dead, doesn't it?'

'We don't yet know if it's your husband,' Geraldine replied. 'I'm sorry to have to put you through this painful process when it's still only a possibility at this point, but we need to make sure.'

'I can't believe it. I can't believe it,' Jeannie replied. She stared ahead without seeming to register anything, as though afraid she would fall apart if she moved.

Gently, Geraldine asked for a toothbrush or a comb from which a trace of John's DNA could be extracted. Jeannie rose to her feet and glided silently out of the room. She was gone for some time. When she returned, only her reddened eyelids betrayed the fact that she had been crying. She was clutching a comb. Without a word Geraldine held out an evidence bag and nodded at Jeannie to drop it in.

'You'll let me know, won't you?' Jeannie murmured. 'It might not be him. He might have had an accident, or lost his memory, or...' Her voice petered out into a half-suppressed sob.

'Is there anyone who can keep you company while you're waiting?' Geraldine enquired before taking her leave. 'This is a difficult situation to cope with all on your own.'

Jeannie shook her head. 'I don't want to worry anyone

unnecessarily,' she replied. 'I'd rather know for sure before I talk about it. I think I'll just wait.'

Having promised to contact Jeannie the minute she had heard from the forensic team, Geraldine left. There was nothing she could do for Jeannie but confirm the identity of the body as quickly as possible.

'Don't worry,' she said to Jeannie, turning to address her on the doorstep. 'We'll be in touch very soon.'

Jeannie nodded uncertainly and let out a tiny whimper as she closed the door.

9

WHILE THEY WERE WAITING for confirmation of the identity of the dead man, Geraldine took a team to the bank where John Hodgson had worked to see what they could find out from his colleagues. In the unlikely event that he was not now lying in the mortuary, he was nevertheless missing and his whereabouts needed to be investigated. The branch of the bank where John had worked had been closed for the morning while the police team spoke to the staff. They all looked appropriately sombre, but no one appeared to be particularly upset. Reading through the statements, Geraldine had the impression that a rumour must have been circulating about the future of the branch now that the manager had gone. Most of the people working there seemed to be more concerned about their jobs than about what had happened to John.

Geraldine decided to question the deputy bank manager herself. Aidan Barnet was a small sandy-haired man who looked too young to be acting manager of the branch. He scurried over and led her into a small, neat office where he invited her to take a seat. Smoothing invisible creases in the jacket of his old-fashioned pinstriped suit, he stared at her with piercing green eyes, a resolute smile failing to hide his nerves.

'You're here about John, aren't you?' he enquired, raising a delicate white hand to his lips as if trying to control his quavering voice.

Geraldine nodded. 'Yes, that's correct. He's been reported missing and we're looking into his disappearance.'

The deputy manager opened his hands in an expansive gesture. 'If there's anything I can do to assist your investigation, anything at all, don't hesitate to let me know. Although I'm not sure what more I can do,' he added plaintively. 'I've been rather thrown in at the deep end since he went missing and it's been mayhem here. I mean, we have our procedures, but everyone's all over the place. People are saying he was mugged and fought back. That would be just like John. He didn't take shit from anyone. You know he used to box when he was younger?' He shook his head morosely. 'You wouldn't think anyone could get the better of him in a physical confrontation. I dare say that's what he thought. I suppose that's what got him killed?'

Geraldine remembered what Jonah had said about the victim's muscle turning to fat. That description fitted an older man who had boxed in his youth.

'We're investigating a possible suspicious death, but we haven't yet received confirmation of the identity of the victim.'

'Well, whoever it is, I hope you catch whoever did it and see them convicted for murder. I know everyone's saying he was mugged, but that's still murder even if it wasn't planned, isn't it? I mean, he's still dead and someone killed him.'

'What makes you think he was the victim of a mugging?' Geraldine asked, concealing her dismay.

It was increasingly difficult to keep anything from the public, even for a few days, while the police were still sifting through evidence and not yet ready to make a statement.

Aidan shrugged. 'It's not just me. It's what everyone seems to think. It's all over everywhere. Check the local residents' pages on social media,' he added earnestly. 'I suppose someone saw something about it on the local news and now everyone here's talking about it and posting online. You can't expect people not to be interested in something like this,' he added with a slightly defensive air that made Geraldine suspect he had played a part in spreading the rumour.

She nodded. 'I can imagine,' she murmured, doing her best to conceal her frustration.

Once one local reporter discovered a man had apparently been killed by a mugger, the media would go into a frenzy. Headlines like: 'Mugged to Death' and 'Violence on the Streets' would be posted regularly, followed by polemics against the police, the council and anyone else in any position of authority. 'What are the police doing about it?' the reporters would demand. 'How many more murders will it take before action is taken?'

Despite his expressions of concern about his manager's disappearance, Aidan had no information that was likely help the police.

'I hope you catch whoever did it,' he said as Geraldine took her leave.

That refrain was repeated by everyone working at the bank. It seemed to be all some of them had to say. In the car on the way back to the police station, Geraldine and Sam discussed their morning's work which, in Sam's opinion, had been a complete waste of time. No one he had spoken to had anything to add to what the police already knew, and most of the employees at the bank had merely parroted what they had heard or seen online or in the media.

Sam agreed with Aidan. 'There's no doubt about it,' he said firmly. 'It has to be a murder charge. All this talk about a mugging going wrong is just a distraction. If someone is violently attacked and killed, then it's murder, whether the attacker set out to kill the victim or not. Hodgson was fatally stabbed, for Christ's sake. He was attacked with a knife and stabbed to death. How is that anything but murder?'

'No one's going to argue with you about that, Sam, but we're not the judge and jury. Our job is to find out who's responsible and make sure they stand trial.'

'For murder.'

Geraldine nodded. 'Yes, that's almost certainly going to be the charge, but it has to stick. What we need to do is not only find the killer, but gather enough evidence to guarantee a conviction. The case has to be watertight so no defence counsel, however crafty, can get the suspect off. Believe me, there's nothing more galling than seeing a villain you know for a fact is guilty walk free on account of some legal technicality. It happens more often than you might think. So let's have less sounding-off and more solid detective work. Everything we do has to be strictly by the book. There's no room for cutting corners or making assumptions, however reliable or obvious they seem. Every detail of the case has to be corroborated with irrefutable evidence. Remember, if we do a poor job, or fail to close a single loophole, a killer could walk free. We can't let that happen.'

Back at the police station, Geraldine sat down at her desk and read through the answers the bank employees had given to a standard set of questions. She studied them closely and, out of all the reports, only one small point struck her. It was a detail so trifling she almost failed to notice it. She thought it was probably of no consequence but, having noticed it, she decided to follow it up. Years of experience had taught her there was no way of knowing whether a seemingly trivial remark might prove unexpectedly significant. More than once she had worked on a case where a chance remark had resulted in a lead that ended up solving the case. So noticing that one of the staff at the bank had mentioned in passing that she thought the manager had seemed slightly distracted recently, Geraldine decided to find out whether anything lay behind that remark. Reading the notes again, she saw that the employee had said the manager had possibly been depressed. Geraldine summoned the constable who had questioned that particular bank employee to see if she could add anything to her report.

'Did you ask her to explain what she meant when she said the manager was distracted? Did she say what he was distracted about or why she thought he was depressed?'

The constable shrugged, but she looked anxious and licked her lips nervously. 'I asked her if she had anything to add but she said she hadn't and she said it wasn't important. She didn't seem comfortable talking about her boss, so I didn't think it appropriate to press her,' she added defensively. 'It's not like she was a suspect or had witnessed a crime.'

Geraldine was tempted to reprimand her colleague for dismissing the matter so lightly, but the constable hadn't really done anything wrong. Letting her go, Geraldine checked on the bank clerk. Close to retirement, Eileen Simms had been employed at the bank for nearly nine years, during six of which John Hodgson had been the branch manager. Having worked at the same branch for some time, Eileen and John might have known one another quite well. Geraldine decided to speak to her and find out what else she could tell them about the missing manager.

'Leaving no stone unturned,' Geraldine's colleague, Ariadne, said with a faint smile, when Geraldine explained why she wanted to speak to Eileen.

Geraldine nodded. She was privately pleased with her reputation for being thorough in her investigations.

'No stone unturned,' she agreed as she hurried away.

She knew she was probably being paranoid, as well as arrogant, in refusing to rely on a colleague's report. But, ultimately, tracking down every possible scrap of evidence was all that mattered. If there was a detail that the constable had failed to uncover, Geraldine was determined to find it.

10

DANIEL BRUSHED HIS HAIR off his forehead with the back of his hand. His long fringe flopped forward again as he leaned over to smile lazily at the woman who was lying beside him. Gazing adoringly up at him from her comfortable nest of crumpled sheets, she reached out and stroked his cheek with one manicured finger. At the same time, she wriggled her hips and let out a low moan of contentment through pursed lips. Although he judged her mannerisms affected, it soothed his battered ego to be regarded with such devotion after he had been rejected by a series of younger women. For some unfathomable reason, he never had much luck with women his own age. He was only thirty, yet all of his once-close circle of friends were settled with long-term girlfriends or wives and no longer interested in going out as a group of lads. Some were even fathers. While the thought of shouldering such responsibility terrified Daniel, he envied them their steady relationships. Unaware of his feelings, his friends would goad him. 'Time you got yourself a partner,' they would tell him. 'You can't play the field forever.' Their banter was kindly meant, but he would squirm inwardly as he protested that they were all too young to be hitched.

Despite the care he took over his appearance, regularly working out and watching his diet, romance seemed to elude him. He knew he was reasonably good-looking, with fair hair, straight nose, chiselled chin and blue eyes. Not only that, but he had a steady job with a decent salary and prospects for promotion to area sales manager. All things considered, he was as eligible as the next man and more of a catch than most, yet all the women he approached seemed to be either in relationships or else just not interested in him. He had begun to wonder whether he came across as desperate. His luck had finally changed when he had bumped into a woman who had slipped into his life without any fuss and was now eagerly sharing his bed. Technically, it wasn't his bed; she insisted they meet in anonymous hotel rooms. He didn't object. It saved having to keep his lodgings tidy.

At first, he had looked forward to their clandestine trysts. He knew she was only being stealthy because she didn't want her husband to find out about their affair. Nevertheless, there was something exhilarating about the secrecy of their encounters that seemed to add an additional frisson of excitement to the liaison. The thrill of the risk soon palled, not least because he didn't really care one way or the other if their affair was discovered. She was the one who insisted her husband must not find out and, seeing as she paid for the room, he was content to accept her conditions. Overnight, she had waved away his loneliness like a fairy godmother. When he had mentioned this to her, she had scowled.

'Less of the mother,' she had muttered petulantly, turning her head away from him.

He had laughed at her for being so sensitive and told her it made no difference to him if she was twice his age, he still found her beautiful.

'I'm nowhere near twice your age,' she had retorted peevishly.

She was right. There was actually only seventeen years between them for four months of the year, as she had pointed out, sounding a little aggrieved, as though it was his fault she was older than him. The age difference didn't worry him, but she was clearly uncomfortable with it, so he hadn't mentioned it again. If he was honest, he could understand why it might bother her. She was fine for now, but in three years' time she would hit a landmark birthday. When he was in his mid-thirties would he want to be screwing around with a woman of fifty? When he was forty, she would be getting on for sixty. She was nearly the same age as his mother, but he pushed that thought to the back of his mind because it felt weird. Besides, anything could happen and it was hardly likely their affair would keep going for much longer.

He realised he would probably be the one to end it, unless she became anxious that her husband would discover her infidelity. At first gratifying, after a while her enthusiasm in bed started to make him feel self-conscious.

'I never understood why people make such a fuss about sex until I met you,' she told him, fluttering her eyelashes and pouting in what he could only assume was an attempt to look seductive. 'You really are a sex god.'

'I'm really not,' he had demurred awkwardly, wishing she would stop being so crass in her flattery. Whatever else he might be, he knew he couldn't claim to be a sex god.

Still, it was gratifying to be so admired, even when her adoration made him cringe. *Poor thing*, he thought, *she really has been starved of affection in her marriage.* If she was cheating on her husband, that was her responsibility, not his. Far from behaving badly, he told himself, he was doing a good deed, giving the poor woman some crumbs of comfort in her miserable life. Everyone deserved some attention and, really, what harm was he doing? It was hardly his fault if she was besotted with him. Could he help it if she found him irresistible? Buoyed up with a newfound confidence, he was already looking around for a more serious relationship with someone closer to his own age. He would wait until he found a proper girlfriend, someone he might potentially settle down with, before telling his current flame it was over between them. He wasn't cruel. He would let her down gently. But when the time came, he would be resolute. Relationships ended all the time. No amount of pleading or arguing would sway him. In the meantime, he was content to let things drift along as they were until he found her replacement. He already had his eye on someone.

Disentangling himself from her limbs, he wriggled away and sat up, but she slapped her hand on his chest and pushed him down against the pillow again. She was giggling, but he no longer found her demonstrations of affection entertaining. Pushing her firmly aside, he scrambled out of bed before she could grab hold of him again and stop him.

'No!' She pouted. 'Where are you going?' He couldn't tell if she was genuinely upset or putting on a performance for his benefit. Either way, it was annoying.

'I have to get back to work,' he said, reaching for his clothes.

'Don't go yet.'

She flung the covers aside to reveal her naked body, spread-eagled on the sheet. As though daring him to resist, she slowly opened her legs and began touching herself, moaning softly. Her head was thrown back against the pillow and her eyes appeared to be closed, but he was almost sure they were open a fraction so she could watch him.

He stood up and pulled on his trousers. Once, he might have been swayed by her cajoling, but she had enticed him so many times he had become immune to her antics.

'Stay with me,' she pleaded. Her belly was nearly as white as the sheet, while her arms and shoulders and legs were tanned from a recent holiday with her husband. The reminder that she was another man's wife hardened his resolve to leave. Far from seducing him, she was beginning to repulse him.

'My lunch hour is over,' he said curtly.

'Can't you take a longer break? You work too hard,' she wheedled, rolling over on to her side and patting the space on the bed beside her.

He wanted to tell her it was all over between them and he was going to walk away from her forever. Instead, he heard himself insist cravenly that it could cost him his job if he was late again.

His boss was a clock-watcher and punctuality wasn't one of Daniel's strong points.

'You won't need to be patient for much longer,' she said, half sitting up in bed and leaning on one elbow. In that position her belly looked flabby and he tried not to stare at it. 'I've got a plan. You'll soon be telling that boss of yours where he can stick his job.'

'I don't know what you mean.'

'You don't need to know,' she replied. 'But I can promise you we won't be meeting in secret for much longer. I have plans for us, my love. Just wait and see.' She fell back on the bed, laughing.

Muttering to himself that he didn't have time for this nonsense, he left. The sound of her laughter cut off abruptly as he closed the door firmly behind him.

11

RETURNING TO THE BANK, Geraldine asked to speak to the employee who had given a slightly ambiguous response when questioned about the missing manager. She was taken to a small meeting room where she waited impatiently for Eileen to appear. After a short delay, she was joined by a woman who sat down abruptly without uttering a word. Eileen had straight grey hair which she wore down to her shoulders. Pursing crimson lips, she peered sternly at Geraldine through black-framed glasses.

Geraldine introduced herself and confirmed that she was speaking to Eileen Simms.

'That's correct,' the woman barked, staring at Geraldine with a disapproving expression. 'I hope this won't take long,' she added. 'We're very busy at the moment, with everything that's been going on.' She sounded as though she was accusing Geraldine of having caused the problems the branch was experiencing. 'All these interruptions and interviews are making life even more difficult for us, as though we're not facing enough problems as it is with Mr Hodgson going off so suddenly.' While she was voicing her complaint against the police enquiries, Geraldine noticed a tiny smear of crimson lipstick on her upper front teeth.

Without any further preamble, Geraldine asked her to explain what she had meant by her remarks concerning her missing colleague's state of mind. At first, Eileen prevaricated. Insisting that she hadn't been implying anything at all, she blustered and claimed she had no idea what Geraldine was talking about, but Geraldine pressed her to clarify her comment.

'You told my colleague you thought John might have been depressed,' she reminded Eileen.

'Not exactly,' Eileen replied, dropping her gaze but still contriving to look belligerent. 'Certainly he didn't strike me as depressed. Not so as anyone might worry about him.' She hesitated before adding that he had just seemed a bit forgetful recently. 'It wasn't like him at all. I mean, he was always so precise and pedantic about everything, only for the last month or so he'd started to seem almost slapdash. It wasn't as if he didn't care about the work, but more as though he had something else on his mind. And he became quite tetchy, which also wasn't like him at all. I wondered if he was worried about something. But it was only an impression I had and I could be completely wrong. I wouldn't want you to quote me on it and if you ask me to make another statement, I'd really prefer not to.' She sighed. 'Honestly, I wish I'd never mentioned it at all. If I'd known it was going to cause such a fuss, I would have kept my mouth shut. I'm sure it's nothing, really. Only, when you've worked with someone for years, you notice these things.'

'And I'm sure you're very observant,' Geraldine said, hoping her praise didn't sound insincere as she tried to encourage Eileen to talk. 'Can you be more specific about these things you noticed?'

But Eileen would not be drawn, only repeating that she had thought John had seemed preoccupied.

'Were you aware of anything that might have prompted his unexpected preoccupation?' Geraldine enquired, choosing her words with care.

Eileen hesitated before replying that she wasn't aware of any problems John might have been experiencing. Geraldine pressed her again, pointing out that it would only help the missing man if the police were fully apprised of his state of mind before he disappeared. Eventually Eileen admitted that the change in his attitude might have coincided with one of her other colleagues leaving the bank.

'I'm not saying anything was going on between them,' she added quickly.

Once again, Geraldine requested clarification. 'By "anything going on", are you suggesting they might have been having an affair?'

'I never said that,' Eileen replied quickly, pursing her lips waspishly as though she disapproved of the idea that Geraldine had put forward.

Geraldine asked for the other woman's name and whether Eileen knew why she had left the bank.

'You'd have to ask her that,' Eileen replied. 'I've no idea what was going on between them, if anything, and if I knew I wouldn't want to say. I can tell you she was a flirty blonde, if you know what I mean, but I'm not one to gossip.'

Geraldine kept her own counsel about that.

'And now,' Eileen went on, rising decisively to her feet, 'if you've quite finished, I really do need to get back to work.'

A little research disclosed that a young blonde bank cashier named Lily Transom had quit her post at the bank two months earlier. No one had yet questioned her about any relationship she might have had with John Hodgson. Geraldine traced her to another branch of the bank where she had a similar post, this time in Liverpool. She didn't appear to have been promoted, suggesting there might been a reason for her wanting to leave John's branch of the bank in York. Geraldine called the Liverpool branch and asked to speak to her and a moment later a young woman came to the phone.

'Hello, this is Lily,' she said. 'Who am I speaking to?'

Geraldine explained the reason for her call.

'I don't understand. Who did you say you're calling about?'

Geraldine went over the situation again.

'You're saying the manager from the York branch is missing?' Lily asked when she finally grasped what Geraldine was talking about. 'I'm sorry, when you said John Hodgson, I didn't immediately twig who you were referring to. He was the manager at York when I was there, but we didn't have much direct contact.'

This did not sound like a woman who had been having an affair with John Hodgson, but Geraldine wondered if Lily was covering up how close she and John had been. She enquired why the bank cashier had requested a transfer to Liverpool.

'Oh, I put in my request for a transfer about a year ago,' Lily explained, readily enough. 'It's taken ages, but these things always do.'

'Why did you want to leave York?'

'It's my husband's job. He moved to Liverpool ten months ago. It's a huge promotion for him,' she added cheerfully. 'Anyway, we decided the best thing was for us to up sticks and move to Liverpool and that took ages. But we're all sorted now, with both of us living and working in Liverpool, so it was worth it in the end. I'm sorry, why do you want to know?'

Cautiously Geraldine enquired how well Lily had known John Hodgson.

Lily hesitated. 'Well, I knew him, of course, while I was working in York.'

'Were you close?'

There was a slight pause before Lily answered and Geraldine could almost hear the young woman frowning at the other end of the line. 'Close? I'm not sure what you mean by that. We worked in the same branch of the bank so we had dealings with one another from time to time, just in passing, you know. I'm not sure I ever really had a conversation with him, but he seemed like a nice man. I don't have any complaints against him, if that's what you're asking. There was never anything improper about the way he behaved towards me and I never heard anyone else complaining about him. Honestly, I hardly knew him. There are other people who would be better placed to help you. I mean, if you're looking for people who actually knew him and might be able to tell you something about him, I think Eileen would be your best bet. Have you spoken to her? Eileen Simms. She was his right hand. And there was Aidan, the deputy manager. I'm sure they'd both want to help you. But I'm not sure what I can tell you that you won't already know. As far as I was aware, he was happily married. At least, I know he was married. I couldn't really tell you anything about his personal life. Like I said, we never really spoke much. I hope you find him.'

Thanking Lily for her help, Geraldine ended the call. She put a cross against Lily's name on her list, before thoughtfully adding a question mark after Eileen's name. She wondered whether Eileen had really been impatient to return to work or if she had been eager to avoid uncomfortable questions.

12

GERALDINE WAS STRUGGLING TO feel positive; as the senior investigating officer on the case, she was frustrated by their lack of progress. She really needed to work out a clear plan, but her mind was filled with so many different potential leads it was difficult to decide what to prioritise. Ariadne was encouraging, but her support didn't help.

'We need a definite lead, not platitudes,' Geraldine grumbled. 'I'm sorry, I don't mean to sound harsh. I know you're right and we have to be patient, but we just seem to be going round in circles.'

Later that afternoon, Ray called Geraldine from the front desk again.

'What's up?' she asked.

'There's a young lady here asking to speak to whoever's in charge of the street mugging case. She says she might know the victim.'

'She knows something about what happened to John Hodgson?'

'Well, no,' Ray replied, sounding puzzled. Geraldine had a mental image of him scratching his square head. 'That's not exactly what she's saying. I think you'd better see her.' He paused and lowered his voice. 'She's a very *young* lady.'

Heaving a sigh, Geraldine closed the report she was rereading and headed towards the front desk. Ray met her eye and nodded at the row of chairs facing the reception window where a girl of about sixteen was seated, twiddling her fingers and gazing nervously around. Even from a few feet away, Geraldine could

71

see the girl's hair had been badly bleached until it resembled dirty yellow wool and her dark eyes peered out from thick rings of smudged black eyeliner. If she hadn't looked so wretched, her appearance would have bordered on comical. As Geraldine approached her, she saw that the girl was not as old as she had at first appeared, and was possibly as young as thirteen. Her shoes were scuffed and her school uniform looked shabby. She gave the appearance of a child who had been neglected but Geraldine reserved judgement, aware that teenagers sometimes chose to look scruffy against their parents' wishes.

Greeting the girl with a friendly smile, Geraldine sat beside her and introduced herself. 'I understand you asked to speak to me?'

The girl looked up and stopped fidgeting with a loose thread on her skirt. 'Are you in charge here?' she demanded, sounding almost aggressive.

Realising the girl was frightened, Geraldine answered gently. 'I'm part of a team working on the investigation into a recent tragedy.'

'You mean the man who was killed?' the girl said. 'The one who was stabbed?'

Geraldine nodded. Wondering where this was leading, she asked the girl's name, and whether her parents or her guardian knew she was there. The girl muttered that she was called Daisy. She lived with her mother and no, her mother didn't know she was there. She didn't want her mother there as a chaperone while she was telling the police what she knew. Geraldine asked her age. Daisy prevaricated and blustered for a moment before admitting she was fourteen.

'I'm afraid I can't speak to you without—' Geraldine began, but the girl interrupted her.

'I can tell you his name. The man who was killed.'

Geraldine was keen to hear what she would say next, but after her initial outburst, the girl hung her head and was silent.

'Don't you want to know?' Daisy asked at last when Geraldine continued to sit patiently waiting for her to speak.

Cautiously Geraldine pointed out that she wasn't able to question a girl of Daisy's age without a responsible adult present.

'Aren't you responsible?'

'It means an adult who is responsible for you,' Geraldine explained, afraid she would scare Daisy away before she revealed what was on her mind. It was possible she had useful information to share.

Daisy shrugged. 'You don't have to question me,' she pointed out. 'I could just tell you. That's what I came here to do. You could just listen.' She swore. 'Why do adults never listen?'

Geraldine hesitated. Having attended training sessions on how to question underage witnesses sensitively, she was aware that she ought not to continue without contacting Daisy's mother or another appropriate adult. At the same time, she had the impression that Daisy had come to the police station impulsively and she might decide to leave on another whim. As Geraldine tried to decide what to do, Daisy cleared her throat theatrically.

'It's my father,' she blurted out. 'Peter Selby. He's the man you found. He hasn't been home since Monday, so it's obviously him. It's the second time this has happened to him.'

Geraldine was careful not to react, aware that Monday was the day the unidentified victim had been killed. What Daisy had said didn't make sense and she waited to hear what else the girl would say.

'I mean,' Daisy added sullenly, 'he was almost mugged once before, just a few days ago.'

'What do you mean, he was almost mugged?' Geraldine couldn't help asking.

'That's what he told my mother. Not me, he wouldn't talk to me, not about anything important, anyway,' she said sourly. 'But I heard them talking about it in the kitchen. They didn't know I was listening. He said he had been nearly mugged but the attacker ran off. And now he's gone. Vanished.'

'Do you mean you haven't seen your father since Monday?'

'I just said that.'

'Where's your mother?'

'At home,' Daisy replied. 'So, you see, that man who was mugged, I know who he is. Who he was, I mean. He's my father. It's got to be him. Whoever killed him, they came back for him after the first time to make sure he couldn't identify them.'

Geraldine decided to drive Daisy home and speak to her mother. Daisy went with her readily enough, although she was disappointed to discover they wouldn't be travelling in a police car. She gave Geraldine her address and they drove to a new estate in Huntington.

'This is it,' Daisy called out as they were about to drive past a smart red-brick house.

They drew up on the street as there were two cars parked on the drive outside the double garage attached to the house. Daisy led the way along a wide curved driveway, bordered by high hedges. The house appeared to be well maintained and Geraldine wondered at Daisy's neglected appearance in the face of her parents' ostentatious affluence. She had little time to speculate before the front door was opened by a tall elegant woman of around forty whose eyes darted anxiously from Geraldine to Daisy.

'Where have you been?' she cried out. 'Do you know how late it is? I've been going out of my mind with worry. Why didn't you answer your phone?'

'It's hardly late,' Daisy scoffed. 'Why do you make a drama out of everything? I'm not a child.'

'You shouldn't stay out so late without at least letting me know where you are.'

'It's hardly late,' Daisy repeated sullenly.

As the exchange seemed to be escalating into a row, Geraldine stepped forward and introduced herself.

'Oh my God,' the woman murmured. Looking aghast, she spun round to face Daisy. 'What have you done?'

'Typical,' Daisy protested. 'My mother always thinks the worst of me. I've done what you should have done two days ago.'

'Shall we go inside?' Geraldine suggested.

As they went in, Daisy turned to glare at her mother before running upstairs. With an apologetic shrug, Christine led Geraldine across a hallway into a bright, spacious living room at the front of the house. It had a large bay window looking out on the garden at the front and an impressive gas fireplace set in an ornate tiled surround. At the far end of the room was a dining area from which the back garden was visible through patio doors. Resisting an impulse to admire the house, Geraldine accepted an invitation to sit down, and proceeded swiftly to the reason for her visit.

'Daisy told us her father's not been home since Monday?'

Christine looked down, but not before Geraldine had glimpsed her apprehensive expression. 'So this isn't about Daisy?' she asked, rapidly recovering her composure and muttering her thanks to Geraldine for bringing her daughter home. 'I hope she hasn't been too much trouble. She can be – that is, her behaviour can be challenging.'

Geraldine explained that Daisy had gone to the police station to report her father was missing.

Christine confirmed that her husband hadn't been home for three days.

'You haven't reported him missing yourself?' Geraldine enquired. 'Why is that?'

'I thought he'd be back,' Christine answered a little too smoothly. 'I thought maybe he had a work conference or something and I'd forgotten.'

'You didn't try to contact him?'

Christine gave a helpless shrug. 'Of course I tried, but he wasn't answering his phone. He usually turns it off or silences it when he's working, or he switches it to airplane mode when he's at a conference. I just thought he was working,' she concluded lamely, as though even she didn't believe the words coming out of her mouth.

'Does he often go away without telling you?'

'No, but like I said, I thought he'd probably told me and I'd forgotten.'

'Do you often forget things?'

'No more than anyone else.'

'How often does he go away?'

'Not often,' Christine replied.

'What made you assume he was at a conference?'

'I couldn't think where else he would be.'

'What does he do?'

'He's an estate agent. He works for a nationwide chain,' Christine replied, mentioning the name of a large estate agency.

'How often does he go away to conferences?'

'Not often. Once a year, usually. I thought it was odd, so I phoned all the local hospitals, in case he'd had an accident, but no one had any record of him being brought in. I was going to call the police station to report him missing if he didn't turn up soon.' She shrugged. 'I didn't really know what to do. Nothing like this has ever happened before,' she added, unaware that she was now contradicting herself. 'I'm sure everything's okay,' she insisted, forcing a smile. 'That is, I'm sure nothing terrible has happened to my husband. I'd know if it had.' She paused before adding in a low voice that he wasn't the sort of person to whom bad things happened.

Geraldine didn't point out that Christine's daughter didn't appear to share her optimism, nor did she mention that terrible things happened to the most unlikely people, sometimes in the most unexpected ways. Having asked for Peter's toothbrush, which Christine handed over without demur, Geraldine made a note of Peter's approximate height and build and, with a slightly

SILENT TIES

blurry picture of him in her pocket, she left. An image of Daisy's haunted face lingered in her mind, contrasting sharply with Christine's studied composure.

13

AT FIRST SHE WAS too exhilarated to relax. Alone in her room, she replayed what had happened in her mind, over and over and over again. It was like a drug. She couldn't stop thinking about it, not that she tried very hard. She wanted to dwell on her triumph. The more she thought about it, the more convinced she was that her actions had been positively heroic. Other people would accuse her of wrongdoing and tell her she had no right to mete out justice. But far from feeling ashamed of what she had done, she exulted in her newly discovered power. She had endured his persecution for too long and he deserved everything that had happened to him. If she hadn't put an end to it, she told with herself, he would almost certainly have gone on to abuse other vulnerable girls. That alone justified her actions.

Once the initial flush of elation had worn off, she became anxious. There were moments when she was so scared it was difficult to hide her feelings. During the day she had to force herself not to break down in front of other people. To confess would be weak and she was desperate to cling to her newfound strength. She had been a victim for long enough. It didn't help that she was awake most of the night. She was exhausted, but every time she closed her eyes and began to drift off, she saw his face. Sometimes he was leering at her, reaching out to grab her, while at other times he fixed his eyes on hers and called out to her to help him. They both knew that was never going to happen, not after what he had done to her.

When she finally managed to get to sleep, she was disturbed by weird dreams and woke feeling hot and sweaty. She could still feel the hard surface of the wall pressing against the back of her head as he pinioned her against it, his wet mouth on her lips, muffling any sound she made. In her nightmares she tried to scream, but she couldn't make a sound, while other people walked past, ignoring her plight. She wasn't sure why she was so agitated now it was all over and she knew he would never touch her again. It wasn't as though she had done anything wrong. On the contrary, she had only done what any right-thinking person would have done in her situation. If she had to blame herself for anything, it would be for waiting so long to fight back. The fact was, he'd had it coming, and she had nothing with which to reproach herself.

All the same, she determined to keep quiet about what had happened, even though he had deserved it. Defending herself with violence against a cruel monster might be morally acceptable, if not downright necessary, but she suspected other people might not see things the way she did. In fact, she had an uncomfortable feeling no one would openly agree with her point of view, even though they might secretly believe she had done the right thing. The world was so twisted, it was a wonder anyone stayed sane. People tolerated petty injustices for so long that in the end they lost the ability to distinguish between what was right and what was wrong. Life shouldn't be like that. There were times when you felt you had been pushed so far, you just had to retaliate. She wished the feeling of satisfaction at having eliminated the threat was permanent. Right now, it felt as though she was the one being punished and that wasn't fair.

She sighed and picked at the frayed edge of her sleeve. Her mother was always nagging her to stop finding loose threads and pulling them, but there was something reassuring about how easily the jumper came apart. That, at least, was something she could control. It was fun watching the stitches slip off.

Knowing that her mother would be vexed made it all the more enjoyable. The entire left cuff would soon vanish, leaving only a line of wool with tiny kinks in it at the edge of the knitted sleeve. Before long the sleeve of her shirt would be uncovered all the way up to her elbow. She could probably demolish the entire sleeve of her jumper in a few seconds with just one long tug, but she wanted to take her time and savour the sight of the yarn gradually unravelling. She pulled one more stitch undone. The jumper would soon be unwearable and she didn't care. She hated her school uniform. It was ugly and itchy. If her mother wanted her to wear it, her mother would just have to buy her a new jumper. She always bought second-hand anyway, as though her only daughter wasn't worth the cost of new uniform.

Remembering what she had done and the shocked expression on his face, she felt a bubble of laughter in her throat. It served him right. He would never do anything to upset her again. She unwound another row of knitting on her sleeve very slowly, stitch by individual stitch, and smiled to herself, knowing she was safe. Adults might think they could control every aspect of her life, but they were wrong. She had been browbeaten for long enough and now she was breaking free and taking control of her own destiny. She had begun and in future there would be no holding back. From now on, no one would ever bully her into submission again. She ought to be happy, but if anything she was even more miserable than before. The world was a horrible place and she hated it and everyone in it. Adults were constantly hectoring her without ever listening to what she had to say. It was *her* life, but no one ever bothered to ask her what she wanted to do. One day soon, all that would change, because she was only just beginning to fight back, but for now she would have to be content with knowing that they would never find out what she had done. Scowling, she pulled at another row of stitches on her sleeve.

From downstairs, she heard her mother calling, as if she actually expected Daisy to trot downstairs and sit at the table and eat her dinner like a good little girl. Swearing to herself, Daisy turned her music up and flung herself on her bed, alone with her momentous secret. There was no one in whom she could confide and, now that she was over the initial flush of success, her victory felt empty.

14

THE DETECTIVE CHIEF INSPECTOR gazed sternly around the assembled team who were waiting anxiously to hear that morning's update. As they all fell silent, she nodded and cleared her throat. As usual, she was immaculately dressed in a trouser suit that looked expensive. Rumour at the police station had it that her husband was a very highly paid executive for some global corporation, although no one seemed to know exactly what he did or who he worked for. As a rule, Binita appeared calm and well-groomed, but Geraldine felt there was something awkward about her demeanour that morning. She couldn't help noticing that the senior officer's hair looked slightly dishevelled, as though she had been running her fingers through it in exasperation, and her expression was frantic rather than composed.

Looking worried, she announced that she had summoned the team together to discuss the latest update on the victim. 'We have a match,' she said, sparking a ripple of excitement among her colleagues. 'We have received confirmation that the dead man is John Hodgson, the bank manager who's been missing since Monday, the day his unidentified body was discovered. He could have been the victim of a fatal mugging, although as yet we have no witnesses and no CCTV to substantiate that theory. Until we have more definitive evidence, we're treating this as a murder investigation.'

'Mugged or murdered,' Ariadne pointed out, 'it's still an unlawful killing.'

'It could have been a premeditated attack that was deliberately planned to look like a random mugging,' Geraldine added.

'That's what we need to find out,' Binita said. 'Now,' she fixed her penetrating stare on Geraldine, 'we need to inform his wife and see if she knows anything more than she's already told us about her husband's death. You questioned her about her reporting his disappearance, didn't you?'

Geraldine nodded, understanding that, not for the first time, it fell to her to share the news of a murder with the victim's family. She took Ariadne with her, not only to help support the widow, but also to observe Jeannie's reaction to the news. As they drove slowly to the side turning off Blossom Street where John had lived, Geraldine was silent, mulling over how to approach the task. Inside the neat house with its colourful front garden they would find a shocked and grieving innocent woman or a callous and calculating murderer. Aware that the truth about the widow might not be obvious, she rang the bell, determined to miss nothing. Jeannie came to the door almost at once. Her shoulders drooped and her hair, previously tightly curled, was unkempt, but her face was fully made up with thick foundation, mascara and eye shadow, and scarlet lipstick. She was dressed in a short black leather skirt and a low-cut tight white jumper that exposed a deep cleavage.

'I was just about to get my hair done,' Jeannie said, reaching up to pat her unruly curls.

Privately, Geraldine thought the looser curls suited Jeannie.

'We're going to have to ask you to wait for a moment,' Geraldine replied. 'There's something we need to tell you.'

'If it's about John, it'll have to wait,' Jeannie said a trifle sharply. 'My appointment's in ten minutes and I'm going to be late if I don't hurry.'

Geraldine blocked the doorway and gently insisted that Jeannie go inside and sit down.

'I really don't have time for this right now. Can you come back later?'

'I'm afraid this can't wait.'

'Oh dear,' Jeannie said, with a nervous smile. 'You make it all sound terribly serious.'

Given that her husband had been missing for three days, Geraldine found Jeannie's response rather surprising. Clearly she was in denial and blocking out all thoughts of what might have happened to John. With an impatient sigh, Jeannie turned and led the way inside.

'Very well,' she called out over her shoulder. 'But unless you can make this really quick, I'll have to phone my hairdresser and tell her I can't make my appointment. I really don't want to have to do that,' she added plaintively.

'There's no easy way to tell you this,' Geraldine began cautiously, once she had persuaded Jeannie to sit down on one of the armchairs in the old-fashioned living room. 'I'm afraid your husband was mugged early on Monday morning and he died from his injuries. He would have lost consciousness almost at once,' she added, parroting a standard phrase. 'He wouldn't have suffered.'

Actually, they had no way of knowing how much John had suffered or whether he had been aware of what was happening to him. Geraldine paused, observing Jeannie's reaction to the news. Jeannie sat motionless and dry-eyed, staring at Geraldine as though she didn't understand what she was saying.

'Is there someone who can come and sit with you?' Geraldine asked gently. 'Do you have a friend or a neighbour you can call on?'

'No, no, we won't tell anyone,' Jeannie replied, staring around with a wild expression. 'They don't need to know. No one needs to know. Let's just keep this between ourselves, shall we?' At which point her face crumpled and she dropped her head in her hands. 'What shall I do?' she wailed. 'What shall I do? I'll be all alone. How am I going to manage? Oh, why has this happened? Why? Why? I don't understand.'

Her shoulders shook but, with her head still in her hands, Geraldine couldn't see her face. She wondered whether Jeannie was genuinely shocked by the news or if she was hiding her face to conceal a very different reaction.

'I'm sorry, but I am going to have to ask you a few more questions,' she said after a few moments. 'I can come back later if you need some time to process the news. A family liaison officer will be with you shortly to support you. In the meantime, is there someone you would like to be with you?'

Jeannie shook her head. She dropped her hands and looked up. Her expression was blank and her eyes remained dry, but when she spoke her voice was trembling with emotion. Geraldine thought she sounded angry. It wasn't an unusual reaction for someone in Jeannie's situation.

'What good can that do?' she hissed. 'You just told me my husband's been murdered and all you can do is offer to send someone to sit with me as some kind of babysitter. I don't need anyone. Not now. Not unless you can bring him back to me.' She stood up. 'Now, if you don't mind,' she went on in a curiously clipped voice, 'I'd like you to leave my house.'

'We'd like to ask you a few questions before we go.'

'Oh, go on then, ask your questions if you must,' Jeannie replied, resuming her seat with an air of angry resignation. 'I can see I'm never going to get rid of you until you're satisfied. Although this is the last thing I need right now. I just want to be left alone.'

As it turned out, it didn't take long because it quickly became apparent that there was no point in trying to question Jeannie. She responded to every question with the flat statement that she had no idea.

'She had no idea where her husband was going when he was mugged. She had no idea who might have attacked him. She had no idea if he had any enemies. She had no idea if her husband had been worried about anything lately. She behaved like someone under caution replying "No comment" to every question,' Geraldine grumbled as they drove away.

'Was she hiding something, do you think?' Ariadne asked.

Geraldine shrugged. 'It's difficult to say. What do you think?'

'She was certainly in a hurry to get rid of us. I don't think that's entirely unreasonable, if you believe her when she said that nothing makes any difference to her now he's dead.'

'You'd think she'd want to help us find who did it.'

'I know, but if she believes it was a stranger, a chance mugger, then I suppose it's fair enough that she would think there's nothing she can say to help us trace the killer.'

Geraldine was still fretting about Jeannie when she reached home that evening. When Ian asked her about her day, she couldn't help venting her irritation.

'It's impossible to gauge what she was feeling,' she admitted. 'She struck me as a bit of an odd fish.'

Ian smiled grimly. 'There are a lot of them around,' he said.

Geraldine seized a cushion and swung it at him, laughing. 'Why are you looking at me?'

'If that's a new technique you're trying out for questioning suspects, I'm not sure it will get you the results you want,' Ian replied. Grabbing the cushion from her, he leaned over to kiss her.

'Well, I'm not sure you're right about that,' she laughed, putting her arms around him and pulling him closer. 'I'd say this was a pretty satisfactory result.'

15

THE FOLLOWING MORNING, GERALDINE stopped for a quick chat with Tom's childminder about the disturbed night he had passed. The childminder agreed that it was probably because he was teething and reassured Geraldine that she would keep an eye on him and call her if she was concerned. After that brief delay, Geraldine was held up in traffic and arrived at work ten minutes late to be instantly summoned by the detective chief inspector. Feeling a little aggrieved at the anticipated reprimand, she entered Binita's office preparing to defend herself. Binita's welcoming smile took her by surprise. Caught off guard, Geraldine hesitated.

'Come in,' Binita said, gesturing to Geraldine to take a seat. 'I've been reading the reports and want to hear how you feel the investigation is going, and in what direction you think we ought to be heading.'

'I appreciate you want to be kept up to speed about what's happening and it does all seem to be a bit of a muddle at the moment,' Geraldine admitted. 'But I think it's too early to do anything more than speculate.'

Binita nodded. 'Well, we're in the early stages and still gathering information.'

'There is one thing I wanted to raise with you,' Geraldine said. 'Peter Selby is still missing. It might be there's no crime to investigate, but his daughter claimed he told her he was almost mugged, didn't she?'

'You spoke to the Selbys' daughter, didn't you? What did you make of her statement?'

Geraldine thought for a few seconds, wondering whether she was in trouble for questioning an underage witness alone. 'She seemed overwrought. I had the impression she came here on impulse. I tried to set up a chaperone before questioning her, but she resisted that suggestion and became quite defiant. When I explained to her that we ought to have a responsible adult present before I could question her, she pointed out that I didn't have to question her at all as she had come here to tell me something and all I had to do was listen to her. I mean, what she said made sense, but she was definitely belligerent. I decided to let her have her say and tell me what was on her mind because I was afraid she might walk out at any moment, she was so jittery. I think she was quite possibly unreliable and I'm not sure we should lend too much credence to anything she said. All the same, I'm just wondering if it's a coincidence, these incidents being brought to our attention so close to one another. Is it possible John and Peter were victims of the same mugger?'

'We're talking about a fourteen-year-old girl whose father's allegedly disappeared. It's hardly surprising she was upset and she was quite possibly exaggerating what had happened with this near mugging of her father, which in any case sounds unlikely.' Binita suggested Geraldine see whether Christine was able to corroborate her daughter's claim that a mugger had approached Peter. 'He would presumably have told his wife as well as his daughter, if it's true.'

Geraldine pointed out that Daisy only knew about the alleged incident with her father because she had overheard him talking to Christine about it. Still, as far as they were aware, Peter had not actually been assaulted.

'You don't think hearing about the attack on John might have given Daisy the idea of reporting that her father had met a mugger?' Binita asked.

'I agree that a fourteen-year-old girl, disturbed by her father's disappearance, might well seize on any explanation that offered itself, rather than acknowledge that her father had abandoned the family. All the same, we ought to make sure there's nothing connecting the two men.'

Before setting off to speak to Christine, Geraldine joined Ariadne in the canteen for a coffee. As they sat down, she admitted she was finding the case a little too confusing for comfort. It was possibly conflating unconnected incidents, but one man had allegedly been nearly attacked before he disappeared, while another man had been fatally stabbed.

'Is it a coincidence? Could the two events be completely unrelated?' she asked Ariadne. 'I told the DCI we should look for a connection between John and Peter. Are we looking for one violent individual picking on random victims? A crazed addict or a psychopath? Or is this something more targeted? What do you think?'

She blew the froth on her cappuccino to one side and took a sip.

'The two are probably unrelated,' Ariadne replied, speaking slowly and clearly considering her response. 'But I agree it's a bit of a coincidence, Daisy mentioning that her father was nearly attacked just around the time when John Hodgson actually *was* killed. I mean, it seems a bit odd that both incidents happened on Monday morning.'

'One attack and one suspected attempt,' Geraldine corrected her. 'It's possible the news about the attack on John Hodgson gave Daisy the idea and her father was never really threatened with a knife at all.' She sighed. 'It's a bit of a mess, isn't it? Let's hope Christine Selby can shed some light on Daisy's claim about her father's mystery assailant.'

'At least we've identified the dead man,' Ariadne said. 'I dare say Peter Selby will show up oblivious to the furore and we'll discover that nothing untoward went on there at all. Didn't his wife say he might have just gone to a work conference or something? And the story his daughter spun about him nearly being attacked will probably turn out to be a bit of teenage fantasy inspired by a news item about John Hodgson.'

Geraldine nodded. She wished she could be as sanguine about Peter and his family as her friend was, but something about Daisy had struck her as unsettling although she couldn't say what it was. She tried to dismiss it as normal erratic behaviour from a teenage girl, but something about Daisy seemed off. As she drove back to the smart house in Drakes Close in Huntington, she wondered about the relationship between Christine and Daisy. Finally, she decided it must be the contrast between the well-groomed mother and shabbily turned-out daughter that had made her think something was out of kilter in the household. She reminded herself of something her own sister was fond of saying, that teenagers were 'a law unto themselves'. Daisy had certainly struck her as an independent-minded young person. Probably Christine had tried and failed to persuade Daisy to pay more attention to her appearance. The girl probably did, in her own way, as she had taken the trouble to dye her hair, however badly, and smear horrendous make-up on her eyes. With a sigh, Geraldine decided to put the girl with her haunted face out of her mind and focus on what Christine had to say about her missing husband.

As Geraldine was leaving the police station, they received notification that Peter Selby banked at the branch that had been managed by John Hodgson. That meant it was possible the two men had met, possibly more than once. They might even have known one another, but with John dead and Peter missing, neither of them could be asked about any relationship they might have had. The police would have to find another way to investigate what, if anything, had happened between John and Peter. Ariadne went to the bank to ask Eileen how often Peter had visited the branch in person and whether he had ever had a meeting with the manager. A constable accompanied her, tasked with requesting access to the bank security film which might give some indication of how often Peter had visited the branch while John was there. Meanwhile, Geraldine went to have another word with Christine. She was determined to find out if Peter's wife was concealing information about John and Peter. Even if Christine wasn't deliberately hiding anything, she might unknowingly be aware of something that would help them. If so, it was Geraldine's job to discover that missing piece of information. Any lead would be welcome because, at the moment, the investigation was floundering.

16

STILL PONDERING WHAT TO say to Christine, Geraldine drove out to Huntington and pulled up near the Selbys' house in Drakes Close. The weather was mild and she wriggled out of her jacket and dropped it on the back seat before climbing out of the car and making her way to the house. When she rang the bell, the door was opened almost at once, as though Christine had been expecting someone to call. Geraldine wondered if she had been waiting for Peter to turn up, although she looked anything but optimistic. She had clearly been crying, but now her bloodshot eyes held a bleakness that suggested she had given up hope that her husband might still be alive. When she saw who was on the doorstep she flinched slightly before recovering her self-control and she hesitated briefly when Geraldine suggested they go inside. As soon as the front door closed behind them, Christine's composure shattered. Her stony expression fragmented and she stared at Geraldine eagerly. Her lips quivered and her voice wobbled as she snapped out a series of questions.

'What is it? Do you have any news? Is it him? Is Peter dead?' A flicker of alarm flashed in her eyes as she asked Geraldine to confirm that her husband's body had been found, but Geraldine thought she looked terrified, rather than upset.

'I'm afraid we don't have any news of your husband,' Geraldine replied gently.

'But the body—' Christine stammered. 'You took his toothbrush, so you must have thought it was him. It must have been him. Where else could he be?' She turned away and covered her face with her hands, although she didn't appear to be crying. Geraldine waited. After a few moments, Christine turned to look at her again. Her eyes were dry. 'So what happens now?' she asked. 'If that's not him, where is he? When are you going to find him? I don't understand what's going on. I know you've found him, so why can't I see him?'

Geraldine insisted they go to the living room and sit down before they continued. Once they were settled, she watched Christine closely as she asked her whether she recognised the name John Hodgson. Looking faintly puzzled, Christine shook her head.

'John Hodgson?' she echoed, frowning. 'What's he got to do with Peter? Is he – did he kill him? Is that the man who attacked him?'

'We don't know where your husband is,' Geraldine repeated patiently.

'But where is he?' Christine burst out. 'Tell me he hasn't been killed.'

'Please,' Geraldine replied, 'we'll be done much more quickly if you just answer my questions. I'd like you to think carefully before answering. Does the name John Hodgson mean anything to you?'

Christine shook her head helplessly, saying that she had never heard the name before. Geraldine continued to watch her thoughtfully. Christine appeared convinced that the body identified as John Hodgson had belonged to her husband. Geraldine understood the bewildered woman was desperate to discover a definitive answer to the mystery of her husband's disappearance. Perhaps anything would be preferable to the uncertainty she had been enduring since his disappearance four days earlier. But it seemed neither of them could give the other the information they needed to hear.

'Is this John Hodgson the dead man whose identity you were looking for?' Christine asked looking bemused. 'I don't understand what that's got to do with Peter or why Peter's been missing for so long. He would never have stayed away all this time without contacting me. He wouldn't do that. He would never abandon us. Never, never. You've got this all wrong, you must have.' She paused for a second. 'Do you think he's lost his memory and is wandering around, not knowing where he is or who he is? Oh, why don't you find him and bring him home? Where is he?' She broke down in tears.

Geraldine wondered whether Christine was trying to convince the police or herself that her husband was loyal to her. She considered sharing the information that John was a murder victim who had managed the local branch of Peter's bank. Christine would read about the murdered man soon enough in the media. But she couldn't see any benefit in passing on that information to Christine yet, so instead she mumbled a few generic platitudes about making progress with the investigation. As she was ready to stand up, Christine detained her, admitting that she was worried about her daughter. She stared at Geraldine and this time her anxiety was impossible to misinterpret.

'It's understandable that Daisy would be worried about her father going missing,' Geraldine began, but Christine dismissed her comment with a wave of her hand. She looked utterly forlorn.

'Oh, I don't think she's bothered about him. She's not interested in him or me.' She frowned. 'She was always such an affectionate child when she was younger, but recently she's changed. I know that's supposed to be part of growing up and parents need to be understanding and patient, but she's like a completely different person. I hardly recognise her any more. The school tell us it's just a phase that will pass. If that's true, I can't wait for her to grow out of it. She's—' She broke off. When she resumed speaking, her voice had dropped to a whisper. 'She's become a monster. I know that's a terrible thing for a mother to say about her own daughter, but—' She broke off again and shuddered. 'If we were living a hundred years ago, I think I'd believe she's possessed by a demon. I'm not sure that I don't actually believe that now.'

Geraldine had heard a similar complaint from other mothers, including her own sister, Celia. Geraldine's niece was taking a gap year before going to university but, before finishing school, for several years she had behaved towards her parents with a hostility which Celia had found unnerving. But dealing with teenage angst was not part of Geraldine's job. As tactfully as she could, she extricated herself from the conversation.

'Is there someone you can talk to?' she asked Christine. 'You have a lot on your mind right now and you're having to deal with it on your own while your husband's – away.'

Christine bridled. 'I do have a friend I talk to,' she said defensively. 'And now, if you've quite finished with your questions, I need to get to the shops before my daughter comes home.'

'I hope Peter turns up very soon.'

'Yes, there must be a logical explanation for his absence,' Christine agreed, but she didn't sound convinced.

Geraldine stepped outside and swore under her breath. It had started to rain and she had left her jacket in the car. As she hurried along the pavement, the light rain turned into a heavy downpour. Brushing drops of water off her hair, she drove back to the police station with uncomfortably wet shoulders, pondering what Christine had told her about Daisy.

Ariadne was there, waiting to hear what had happened.

'Give me a chance,' Geraldine laughed, when Ariadne accosted her. 'I haven't even written up my report yet. How about I meet you in the canteen in five minutes and you can tell me what you make of it?'

'It's only going to take you five minutes to write up your report? So there's not much to tell, then.'

Geraldine sighed. Ariadne was right. She hadn't found out anything new from Christine. All she had achieved was to waste time and get herself damp in the process. The interview with Christine seemed to have raised more questions than it had answered. What she had said about her daughter bothered Geraldine, perhaps more than it should have done. Clearly something had been troubling the girl before her father had disappeared. Geraldine wondered if this was merely a case of teenage malaise or whether she ought to try and discover whether there was another cause for Daisy's unhappiness.

'Teenagers are tricky,' was all Ariadne said when Geraldine shared her concerns.

'Tricky in what way?'

Ariadne shrugged. 'I don't mean they're tricky to deal with for procedural reasons, although there is that too, of course. What I meant was, you can't always rely on them to be – well – I don't know.'

'Truthful? Mature?' Geraldine suggested with a smile. 'Unlike adults who are always completely rational and sensible and always on the level?'

Ariadne smiled. 'You know what I mean. I wouldn't start trying to question a teenager unless you're sure it's absolutely necessary. It's almost inevitably going to end up being more trouble than it's worth.'

Geraldine nodded thoughtfully. One day she and Ian would be living with a teenager and the prospect made her anxious. She hoped they would prove equal to the task.

17

HAVING SATISFIED HERSELF THAT she was alone in the house, she slipped into the garage. They called it 'the garage' and told the insurance company that both cars were kept locked up in there overnight, although they always left them on the drive. It was a relatively innocent lie and a plausible one, because there was easily enough room in the garage for two cars. That was to say there would have been plenty of space, had they taken the trouble to clear the garage out. It was crammed with old furniture and junk of all shapes and sizes, essentially garbage accumulated over years of hoarding and neglect. Most of the contents were now obsolete or too spoiled by time and grime to be rescued, but they remained there, stored in the garage, just in case they were ever needed again. Some were too bulky to be readily disposed of, while others were too damaged to be of any further use to anyone and were waiting for an unspecified day when they could be taken to the dump.

Gazing around, she barely registered an old leather sofa, its stuffing leaking out from a threadbare cover, almost hidden under a heap of bric-a-brac; an obsolete pram with rusty wheels, hardly visible through a veil of thick cobwebs; a tall wardrobe with a broken door looking dangerously unstable; a row of chairs stacked untidily along one wall; two dusty metal filing cabinets, scratched and dented; and a multitude of smaller odds and ends: a lidless shoebox of faded photographs, chipped ornaments, souvenirs from holidays abroad, an incomplete set of crockery, a broken nutcracker and much more. Some items were so rusty and dirt encrusted it was difficult to discern what purpose they had once served. The floor was black with ground-in filth and the walls, once whitewashed, were streaked with dirt.

A battered chest freezer in one corner drew her gaze like a magnet. She stared at it through narrowed eyes, recalling its contents with a faint shudder. A long, deep scratch on its side seemed to leer at her. The freezer was not plugged in. She wasn't sure whether the rubber around the lid still formed an airtight seal and, if so, how rapidly it would deteriorate, hardening and finally decomposing, allowing air to creep in and out. Without heating, the garage was permanently chilly, but eventually a putrid stench would start to permeate the dusty air. Before that happened the contents of the freezer would have to be disposed of, but she hadn't yet worked out how to do that. It seemed impossible to manage it by herself, yet she couldn't reveal the contents of the freezer to anyone else without incriminating herself. Somehow she had to remove the corpse discreetly, before it was discovered. She was already working on a plan to make sure the freezer couldn't be opened before it was crushed, but it wasn't going to be easy.

Glancing at her phone, she shivered. There was no time to waste. Whatever else happened, she couldn't afford to be spotted hanging around in the garage. Her presence might arouse suspicions about her motive for going in there and it was imperative no one else had a reason to start snooping around. To other people the garage must continue to appear nothing more sinister than useful storage space, a repository of unwanted possessions, the detritus of a failing family. Fortunately, all the filthy discarded clutter made it an uninviting space and hopefully no one would be in any hurry to explore it. Before it was eventually cleared, the macabre contents of the freezer had to be gone.

Turning, she nearly tripped over a dusty metal tray of cutlery. Mismatched knives and forks and spoons, probably untouched for decades, rattled against the sides of the container. Startled, she recoiled and barged into a filing cabinet. A pile of lever arch files slammed to the floor with a resounding crash, sending up a cloud of thick dust. Alarmed, she glanced over at the freezer with its ghastly contents. The phrase 'dust to dust' flitted into her mind and she felt suddenly sick. It would be a disaster if she threw up, leaving unmistakable evidence that she had been snooping around in the garage. The police might even be able to analyse her vomit and determine the date of her latest visit. Gathering herself together, she stumbled out of the garage before anyone found her there.

Running into her house in a panic, she locked herself in the downstairs toilet. Staring in the mirror, she was relieved to see that her appearance hadn't altered. She scowled, then grinned, and was reassured that outwardly nothing had changed. She continued to stare at herself, trying to read the expression in her eyes. Was this the face of a murderer? She puckered her lips and batted her eyelids in a parody of youthful innocence. Carrying out the first step had been unexpectedly easy. Now, attention to detail was essential if she was to get away with it in the long term. So far so good, no one had the faintest suspicion who was responsible for his disappearance. She was determined to ensure that never changed, but she still had the contents of the old freezer to deal with. An idea was beginning to formulate in her mind, but she would have to be careful. Basically, if she could somehow stick the freezer lid down, no one would spend any time trying to force it open before disposing of it. There was, ostensibly, nothing of any interest in the shabby shell, and certainly nothing worth saving. People who did house clearance were interested only in converting stuff into cash.

A battered old freezer with rotting contents would be of no interest to anyone. Just to make sure, when she stuck the lid down, she would think of something to make it appear completely worthless. If she could completely smash the mechanism in an obvious way, that might help. She would need to study the appliance and it might take some planning, but she was confident it wouldn't be difficult. Above all, she remained convinced it was worth all the effort. She had never anticipated murder could be so exhilarating. It was giving her much more pleasure than just that single rush of power she had experienced when her victim had succumbed, although that had been thrilling in itself. But she was discovering that the benefit continued long after the event. It no longer bothered her to be alone with her memories. Reliving the moment in her imagination was almost more satisfying than the act itself and she could do that any time she wanted. In fact, she could see no downside to murder. She smiled at the irony that causing death was life-affirming. She wondered why more people didn't turn to it as a hobby. Of course, it was possible they did, but she suspected most people were too scared to try it. Committing murder required guts as well as cunning. Fortunately, she was blessed with both.

The appliance wasn't working, but sooner or later he must suffocate in his living coffin, as long as no one released him while he was still alive. She had waited, watching over him as long as she dared, hoping he was dead, but eventually she had felt obliged to leave or risk being discovered. If only there had been a lock on the freezer or some way of preventing it from opening without anyone noticing. Now, after nearly a week, no one had mentioned finding a body in a disused freezer. It was such a dramatic story, the media would have splashed the story across the front pages of the local newspapers and shouted about it on the local news channels, if he had been discovered. Sooner or later house clearance people might be called in to remove the disused appliance and, when that happened, it was imperative the top of freezer didn't fly open.

She regretted having killed him in that stupid way, leaving the body somewhere it could be found. She ought to have thought it through and maybe taken him for a walk along the river and shoved him in the water, rather than pushing him into an abandoned freezer. At the time, she tried to reassure herself that his death would look like an accident, but on reflection that seemed unlikely. If she was honest, she had to admit that she had acted on impulse. All she had to do was ensure no one could open that freezer. How she was going to manage that was another question, because once the lid of the freezer was stuck shut, there would be no going back. After that, no one could possibly believe his death had been an accident.

She wondered if it would be better, after all, to just leave it as it was and let the discovery of the body play out. The more she thought about it, the more sensible it seemed to simply do nothing. Even if the police suspected foul play, there was no way they could prove she was responsible for what had happened. In the absence of any evidence, they would be forced to conclude that his death was an accident and drop any investigation.

Satisfied that she would get away with it, she sat down on the toilet and began to relax and allow herself to speculate about the future. Her next victim would have to be as trusting as her first. Whether or not they deserved to die at her hands was hardly the point. Everyone had to die one day. Her conscience was clear.

18

WHILE SHE WAS WAITING for Ariadne to join her in the canteen, Geraldine read a few statements from bank employees that she had not yet had time to study carefully. A single sentence struck her and she paused, spotting a potentially interesting snippet of information. A woman working in the bank had mentioned that she thought John had been having an affair with a customer. It didn't escape her notice that this was the second such accusation she had seen levelled at the dead bank manager. Ariadne had not yet arrived, so Geraldine hurriedly called the young constable who had taken down the statement.

'It's only a rumour,' the constable stammered, seemingly daunted by the call. 'That is, she said it was just a rumour. It might not be true. Apparently there are always rumours going round at the bank about different members of staff. I guess it must be a pretty boring place to work,' she added with a nervous laugh.

Irritated by her young colleague's flippancy, Geraldine bit back a harsh response.

Ariadne arrived just as Geraldine was ending the call.

'You were young and inexperienced once,' Ariadne pointed out when Geraldine railed about her discovery.

'But never lax about possible leads,' Geraldine snapped.

'There's being alert and there's being overly suspicious. It's hardly what you might call a lead,' Ariadne pointed out. 'I mean, there's not much to go on, is there? It's not as if everyone at the bank mentioned this alleged affair. A scrap of hearsay from one source – probably an unreliable one – about a rumour that probably isn't based on anything concrete.'

'It may not be probable but it's not impossible,' Geraldine said, raising her eyebrows to emphasise her point. 'Since when did we neglect to follow up something because it might not turn out to be significant? What if it is?'

'I get it that you're frustrated. We're all feeling frustrated by our lack of progress, but I don't think you can accuse anyone of being lax.'

On reflection, Geraldine was pleased that she hadn't reprimanded the constable for an understandable oversight.

'We're none of us perfect,' she muttered and Ariadne acknowledged the comment with a smile.

Ariadne had cast an eye over Geraldine's report, which wasn't very illuminating, and they discussed that briefly. While not being exactly unhelpful, Christine had not told them anything new. Peter was still missing and Christine had no idea where he had gone. Meanwhile, although it was admittedly a very tenuous lead, Geraldine was keen to go to the bank to follow up the hint that John might have been having an affair. If the rumour could be substantiated, there was a chance it might throw up a new lead.

'So one door closes,' Geraldine said.

Ariadne nodded, smiling. 'I know, I know. And we can't afford to leave a single stone unturned.'

'Exactly. We both know the most improbable lead can turn out to be the one that cracks a case wide open. Let's hope this statement proves more helpful than anything Christine had to say.' Geraldine paused. 'I still think she might be hiding something, but I've no idea what.' She shook her head. 'There's definitely something wrong about the relationships in that family.'

'Could that be because they have a rebellious teenage daughter?' Ariadne asked with a smile.

'Maybe,' Geraldine conceded.

In spite of their work pitting them against some of the most evil members of society, Ariadne sometimes reminded Geraldine of Ian who seemed able to remain relentlessly optimistic about human nature. One of his favourite expressions was that everything would turn out all right in the end. Even though Geraldine found his optimism naïve, she never challenged him about his belief. Ian's positivity was sometimes the only thing that kept her from feeling overwhelmed during the course of an investigation. In the face of the iniquity that often seemed to hem her in, his cheerfulness was like a lifeline drawing Geraldine out of the darkness that sometimes threatened to engulf her.

'I wish I shared your good opinion of the human race,' she now said to Ariadne, although she was thinking of Ian.

Ariadne smiled. 'I know, you're not a pessimist, you're a realist and I'm a naïve fool. Well, I'll take my naïveté over your realism any day.'

Geraldine chuckled. 'Now, I'd better get going or I'll miss the bank. I want to find out more about this latest rumour.'

'Is it significant, do you think, that we've come across two different accusations about John having an affair?'

Geraldine shrugged. 'It could just be office gossip. It's difficult to tell what's significant and what isn't.'

The woman who had given the statement in question to Geraldine's colleague was called Emma Burley. She was twenty-four and had worked at the bank for two years, claiming to like her job very much. When questioned further, she had admitted that she liked it there because she felt relatively secure in her job. She was saving for a wedding and keen to earn as much as she could over the course of the next year. That much Geraldine gleaned from the statement Emma had already given. She returned to the bank and asked for Emma and, after a short delay, was escorted to a small meeting room where she was greeted by a pretty young woman with soft blonde curls, blue eyes and a healthy complexion.

Emma was polite but clearly apprehensive as she enquired why Geraldine had asked to see her. 'I gave a statement to one of your colleagues a few days ago. I haven't got anything else to say. Really, I should be working,' she added, her eyes flicking to the door.

Geraldine asked her straight away about the rumour concerning John's affair. Emma looked uneasy. Her welcoming smile vanished and she claimed she didn't know what Geraldine was talking about. When pressed, she became defensive.

'For goodness sake,' she exclaimed. Her friendly air had gone and she sounded irritated. 'It was just a passing comment. That police officer had no business making such a to-do about it. Now, if you've finished, I really do need to get on.'

Geraldine didn't stir but gazed firmly at the young woman. 'I'm afraid I'm going to need a little more than that from you,' she said softly. 'Tell me, is there any reason why you're so reluctant to talk about this? Were you involved with John Hodgson yourself?'

As Geraldine had intended, Emma became more forthcoming in her indignation, protesting that the affair had been with a customer, not with any employee at the bank, all of whom were, according to her, consummate professionals.

Apart from the manager, by your own admission, Geraldine thought, but she kept that opinion to herself.

Emma insisted she had no idea who the customer might be and was reluctant to reveal the source of her information. Only when Geraldine pointed out, in no uncertain terms, that Emma was obstructing the police in a murder inquiry did the young woman lose her air of stony composure and admit that she had heard a hint of the rumour from Eileen.

'It was the Christmas party,' Emma explained. 'She was tipsy, and I'm not sure she'll even remember what she said. But you can't say anything to her. If she finds out I talked about it, she'll make my life hell. Seriously, you can't say anything about this to anyone. I should never have mentioned it. It's just a bit of idle gossip and probably not true anyway. Eileen's a bored middle-aged woman who likes to invent drama. I'm sure there was nothing going on.'

Geraldine thanked Emma. Without making any commitment, she assured Emma that she would do her best to keep her name out of the ongoing enquiry.

To begin with, Eileen was even more guarded than Emma had been. Older and fiercer than her young colleague, Geraldine appreciated that it was going to be difficult to force her to share what she knew. Eileen robustly denied knowing anything about an allegation that her former manager had been having an affair with a customer.

'With a customer? That's a disgusting suggestion,' she retorted, as though Geraldine had suggested John had been illicitly involved with a child. 'If you'd known the man, you would never entertain such an idea, let alone spread it around. He was very professional in all his dealings with the public. I can't believe anyone would say such a thing.'

'I'm sorry,' Geraldine said, 'but we've been led to believe you said it yourself.'

'Who told you such a blatant lie?'

'I'm not at liberty to reveal my source.'

'In other words someone's slandering me and is too cowardly to come out and say anything to my face, because they know it's not true. Tell me, how am I supposed to defend myself if my accuser insists on remaining anonymous?' She glared at Geraldine. 'How do I know you're not making up this preposterous story yourself?'

Quietly, Geraldine reminded her that Eileen herself had mentioned a change in John's behaviour after their colleague Lily had left the branch.

'She wasn't a customer,' Eileen snapped.

Geraldine enquired whether Eileen had been romantically involved with John Hodgson herself. Afraid Eileen might lose her temper, Geraldine was relieved when she burst out laughing.

'You are joking, aren't you?' Eileen spluttered. 'John Hodgson was a happily married man. He was hardly likely to be romantically interested in an old fuddy-duddy like me. No, I'm afraid you're barking up the wrong tree there, Inspector. Sadly, I've never been the object of any man's desires or any woman's either, come to that.'

Even when Geraldine pointed out that she was investigating John's murder and appealed to Eileen's sense of justice and threatened her with a charge of obstruction, Eileen refused to open up. Either Emma – or an inebriated Eileen – had fabricated the allegation of an affair or Eileen's loyalty to John was unshakable. But there might be other ways in which to investigate the story. In the meantime, Geraldine was unwilling to let Eileen believe the police had finished with her. Warning Eileen that she might want to talk to her again, Geraldine left. She had wasted enough time on a potential witness who refused to help the police with their enquiries.

'Perhaps she was just inventing or passing on some unfounded gossip,' Ariadne said when Geraldine was back at the police station venting her frustration. 'It's possible she really doesn't know anything about any affair.'

'Yes,' Geraldine conceded irascibly. 'It's possible nobody knows anything about anything. But somebody must know something and whoever it is, and whatever it is, we're not going to rest until we find out what it is.'

But she agreed that Eileen appeared to be nothing more than an unreliable source of malicious gossip.

19

SHE WAS AT HOME by herself with nothing to do but lie around feeling alternately bored and agitated. It was excruciating, because she had all this time to herself and she couldn't even rest. She wanted to loosen up and forget about her current problems, but that seemed impossible. She wondered whether to go out. That might help to take her mind off her situation, but it was supposed to start raining and, in any case, she had nowhere to go. With a shiver of anticipation, she went into the living room, took out one of the crystal tumblers and poured herself a large glass of whisky. As she raised the glass to her lips the pungent aroma reached her, spicy and faintly earthy. Taking a preliminary sip, she closed her eyes as the liquid stung the back of her throat and a satisfying warmth spread across her tongue. She had taken to drinking at home whenever she was alone, but she was unused to spirits and she didn't really like wine. Drinking something she didn't like seemed a poor way of trying to wipe out the pain of her existence. She wondered whether it was time to look for something stronger to dull her overactive brain before her thoughts could drive her mad.

She took another gulp of whisky and another, and felt the alcohol making her lightheaded and sleepy and slightly queasy. Sprawled on the sofa she leaned back and tried to relax, but a familiar sound reverberated in her head as soon as she closed her eyes. She took a further swig straight from the bottle and closed her eyes again. When she opened them, the room was spinning. Having poured herself another generous shot, she carefully replaced the top on the bottle and stowed it at the back of the drinks cupboard before lurching up the stairs clutching her tumbler. Staggering into her room she placed the glass on her bedside cabinet and collapsed on her bed. She was so tired she thought she might drop off straight away, but she couldn't sleep.

The memory of what she had done still electrified her. It kept her awake at night. However hard she tried to stop thinking about it, an echo of the thud when he had hit his head pounded incessantly in her mind. She heard it most clearly when she closed her eyes. Her fingers seemed to feel the rough surface of his jumper as she shoved him, pushing with all her might. She had not yet recovered from the shock she had experienced when he had suddenly lost his footing and toppled over with a deafening din. He had made no attempt to struggle to his feet. Straight away she had suspected he had hit his head and knocked himself out when he fell which, on reflection, had been a stroke of luck. If he had been conscious of what was happening, he would have overpowered her easily. She still struggled to believe what she had done. It seemed almost fantastical that she had succeeded in freeing herself of his unwanted attentions. But she knew she had and knew too that he would never bother her again.

She raised herself up groggily on one elbow. Reaching for the glass beside her bed, she took another sip of whisky, toying with the comforting notion that she had been the instrument of justice. The more she thought about it, the firmer was her conviction that she shouldn't fear retribution when she had really done nothing wrong. She had been the victim all along, not the villain. The realisation that she was blameless lifted her mood and, all at once, she stopped feeling frightened. Perhaps it was the alcohol making her bold, but the future suddenly seemed full of possibilities. After all, having come this far without anyone suspecting she was responsible for what had happened to him, she must be out of danger by now. An opportunity had presented itself and she had taken advantage of it – that was all. It had taken almost superhuman courage to assault him; she could so easily have been the one who ended up being the victim yet again. All she had done was save herself and no one could criticise her for acting in self-defence.

She doubted whether anyone would ever understand her reasons for her actions, but that didn't bother her. As long as no one found out what she had done, she would be safe from judgement and punishment for the rest of her life. And she certainly didn't intend telling anyone. She could be discreet and this was one secret she was never going to share. All things considered, she told herself she ought to be celebrating her victory, not regretting what she had done. Feeling contrite about her success was foolish, because a foul man like him wasn't worth her sympathy. Anyway, she had got away with it. Relief swept through her. Shaking with laughter, she flung her hand up and punched the air. She felt as though she was protected by a shield of invincibility. Killing someone who deserved it wasn't so very difficult after all. This time, when she closed her eyes, she fell straight into a dreamless sleep.

20

CHRISTINE SPENT MOST OF the afternoon preparing a lasagne, her daughter's favourite supper, even though the last time she had made it, Daisy had refused to eat it. When Christine had protested that she liked lasagne, Daisy had stormed noisily out of the kitchen, yelling that her mother had no idea what she liked and she hadn't eaten pasta for years. The sound of her footsteps stomping up the stairs had been all but drowned out by Peter's yelling at her retreating back that her mother had made the supper especially for her and could she please show some appreciation for everything her parents did for her. Daisy had ignored his shouting, which had come as no surprise. It was a while since she had taken notice of anything her parents said or had even bothered to pretend she was listening to them.

'Let her go to bed hungry,' Peter had growled, scowling at Christine, as though any of this was her fault.

He and Christine had settled down to eat their pasta in crabby silence. The lasagne had turned out well, the topping perfectly crispy, but Christine had struggled to swallow a single mouthful. She hadn't dared challenge Peter's unspoken accusation for fear of provoking a row and she knew he was being similarly restrained; they were both conscious that Daisy might walk in at any moment. Although she sometimes made a point of stamping her feet angrily when she was going up and down stairs, she seemed able to move around silently when she chose. Her noisy footsteps was another issue that Peter had regretted raising.

'It's not my fault I have to go to school,' Daisy had cried out furiously in response to his complaint. 'I suppose you want me to just stay in my room all the time and never go anywhere.'

'Don't be ridiculous,' Christine had blurted out. 'You know perfectly well that's not what your father meant.'

Peter had glared at her and snapped at her for interfering, although she had only been trying to defend him against their daughter's unreasonable accusation.

Now Christine had decided to try again. With a lasagne in the oven, she was waiting anxiously for Daisy to come home. When her phone rang, she answered reluctantly.

'Hi there,' Lucy's cheery voice greeted her. 'How's it all going?'

They had known each other for a while. Not having any other friends of her own, Christine had been pleased when Lucy had wanted to spend time with her. They had first bumped into each other at the gym, quite literally, when Lucy had barged into Christine in the changing rooms. Frantically apologising for failing to look where she was going, she had invited Christine to join her for a coffee in the café. Since that first meeting, they had met for coffee at the gym every Tuesday and gradually Christine had begun to unburden herself to her friend, telling her all about her problems with Daisy. Lucy had been sympathetic, assuring Christine that she had experienced similar challenges with her own daughter who had now grown up and left home, having developed into a pleasant and amenable young woman, nothing like the irritable teenager who had lived under Lucy's roof for years. Finding Lucy's experience reassuring, Christine had confided in her with ever more detailed accounts of Daisy's aggressive behaviour.

'She clomps around the house really noisily and refuses to eat with us,' she had complained, while Lucy listened patiently. 'It really helps, talking to you,' she said, when Lucy repeated that her own experience had been similar. 'You make me feel as if my dysfunctional family is almost normal.'

'Either that or we're both off-the-scale weird,' Lucy had laughed.

Christine had joined in, even though she hadn't found Lucy's remark amusing.

'But seriously, every family has its ups and downs and teenagers are just something that has to be endured,' Lucy added, as though she saw through Christine's fake laughter and sensed her true feelings.

At first, Christine had been pleased to find a supportive friend, but after a while she began to tire of Lucy's relentless good humour. She knew Lucy meant well and was only trying to be kind, but her cordial overtures were starting to feel intrusive. Besides, the conversation was always one-sided. Christine confided unreservedly in her friend who listened and responded with a string of inane clichés. Far from comforting, they were irritating. In stark contrast, whenever Christine enquired about Lucy's family, her friend was uncommunicative. When Christine had shown her photos of Daisy and asked about Lucy's daughter, Lucy had not reciprocated.

'Oh, she's all grown up now,' she had replied with characteristic vagueness. Christine didn't even know the name of her friend's daughter.

Trying not to betray her irritation with Lucy for phoning her when she was mentally preparing for Daisy to arrive home, Christine returned her greeting.

'I was worried when I didn't see you at the gym on Tuesday,' Lucy said. 'Is everything okay?'

'Yes, of course. Why wouldn't it be?'

Christine didn't mean to sound dismissive, but she had already been questioned by the police detective that morning, and right now all she wanted was to be left alone to gather her thoughts before Daisy came home. Listening to Lucy spouting inanities, she didn't hear the front door close. The first she knew of Daisy being home was when she heard her tramping up the stairs. With a sigh, Christine hurriedly ended the phone call and put the kettle on before calling up the stairs to Daisy. In answer, Daisy turned her music up really loudly.

Christine hesitated, wondering whether to follow her daughter upstairs, then went back to the kitchen to make herself a mug of tea. While the kettle was boiling she went into the living room and poured herself a nip of whisky. 'Dutch courage,' she muttered under her breath. Having made her tea, she turned the oven right down; the lasagne wouldn't come to any harm if it was left in for a while on a low light. As she settled down, the phone rang. It was Lucy again, wanting to know if Christine was going to the gym the following Tuesday.

'I forgot to ask,' Lucy added breezily.

Christine tried not to let Lucy's good humour provoke her. Life just seemed to be so simple for some people. It wasn't Lucy's fault if Christine found everything difficult.

'I really don't know,' she replied, hiding her irritation. 'Now, I'm sorry, Lucy, but I've got to go.' She hung up without waiting for a reply, relieved that she had managed to hold back an honest response to Lucy's question. Lately she seemed to spend her life struggling to control her temper.

It felt strange being at home without Peter. This was the fourth day since he had gone missing and she was beginning to despair of ever being able to return to normal. Too much had happened and she simply didn't have time for Lucy's fussing. It sometimes felt more like interference than support, even though her friend was only trying to be helpful. Doing her best not to think about Peter and everything that had happened, she turned to putting the finishing touches to the supper before laying the table. Half an hour later, with Daisy's favourite lasagne nicely browned on top and a clean and tidy kitchen, she went upstairs determined to summon Daisy to supper. There was no answer when she knocked on her door and for a horrible instant, she was afraid that Daisy had also vanished. Despite her daughter's insistence that her parents didn't enter her room without her permission, Christine opened the door and, peering in, was relieved to see Daisy lying on her bed, staring at her phone.

'What are you doing in here?' Daisy yelled. 'Get out of my room.'

'I knocked,' Christine stammered. 'I knocked but you didn't answer. I thought – I thought—'

'Well? What did you think?'

Christine almost started crying. With an effort, she managed to control herself and even forced a smile. 'I just came up to tell you that supper's ready,' she said. 'I made lasagne. I know it's your favourite.'

'Get out of my room!' Daisy yelled so loudly she startled Christine, making her jump back. 'And shut my door!'

'I'll leave your dinner in the oven,' Christine called out. 'Come down and get it when you're ready. If you want me, I'll be in the garage.'

'What?' Daisy cried out. 'What are you talking about? Why are you going out there?' As she was talking, she jumped off her bed and darted out of her room to meet her mother at the top of the stairs.

When Christine explained that it was time to start clearing out all the mess in the garage, Daisy scowled at her. 'I thought you were making my supper! I suppose you've changed your mind. That's just typical. Don't you care if I starve? I haven't eaten anything all day. All you ever care about is yourself. You're supposed to be my mother. You're supposed to look after me.'

Christine hesitated. It was tempting to snap that the lasagne was in the oven, and Daisy could go down and help herself to it if she was hungry, but she didn't want to rebuff her daughter in any way. At least Daisy now seemed prepared to talk to her. What was even more encouraging was that she had volunteered to eat the dinner Christine had prepared for her. They might even sit down to a meal together, which would certainly be a step in the right direction. Smiling with relief, Christine said she would go down and get the lasagne out of the oven straight away. Quickly, before Daisy could change her mind, she turned and made her way down the stairs to the kitchen. After a horrendous couple of years, it seemed things might be looking up at last. It felt unreal to be dishing up and calling to Daisy that supper was on the table, but a moment later, she heard her running lightly downstairs.

As Christine had hoped, Daisy sat at the kitchen table with her.

'This is good, Mum,' Daisy said, as they tucked into the lasagne.

As they were eating, Christine's phone vibrated in her pocket. She glanced at the screen and ended the call. Speaking to Lucy could wait, at least until the next day. Right now, she had someone more important to focus on. She wondered whether to ask Daisy about her day, but decided to avoid a subject that might prove contentious.

'That Mrs Proudy seems a bit of a harridan,' she hazarded, hoping to find some common ground with Daisy.

'What's a harridan?' Daisy replied warily.

'It's difficult to explain, but it's not a compliment. A dragon, you could say. The kind of teacher no one likes, anyway.'

'You've got that right. She's a complete bitch,' Daisy agreed and actually smiled at her mother.

Christine was so relieved she almost choked on her mouthful. They seemed to be managing without Peter. She decided it was best to avoid the subject altogether now that she and Daisy appeared to be at peace with one another. Discussing what had happened to Peter could wait.

21

GERALDINE AND IAN BOTH had a day off and they planned to spend time with Tom. It was a while since their last family outing and they had agreed to take a picnic to the park if they could. There had been warnings of heavy rain for the weekend. They hoped the weather report would prove wrong but they woke up on Saturday to see the forecast had been accurate and it was pelting down outside. Forced to abandon their trip to the park they decided to go food shopping instead. Ian was disappointed, but Geraldine didn't mind, and Tom would be just as happy being wheeled around the supermarket in a trolley as he would have been in the park. Another benefit was that they could stock up on food for the week at their leisure. Tom chuckled and kicked his fat little legs and waved his arms, as Geraldine gently manhandled him into his waterproof rain suit. While she was preparing him to go out, Ian packed the changing bag and at last they were ready.

As they were about to set off, Tom let out a grunt and there was an unmistakable smell. With a sigh, Geraldine removed his rain suit and carted him off to the nursery. As she changed his nappy, she thought back to the days when she would only have to put on her shoes and a jacket and grab her bag before going out in the rain. Life had been simpler in so many ways before Ian had moved in with her and Tom had come along, but she dismissed her wistful musings with a shrug, knowing she wouldn't change a thing. Having to mess about before going out was a small price to pay for her new life with her own family.

It was easy to be nostalgic about the freedoms she had lost, but while she had been happy in her work, she had also been achingly lonely on her own at home.

It was chilly for September, with a smell of wet leaves in the air, and Geraldine shivered in the underground car park as they walked to the car. After a long summer, autumn was finally settling in, with a hint of cold days to come. Too young to be discriminating about his environment, Tom seemed to enjoy outings wherever they went. He watched Geraldine expectantly when she strapped him in the car. She bent forward to kiss his head, her pleasure at his excitement tinged with melancholy.

'We're only going to the shops,' she told him, and he kicked his legs and babbled with excitement, as though she was promising him an entertaining ride on a magic carpet.

The car park was almost full but with shoppers arriving and leaving in a steady stream, they were able to find a space without much difficulty. The only advantage of the supermarket being busy was that Tom was cheerfully occupied observing the constant stream of people milling around in the aisles. When any small children passed by, he waved his little hands and squealed with pleasure, making Geraldine and Ian smile. At one point, a little girl of about three stopped by their trolley and made faces at Tom who laughed as he reached out for her with wriggling fingers. The child's mother swept her up in her arms, apologising, but Geraldine reassured her that her young charge's antics had been wonderful entertainment.

After a tiring but productive morning, they arrived home, ready for lunch. No sooner had Geraldine fed Tom and put him down for a sleep than her phone rang. Fearing that she had been called in to work, she answered without checking the screen and was pleased to hear her adopted sister on the line. They chatted for a while, catching up on news of each other's families. Once Celia started on the subject of her children, she talked a lot, and after a while Geraldine's attention drifted. She was only half listening to Celia speaking about her daughter who was off on a gap year.

'She's set her heart on going to Australia,' Celia was saying. 'As far away from us as possible.' She laughed, but Geraldine sensed anxiety and a slight hint of bitterness in her tone as she continued. 'I'm sure it will do her good. She'll learn to stand on her own feet. And Sebastian's got a cousin who lives in Brisbane, so she won't be entirely stranded without support if anything should happen, not that it will, I'm sure,' she added quickly. 'If it wasn't for Charlie, I think I'd struggle with Chloe growing up so fast. I mean, it's like it was only yesterday when she was a sullen teenager, and now she's an adult. Like it's happened overnight.'

Hearing about her niece reminded Geraldine of Daisy Selby and she wondered how Christine and her daughter were getting on in Peter's absence. It was possible he had returned and no one had informed the police. She resolved to check on the Selbys after the weekend and learn whether there had been any developments.

'Geraldine, are you listening to me?' Celia asked.

'Yes, yes, of course,' Geraldine fibbed. 'I wouldn't worry too much about Chloe, if I were you. She seems to have her head screwed on and, like you say, it'll be good for her to experience some independence and learn to stand on her own feet. And she'll know she can always come home if she wants to. That's the main thing. That's all you can really do as a parent. Just have a safe place for her to come back to if she needs it.'

Just then, Ian called her to say lunch was ready and, right on cue, Tom began to yell. Excusing herself, Geraldine ended her conversation with her sister and they hung up after mutual assurances that they wouldn't leave it so long before talking again.

'I don't like to call you too often because you're always so busy working,' Celia admitted, a slightly plaintive note creeping into her voice.

'Call me any time you want to chat,' Geraldine replied. 'I can always tell you if I'm too busy to talk.'

'Or else just not listen to me when we *do* talk,' Celia replied, but Geraldine could tell her sister was smiling. 'Well, give Ian my best and give Tom a big kiss from his aunty. Honestly, Geraldine, did you ever think it would happen? That you'd be a mother, I mean?'

'Honestly? No. Never. But now I really do have to go. Ian's made lunch and Tom's crying. You wouldn't think that one man and one small baby could cause so much mayhem.'

'Tell me about it,' Celia replied. 'Go on, go. And thanks for the chat. You've really reassured me. Let's speak again soon.'

Geraldine smiled as she hung up. She and Ian had never planned to have a child; Tom coming along had been the biggest surprise of their lives. Without intending to, they had become a family and she sometimes struggled to comprehend the wonder of their miracle baby. She knew desertion by fathers was not uncommon, but all the same she wondered how Peter Selby had been able to abandon his wife and child, if indeed he had chosen to leave them. Until he was found, there was hope he might still be alive, but she was almost sorry that the recent victim of a fatal attack had turned out to be John Hodgson. The uncertainty about Peter's fate left Christine and Daisy in a distressing limbo, trapped between hope and grief and unable to deal with either. Geraldine had always felt sorry for families of soldiers who were lost, missing in action. In some ways Christine's situation seemed even worse because, if Peter was still alive, it looked as though it had been his choice to leave his wife and child. The only other possibilities were that he had been injured or had lost his memory, but if either of those were true, it was hard to believe that he would have vanished so completely. Another explanation for his disappearance was that he had been kidnapped, but that seemed even less likely. She sighed, wondering if they would ever find out what had happened to him or if he would remain on the list of persons who went missing, never to be seen again, leaving his wife and daughter stranded between grief and anger.

22

DANIEL WAS RELUCTANT TO answer, but this was the sixth time she had rung him that evening. He considered switching his phone off, but somehow that would feel as though she was still controlling his decisions. He had decided to stop seeing her. Now he had to make it happen. It was time to stand firm and refuse to allow her to influence his life in any way. Gritting his teeth, he accepted the call.

'He's gone, he's finally, finally gone,' she burst out eagerly, before he could utter a word. 'I had to tell you. I couldn't sit on this a moment longer. I'm so excited, I can hardly breathe!' She sounded sloshed or high – or perhaps both.

He couldn't imagine she took drugs, but she might have been prescribed Prozac or something similar. He wouldn't put it past her. More likely she had been drinking. He pictured her face, flushed with excitement, her eyes bright, her thin lips stretched in a broad grin, seeming to split her narrow face in two.

'I can't tell you anything more, not over the phone, because you never know,' she gabbled. 'We have to meet, face to face.' When he didn't answer straight away, her voice rose. She sounded borderline hysterical. 'We need to meet tonight. No, I can't wait that long. I have to see you right now. Tell me where you are and I'll come at once. Anywhere you want, my love.'

Daniel hesitated. What had started out as a lighthearted dalliance had become a real drag. He hadn't told her yet that it was over and he had no intention of seeing her again. On the contrary, he had behaved like a coward, continuing to be attentive and considerate, going out of his way to make her feel special. But the truth was that everything about her was beginning to irk him. She was older than him, for a start. Admittedly, that had been part of her initial allure: the mystique of an older woman, with an aura of sexual experience. That impression had soon worn off. Other than her well-maintained body, she had little to offer. There was nothing particularly striking about her appearance and she seemed to have had precious little education. Either that or she had forgotten everything she had learned in school. Whatever the reason for her ignorance concerning just about everything, she displayed no intellectual curiosity at all. In short, it was impossible to have a decent conversation with her and she wasn't exceptionally pretty. Added to that, she was turning out to be annoyingly clingy and he was starting to regret ever having become entangled with her.

They had met quite by chance at Monks Cross shopping centre about ten months earlier, shortly before Christmas. He had been searching for a gift for his mother when they had both grabbed hold of the same scarf. He had relinquished it at once, but she had insisted he take it, claiming that she had only wanted to look at it.

'At least let me buy you lunch to thank you,' he had offered impulsively.

To his surprise, she had taken his invitation seriously and accepted. That somewhat rash lunch date had led to an affair which he had allowed to drag on for far too long. She didn't suit him at all, but the fact that she was married meant there was no risk the relationship could ever lead to any serious commitment. So he had let it drift on, because that was easier than trying to end it. The affair had its advantages. Her redeeming feature was her adoration. She made him feel dashing and witty, even though he knew she had only fallen for him because he was young and relatively good-looking. Now, if he was honest, he was keen to end their fling, only she had made it clear that she still wanted to see him. She could be very importunate and he had been struggling to free himself from her clutches for a while.

So far her married status had kept her at bay; they had to be discreet and could only meet once a week, at most. But after a while the fun of their secret meetings had petered out and her company alone wasn't enough to hold his interest. It wasn't as if sex with her was all that compelling once the initial glamour of a clandestine affair with a married woman had worn off. Seeming to sense that he was losing interest in her, lately she had become needier than ever.

'What do you mean, he's gone?' he responded. He wasn't interested in what she had to say. He was just prevaricating while he steeled himself to dump her.

'Don't be obtuse,' she scolded him, with what he supposed was intended to be a girlish giggle. 'You know what I'm talking about.' She continued in a conspiratorial murmur, but she couldn't conceal a note of triumph from her voice. 'My husband won't be troubling us any more.'

He was filled with a sudden overpowering sense of dread. 'What's happened? Have you left him?' he stammered, his thoughts whirling. He felt as though he couldn't breathe.

'More like he's left me,' she replied with a curious bark of laughter. She lowered her voice again, as though she was afraid of being overheard. 'He was stabbed by a mugger, and he's dead.' She sounded exhilarated. 'It happened nearly a week ago. I've been trying to get hold of you. Where have you been?'

'I'm sorry for your loss,' he blurted out in a panic.

'Well, I'm not,' she replied cheerily. 'Don't you see what this means? I'm finally free of him and we can be together all the time.'

He stifled a gasp. He thought he had seen something about a stabbing on the local news. 'Are you telling me your husband was killed?' he asked, not quite sure what to make of it. But the implications of her startling news were clear.

He cursed himself for failing to end the relationship sooner, when he could have done so relatively easily. All he had needed to do was tell her the truth – that he had fallen for someone else, a woman twenty years younger than her. He could hardly tell her about Suzie right now, just when she had told him her distressing news about her husband. Not that she sounded upset about it.

'That's why I need to see you,' she was saying. 'There are certain things I want to tell you, but we can't talk about it over the phone. Don't you see? It's all good. We're free, free, my darling, my love.' He shuddered on hearing the terms of endearment flung at him with such confidence. 'It means we can be together all the time.'

He really didn't want to see her but she was insistent, so he agreed to meet her the following day. He thought better of the rendezvous as soon as he hung up. He had agreed partly out of curiosity. There had been something exuberant and, at the same time, curiously furtive about her, when she was talking about her husband's death. Intrigued, he wanted to know what had happened. At the same time, he was aware that he had allowed her to bully him into seeing her again and was afraid he was going to regret the meeting. He considered calling her back to tell her firmly that he was too busy to meet her in person just then and if she couldn't tell him over the phone then her news would have to wait. He contemplated telling her that his job was sending him out of town for a while. He had used that excuse on her before and so far it had always worked. But this time he realised things might be different. There was nothing to stop her offering to go with him. He shuddered. No longer plaintive, she had been gloating, as though she had finally trapped him. For the first time, he felt there was something threatening in her obsession with him.

Taking a deep breath, he rebuked himself for succumbing to an internal melodrama, as if he was a teenager. His erstwhile mistress was just a pathetic middle-aged woman vainly trying to hang on to some private fantasy of her own. Once he had told her in no uncertain terms that it was over, she would no doubt latch on to another unsuspecting victim to prey on. Too late, he had realised she was a predator and what might seem like a joke if it happened to someone else was actually quite horrific for the unfortunate victim. She ought to wear a sign warning young men to steer clear of her. Resigning himself to meeting her one last time, he resolved, again, to tell her in no uncertain terms that it was over. He owed her that, after so long. She could weep and plead with him as much as she wanted, but he would have no trouble standing firm now he had met another woman, a woman he wanted to be with. However desperate or manipulative Jeannie might be, she couldn't control his feelings. He just had to brace himself to withstand her histrionics. Only if absolutely necessary would he be unkind and mention how her body had started to repulse him, but he was prepared to be cruel if there was no other way to convince her he was serious. If she threatened to kill herself, he would tell her that everyone would conclude she had been unhinged by the death of her husband. No one, himself included, could possibly blame him for her suicide. He wasn't looking forward to the confrontation but he had no other choice and it would be worth it to be finally free of her.

23

AFTER LOOKING INTO PETER Selby's financial affairs, Detective Sergeant Naomi Arnold reported that she had been looking into his account at John Hodgson's branch of the bank.

'There's something interesting,' Naomi said, her blue eyes alight with intensity, like a raptor spotting its prey. 'Five hundred pounds was transferred to the account last month and again this month, shortly before Peter disappeared. The money hasn't been withdrawn,' she added, preempting any suggestion that Peter had taken the money and run off with it. 'What's significant is that the transfer was set up by John himself. As the manager of the bank, he could have been acting on someone else's instructions, concealing the source for whoever was paying the money in. We're working with the bank now to try and find out where the money came from.'

'Hopefully from John himself,' Geraldine said. 'That would certainly open up a range of interesting possibilities.'

'What a pity we can't ask him,' Naomi replied with a wry smile.

With a possible link between him and John, Geraldine made finding Peter a priority. Not only would it be good to close the enquiry into the missing man, as it had been bothering her, but there was a chance Peter might be able to help shed some light on who had attacked John. The post mortem had thrown up no new information. There were no defensive wounds or DNA on the body that might lead them to the killer. With the investigative team struggling, to say the very least, Peter might offer them a new lead. But first they had to find him. As far as the police knew, there was still no sign of Peter anywhere. Geraldine phoned Christine to check he hadn't returned home and received confirmation that he had neither been seen nor heard from since the Monday he had vanished. It hadn't escaped anyone's notice that his disappearance had coincided with the murder of his bank manager. The majority of Geraldine's colleagues were convinced the two incidents must be connected and many suspected Peter was guilty of murdering John. It was certainly a plausible explanation for him running off without a word to his wife, assuming she was telling the truth.

'Something's happened to him, hasn't it?' Christine asked wretchedly. 'Why else would he have gone off without a word like that and not even been in touch to let me know he's alive. He's dead, isn't he?'

Having reassured Christine that the police were doing everything in their power to find her missing husband, Geraldine turned her attention to looking for him. A team had been tasked with checking CCTV in the shops and streets around the office where Peter worked, and a further group of constables had questioned his neighbours to find out whether anyone had seen him since he left home. As far as they knew, the last person to have seen him was his wife, Christine, who had spoken to him on Monday morning when he had returned home from his early morning run. After that, she said he had showered and gone off to work. He had never turned up and no one had seen him since then. As far as the police could ascertain, he seemed to have vanished off the face of the earth after leaving home to go to work.

Geraldine started her enquiries at the estate agency where Peter worked. At the smart premises in Spurriergate in the main York shopping area, she found a young man, a middle-aged man and a girl with auburn hair seated at desks, tapping at keyboards. They all looked at her speculatively as she entered.

'Can I help you?' the younger of the two men enquired, straightening his tie and fixing a welcoming grin on his lips. 'Please, take a seat.' Dark-haired and clean shaven, he was wearing a neatly pressed jacket and shirt and looked so young and eager, Geraldine wondered if this was his first day at work.

'I'm looking for Peter Selby,' Geraldine replied, without stepping forward to sit down.

Her gaze flickered around the room, trying to gauge the reaction of each of Peter's three associates. None of them showed any particular interest when they heard the name of their absent colleague.

'Peter?' the young estate agent who had spoken to her repeated. 'I'm afraid he's not in today. But we all work together and are happy to cover for each other. He will have left all your details here. Can I help you?'

'Not unless you can tell me where to find him,' Geraldine replied. 'I'm not here as a customer. When I said I was looking for Peter Selby, I meant that I'm looking for Peter Selby.' She took out her warrant card and held it up.

'Detective Inspector?' the young man read out. 'You're a police officer?'

The girl shook her auburn curls. 'What's going on? Has something happened to Peter?'

The three agents appeared curious, but none of them seemed unduly worried. The young man muttered randomly about how Peter liked to party.

'We think there's a possibility he might be able to help us with an enquiry and we would very much like to talk to him. Do any of you know where I might find him? Please, this is important,' Geraldine added.

The three estate agents shook their heads. The young man who had spoken first looked at the older man. At the same time, the young woman also turned to the middle-aged man. Since he appeared to be in charge, Geraldine approached his desk and sat down.

'When did you last see Peter?' she asked him.

The oldest estate agent introduced himself as Paul and smiled pleasantly at Geraldine.

'What's this about, Inspector?' he asked cheerfully. 'I'm sure we can help you.'

It took a few moments for Geraldine to persuade the estate agent that she was perfectly happy with where she was currently living and intended neither to sell nor to buy a property. Only after refusing to give him her email address assuring him that if she was ever looking to move she would call on him, was she able to persuade him to listen to her. She addressed her questions to all three of them, as a group, in order to save time.

'Very well,' Paul agreed, 'but I'm afraid we're going to have to stop if a client comes in.'

Without a word, Geraldine stood up, walked over to the door, turned the open sign around and pushed the bolt across.

Paul leapt to his feet. 'You can't do that,' he cried out in surprise.

'I'm afraid I can close your offices for as long as it takes me to question you,' Geraldine replied mildly. 'If you refuse to cooperate, I may have to summon my colleagues and have you all taken down to the police station and charged with obstruction. But I'm sure such drastic measures won't be necessary and you'll agree to answer my questions without any fuss. Now, shall we get on and not waste any more time?'

She went over and sat down again and resumed questioning them as a group. Paul seemed duly chastened and listened with apparent close attention, and his two fellow agents followed his example looking equally cowed. They all agreed they had last seen Peter on the Saturday afternoon before he was reported missing. None of them had seen him or heard from him since then, and none of them had any idea where he might be.

Geraldine learned that Peter was friendly and helpful and this was the first time he had failed to turn up for work. The only explanation his colleagues could offer for his absence was that 'something must have happened to him', but none of them had the faintest idea what that might be.

'It's not like him at all,' the auburn-haired girl kept saying, while Paul insisted that Peter was a successful and absolutely reliable agent and not at all the kind of person who could be expected to go AWOL.

'Something must have happened to him,' Paul echoed what his colleague had said, although none of them had any idea what that could be.

Christine had told Geraldine that Peter's work sometimes took him away from home. Wondering whether he had been having an affair and covering up for his absence, she asked his colleagues whether he had attended many conferences.

'Not many,' Paul replied. 'But he did go occasionally.'

The girl mumbled something about Peter enjoying a bit of a jaunt and they all grinned. But they confirmed that he wasn't currently at a conference.

'I'm afraid we don't know where he is,' Paul said.

'He must be ill,' the girl suggested.

'Or had an accident,' Paul added. 'Have you checked with the hospital?'

Trying not to feel discouraged, Geraldine went back to the police station to type up a brief report on her futile visit to Peter's place of work. There wasn't much to tell. While Geraldine was occupied with Peter's colleagues, Ariadne had been busy coordinating the responses to the door-to-door questioning and gathering information from the security cameras around Peter's house. They too had produced nothing new.

24

THE LOCATION FOR THEIR meeting turned out to be a café on the outskirts of town, a run-down place with sticky tables and a grubby floor. It didn't look as though it would pass the most perfunctory sanitary inspection and Daniel wondered how it managed to avoid falling foul of whatever health and safety body governed standards of hygiene in the hospitality industry. He arrived on time to find Jeannie already waiting at a table in the corner, her face almost completely hidden by a scarf and sunglasses. She was facing the wall. Had she not been the only woman sitting by herself, he might not have noticed her and certainly wouldn't have recognised her. He went up to the counter and ordered a tea before shuffling over to the table next to hers and sitting down immediately behind her, as she had instructed him to do.

'We can't be seen together in public,' she had insisted, 'not yet. Not until all this dies down.'

'All what?' he had asked, both intrigued and irritated by her pretending to be a secret agent of some kind or perhaps a fugitive from the law.

She had refused to say any more over the phone. Feeling increasingly like a spy, and also foolish, he had complied with her wishes. Tempted to refuse to meet her, in the end he had been too curious to stay away. Besides, he wanted to tell her to her face that their affair was over. Once he was seated, he waited for her to begin a conversation. If they both appeared to be talking on their phones, she had explained, no one would suspect they were talking to each other. It was a pointless charade as there were only a couple of other people in the café and they were engrossed in a conversation of their own. The blue-haired girl behind the counter showed no interest in any of her customers, but sat gazing blankly at her phone, absorbed in some game or other while no one was waiting to be served.

'I'm glad you decided to turn up,' she murmured in a voice tense with suppressed agitation. 'I was afraid you would chicken out.' Her laugh sounded fake.

Daniel took a gulp of tea and burned his tongue. He fiddled about, fishing the tea bag out with a narrow wooden spill and depositing it on a thin paper serviette.

'What do you want?' he muttered at last, pretending to talk into his phone and trying to hide his embarrassment at their silly expedient.

Hurriedly she explained that she had held no personal animosity towards anyone, but it had been necessary to get him out of the way.

'Get who out of the way?' he repeated. 'Out of whose way? What do you mean?'

She leaned back, half turned towards him and lowered her voice. 'It was me,' she whispered and nodded. 'I did it.'

'What? What did you do?' he stammered into his phone, his voice barely audible. He didn't dare to glance at her. 'I've no idea what you're talking about.'

'It's perfectly clear,' she hissed. 'Stop playing games. You know very well why I did it and what this all means. We want to be together, don't we? Believe me, I wish it didn't have to be like this, but it was the only way. If we hadn't taken matters into our own hands when we did, we might never have been together. He was beginning to suspect.'

'Who? What? Who was suspecting what?'

She sighed. 'Why are you being like this? Think, Daniel. We want to be together, don't we? And there was only one thing standing in our way. So I removed the obstacle. Now we can be together. We just have to wait for a while—'

'No,' he blurted out, horrified. 'Tell me you haven't done anything you're going to regret.'

'Why would I regret it? He was the only thing standing in our way.'

'When you say you removed the obstacle, you mean—' he began, and broke off unable to complete the sentence.

'Yes,' she whispered. 'I did it. I killed him.'

Although he had suspected something like this, he shuddered on hearing her confess.

She sighed. 'I know you're impatient, but I won't keep you waiting long, I promise. We just can't be seen together in public yet, that's all. For the sake of appearances. We don't want anyone to suspect. And then we can be together all the time. We can live together. We can get married. There's nothing stopping us now.'

Daniel stood up, shaking his head, appalled by her casual confession. 'No,' he said, softly but firmly.

She turned round and stared up at him in surprise, and her expression softened. 'It's hard for me too, but it won't be for long. We just have to be patient.'

He took a step back. 'This is over,' he hissed fiercely. 'I'm leaving. I never want to see you again. Don't call me.'

'Wait,' she cried out and he hesitated. She lowered her voice and continued, speaking very rapidly. 'You mean you don't want to hear from me for a few months, that's it, isn't it? I agree we need to be careful for a while. We don't want to arouse suspicion.'

'No,' he replied. 'It's over.'

'I know. I've finished it. He's gone.'

'I mean this is over.' He frowned. 'I'm talking about us. It's over. I never want to see you again.'

'There's no need to overreact. I can see this is a bit of a shock, but it's okay. No one will ever know it was me and you're not implicated in any way. You don't have to worry about anything.'

'You're not listening to me. I'm telling you it's over between us. It was over a long time ago. Over.'

'What do you mean it's over? It can't be,' she protested, her voice rising in agitation. She glanced around fearfully and lowered her voice. 'Sit down. We need to talk.'

He shook his head but he sat back down, feeling irrationally intimidated. If what she had told him was true, he wondered what she might do to him if he crossed her.

'You can't just walk away from me,' she went on in a furious undertone. 'You know what I've done for you. Now I have money, we can do anything we want. We can be together all the time. Don't you see, it's going to be everything we ever dreamed of.'

'Your dreams, not mine. I want you to leave me alone.'

'You know I can't do that. Why are you being like this? We love each other.'

'Do you really think I could love someone like you? If you want to know the truth, you disgust me, with your wrinkled face and your flabby body. As for what you did, I think it's evil.'

'I did it for you.' Her voice was pleading, but he sensed her anger.

'For me? I never asked you to—' He shook his head in disbelief. 'I never asked you to do anything for me until now, but now I'm asking you to leave me alone.'

Jeannie had just confessed to him that she had killed her husband. It sounded crazy, but he was desperately afraid it was true in which case he really ought to go straight to the police. As he considered his response, it occurred to him that she might do the same to him if he crossed her so he kept silent, considering what to do.

'If you tell anyone,' she murmured, 'I'll deny it. All I need to do is tell the police about your obsession with me. I'll accuse you of stalking me.' She glanced around as though ready to start accusing him then and there.

'I never wanted you to do that.' He shook his head. 'How can I trust you after this? What if you get angry with me? Are you going to do the same to me?'

She laughed, a hard, brittle sound. 'How can you refuse to trust the one person who loves you more than anything else in the world? I'd do anything for you, anything. Haven't I just proved that?'

'Listen to me,' he blurted out in a panic. 'I was going to tell you about a week ago but when your husband went missing and then you heard he was dead, I thought I ought to wait, to give you time to process your loss. But I've been planning to tell you for a while. This relationship – us – it's too intense. I never wanted a serious relationship with you. It was only ever going to be a bit of fun. When I suspected you were becoming too involved, I realised it had to end. So now it has. I'm sorry, but I won't be seeing you again.'

Her voice hardened. 'There's someone else, isn't there?'

He knew it was a mistake to hesitate before stammering his denial.

'You're lying,' she snapped, no longer making any attempt to speak quietly. 'You won't get away with this.'

'I'll go to the police and tell them exactly what you told me.'

'Don't be silly,' she chided him. Her playful tone made him shudder. 'Who are they going to believe? A grieving widow or a jealous lover? But let's not quarrel.' She glanced around and lowered her voice, although no one else appeared to be paying any attention to their whispered conversation. 'We belong together. I deserve you after all I've done for you. So you can forget about chasing anyone else. Ever. You love me,' she went on, her tone wheedling now. 'You know you do. So let's stop this nonsense, because we both know we're never going to be able to stay away from each other. We'll give it a month, tops, and then we can arrange to meet as if by chance and pick up where we left off, except this time we won't need to meet in secret. And as far as anyone else will ever know, we'll be meeting for the first time. What's wrong with us getting together? We're both single and we're both free. Come on, cheer up. There's no need to be frightened. We can do this. We have to. Our love doesn't leave us any other choice. We're going to be together forever. The hard part is behind us.'

He started to answer, but there was something manic about her insistence that made him apprehensive about saying too much. Somehow he had to get away from her. Once she had recovered from the shock of losing her husband, she was bound to see reason. Meanwhile, there was no way he was going to risk telling her about Suzie. Frantically, he told himself Jeannie couldn't possibly have killed her husband. It was blatantly a bluff to gain his attention. Perhaps she thought her stupid boast would win his admiration and loyalty. After repeating that it was over between them, he stood up and strode away without looking back. He hoped she wouldn't be able to see his legs were shaking because she was right about one thing. He was frightened.

25

Drakes Close was a cul-de-sac. Ring cameras had been installed on a few properties, but they were directed at their own private entrances not the roadway and very little activity was recorded along there. Residents arrived and departed, post was delivered and a few visitors turned up from time to time. There was nothing of any interest. No one had recorded Peter going out on the Monday when his wife saw him for the last time although, to be fair, he was rarely caught on his neighbours' films. He had installed a ring camera on his own front door, which had unfortunately stopped working a few days before he disappeared. Geraldine wondered if that was another unfortunate occurrence in an investigation that seemed to be throwing up a few such issues. As far as she was concerned, one coincidence in a case was one too many.

The door-to-door questioning had yielded little new information, none of it of any help to the investigating team. One woman thought she had seen Peter, but her account to the constable who had questioned her was too vague to be of any use. Geraldine drove to Drakes Close specifically to speak to her. The constable had dismissed her as too old and confused to remember much, but Geraldine knew that elderly ladies could be a useful source of information. Many of them watched the street outside their houses and noticed everything that went on. Sadly, they often had little else to occupy them. The woman she was going to question lived next door the Selbys. They lived right the end of the street, so anyone who passed by the neighbour's house could only have been going to or from their own.

Geraldine's first sight of the neighbour seemed to bear out the constable's opinion. Minnie was a tiny, shrivelled woman who could have been anything from mid-seventies to early nineties. She greeted Geraldine in a rasping voice.

'Oh, you're from the police, are you?' she enquired, speaking very slowly and enunciating each word carefully, as though she was talking to someone who might not understand straightforward English. 'Well, then, let me see your identification,' she went on, squinting at Geraldine's warrant card which she appeared to struggle to see. 'You'd better come in, then. Come on, don't worry. He won't bite you. Down, Dobo.'

Looking past her, Geraldine saw a small, fluffy white dog stretched out on a cushion. It opened its eyes and closed them again almost immediately, wagging its tail lazily. The command to the dog stay down seemed redundant.

'How old is Dobo?' Geraldine enquired politely.

'He'll be fourteen come November,' his ancient owner croaked.

Minnie led her into a cluttered front room which stank of stale cigarette smoke. A bay window overlooked the street, which was visible through slightly grubby net curtains.

'You don't mind if I light one up, do you?' Milly asked, taking up a packet of cigarettes from the small occasional table beside her chair.

The room being small and airless, Geraldine said she would prefer it if her hostess didn't smoke. Minnie grunted as she replaced the packet on the table, but she didn't remonstrate. Glancing around, Geraldine saw a number of family photographs, some featuring Minnie, others showing a variety of children of different ages. Scattered among the pictures were an assortment of small ornaments: dogs, dancers, shepherdesses, dolphins and other creatures, all seemingly from abroad. Geraldine imagined Minnie's children and grandchildren returning from their holidays bearing random souvenirs to add to the old woman's collection, inadequate offerings to assuage their guilt for abandoning her to the company of one small dog.

'We're trying to establish Peter Selby's movements last Monday,' Geraldine said, as she sat down on a threadbare armchair in which several springs were broken.

Minnie settled herself on another chair, put her feet up on a footstool and nodded her wizened head.

'Oh yes,' she replied. 'Your colleague was asking me about him.'

'Peter from next door. Can you remember when you last saw him?'

Even as she asked the question, she had a feeling it was pointless. The constable had been right in her assessment of the situation. Geraldine sighed. She had often been criticised for failing to trust her colleagues. Delegating responsibility wasn't her forte, at least not at work. When it came to looking after her son, she was happy to defer to a childminder who had a lot more experience with babies and infants than she did.

'Can you remember when you last saw him?' she repeated, raising her voice in case Minnie was struggling to hear her.

A frown wrinkled the woman's forehead and she looked baffled.

'Can you recall when you last saw Peter Selby going past your house?' Geraldine reiterated patiently, but without much hope of receiving a coherent answer.

Minnie shook her head. 'Peter, Peter Selby,' she muttered. 'When did I see him? It was a few days ago. It could have been as long a week ago, it's difficult to say for sure. The days seem to blend into each other when you get to my age. No, wait, my Lizzie came to see me and I don't think I've seen him or anyone else go by since then.'

'When did you see Lizzie?'

'Well, that's just it. Like I told your colleague, I can't quite remember. The days get muddled up, you know. It wasn't long ago but I can't tell you when, exactly. But it'll be on my calendar in the kitchen,' she said, brightening up. 'Wait here a minute and I'll fetch it.'

Geraldine wasn't sure there was much point in continuing with the conversation, but she waited for Minnie to return with her calendar.

'Here it is,' Minnie said when she had shuffled back to her seat, clutching a cardboard calendar dotted with scrawled notes. There were very few entries.

'It's mostly doctor's appointments,' the old woman admitted wistfully, 'but I do write on it when my family comes to see me. Look, there's Lizzie's last visit.' She pointed a gnarled finger at an entry scribbled on the calendar, eight days earlier.

'It was last Sunday, not the one that's just gone, but the one before that, when Lizzie came.'

Evidently Lizzie's visit had been a significant event for Minnie. It wasn't clear whether the old woman remembered why Geraldine was there. She cleared her throat, but before she could pose another question, Minnie spoke again.

'I don't think I've seen anyone go past since then. Not since my Lizzie came. The nurse came to see me, but there's been no one else, apart from your constable and now you. I don't get many visitors so I remember who comes, even if I'm not always clear about the days. But I don't often notice if anyone goes past in the street. I fall asleep a lot,' she added with a moue of regret. 'The girl from next door, and the woman, come and go all the time. I used to see him as well, going home in the evening, although I didn't usually see him go out in the morning. But you know, I've been thinking about it since your colleague came to ask me about him, and I haven't seen him for a while. Not since before my Lizzie came to visit.'

Geraldine leaned forward. 'When you last saw him, was he going out or going home?'

Minnie shook her head. 'I'm sorry, my dear, but I really can't remember. It could have been either one. My memory isn't what it was. I can tell you that they weren't a nice family. I often heard them over the summer, when I was in the garden. Lizzie liked to wheel me out there, said it was good for me. But I didn't like to listen to them shouting at each other. That girl of theirs was the worst; the language she used would make a sailor blush.' She shook her head. 'I'm no nun, but really, it wasn't what you want to hear from a young girl.'

Geraldine said she would see herself out, but Minnie insisted on accompanying her to the door. The little dog opened its eyes and thumped its tail as they passed but it didn't stir from its basket.

'Dobo's getting on a bit too,' Minnie said. 'I can't bend down to pet him any more.' She sighed. 'He's all I've got left now. Lizzie comes to see me every month or two, but she's moved away to London and can't come often, and my other daughter's gone and settled in Australia. She seems to think the life there suits her. She used to invite me to stay but it's such a long way and I couldn't manage it now anyway. You do your best for them, but they all leave you in the end. If anything happens to Dobo, I'll be all on my own. It's a struggle, but I couldn't bear the thought of giving him away. He wouldn't survive without me. I just hope I outlive him. That's what I'm hanging on for, really.'

Geraldine hesitated but there wasn't much to say. All the same, she trotted out a comforting platitude as she left. She wondered whether Tom would choose to live near to them when he grew up so that he could pop in on them and see how they were. After picking him up from the childminder, she went home and put some dinner in the oven before feeding him. It gave her a chill to think that he might move away one day, possibly to the other side of the world.

'Do you think Tom will want to stay in York when he grows up?' she asked Ian as they were eating.

He shrugged. 'Who knows? This is really good risotto.'

He smiled appreciatively at her. She wanted to continue the conversation, sharing her concerns about the future, but she was reluctant to spoil his good mood. So she said nothing about the lonely old woman she had seen that day, instead returning Ian's smile as though she hadn't a care in the world.

'It's good to see you smiling again,' Ian said. 'I thought your investigation was wearing you down.'

'It's a tricky one, but I'm not going to let that ruin our evening. Thinking about work can wait until the morning.'

They both knew she was lying and the investigation would be playing on her mind all evening, but he smiled at her, appreciating her lie was kindly meant. Not for the first time, she thought how lucky she was to have so understanding and supportive a partner.

26

CHRISTINE AND PETER ALWAYS went to Daisy's school together for parents' evenings. That way, they were able to split up and have two consultations at the same time meaning they could see all of their daughter's teachers, even the ones Daisy told them they really didn't need to speak to.

'When I was at school,' Peter had told her and Daisy, 'I used to try and steer my parents away from any teachers I knew would give me a bad report. My mother saw through my plan and then we engaged in this game of bluff and counter bluff, where I told her she absolutely must see the teachers I really wanted her to avoid and then changed to pretend I didn't want her to see them so she would think I actually did.'

He had laughed at his own puerile attempt at cunning and Christine and Daisy had laughed with him. But that was in the days when they all used to get on well together and Christine had felt part of a family.

It felt awkward going to the parents' evening by herself, but there was no help for it. The first few teachers were fairly bland and she wasn't sure all of them knew who Daisy was, their comments were so generic. Next on Christine's list was Daisy's form teacher that year. Christine approached her with some trepidation because of all the staff the form teacher would have the best overview of Daisy's progress, and should have some idea of how she was settling in to Year Ten generally. Mrs Proudy was a skinny woman who blinked nervously at Christine through black-rimmed glasses that looked too heavy for her gaunt face. She was faintly sweaty and her glasses kept slipping down her thin nose.

'You may have noticed,' the teacher began and hesitated, while an uneasy smile flitted across her face without reaching her eyes. 'You may have noticed,' she repeated, glancing down at her notes, 'that Daisy has been experiencing a few problems lately. Her reports from last year suggest this is a fairly recent development and we've been waiting to discuss this with you. I've discussed Daisy's progress with the head of year.' She said this as though the involvement of the head of year held some fearsome significance. 'We would have called you in before, but we decided it made sense to speak to you now, when you're here anyway for parents' evening, to save you coming in twice.' She gave an ingratiating smile, as though she was doing Christine a favour.

Christine didn't point out that dealing with her at parents' evening when the form teacher would have to speak to her anyway was saving both of them time. Swallowing back her apprehension, Christine leaned forward slightly in her chair to indicate she was listening.

Mrs Proudy cleared her throat. 'We wanted to enquire whether there have been any problems at home recently?' the teacher asked, looking uncomfortable, but clearly determined to plough on now that she had broached the subject.

Christine bristled. *Other than her father buggering off without a word to anyone?* she thought, but remained silent. Her husband's disappearance was none of this woman's business. She resented being interrogated about her family relationships by a woman who seemed to be doing a poor job of concealing her dislike of Daisy.

'Has anything happened that might have disturbed her?' Mrs Proudy pressed on, sounding slightly panicky.

'What do you mean, disturbed her? I don't understand,' Christine lied.

She was determined to be as unhelpful as she could without behaving in a way that might appear deliberately obstructive. Aware that she was only allocated a few minutes with the form teacher, she was uncertain whether she actually wanted to hear what the woman had to say. Mrs Proudy's report was evidently going to be disagreeable. On top of everything else Christine had been contending with lately, she wasn't sure she could take much more stress.

'Has she been having any problems at home that might have upset her?'

'I'm not sure I know what you mean,' Christine kept up her pretence, playing for time while she tried to decide how to answer what felt like an implied accusation.

'We're just trying to find out if there's any reason for Daisy's belligerent attitude. Has anything happened that might have thrown her off balance?'

'Belligerent?' Christine repeated dully. 'Off balance?' She forced a laugh. 'You make it sound as though she has some kind of mental problem. I thought she was just going through a phase. Normal teenage angst is what her form teacher said at the end of last term. *She* really knew Daisy,' she added pointedly. 'She said all the moodiness was part of growing up. Puberty, you know?'

'I know what puberty is,' Mrs Proudy replied frostily. 'I've helped many adolescents through problems of all kinds. It's a challenging time for many of them.'

'You only recently met Daisy,' Christine pointed out, conscious that she was sounding plaintive. 'Surely it's a bit early to start forming a judgement about her.'

She refrained from adding that she couldn't imagine Mrs Proudy being very supportive to any of her charges who were struggling.

'I haven't known Daisy for long, but I've seen enough to gain an impression of her state of mind.'

'Is her state of mind really your concern? I mean, you're not a psychologist. With all due respect, I think you should concentrate on my daughter's school work and leave her state of mind to me.'

'Not when it's affecting her work. She needs to understand that Year Ten is an important year for her in terms of her education and her whole future. I'm afraid currently she's simply not focused on her studies. She's not a stupid girl, but if she doesn't apply herself she can't expect to do herself justice in the exams, which would be a great pity.'

'Well, her education is your responsibility and you don't seem to be doing a very good job if she's not going to do well in her exams,' Christine snapped.

She regretted the words as soon as they left her lips, but it was too late to recall them. The other woman's face remained rigid and before either of them could speak again, the bell rang to signal their time was up. Although the discussion was unresolved, Christine was relieved to move on. She was in no doubt that the form teacher felt the same way. After that spiky confrontation, the encounters with Daisy's other teachers passed in a blur. None of her subject teachers said they had a problem with Daisy, although they all reported that she was very quiet in class and a few of them suspected she was coasting and 'could do better', as her school reports always said. Clearly there was a personality conflict between Daisy and her form teacher which was unfortunate. If Christine hadn't been keen to avoid any probing into the situation at home, she would have complained about Mrs Proudy. The woman was callous and supercilious. Thinking about their conversation, Christine swore under her breath. The cheek of the woman, telling her Daisy was belligerent. This was all Peter's fault, she thought bitterly as she left the school.

As though in response to her thoughts, a shrill voice cut into her reverie. 'Christine! Hello! Where's Peter? Are you here on your own?'

She glanced round to see the mother of Daisy's best friend. 'Fiona! How are you?' she responded politely, pretending she hadn't heard the other woman's questions.

Fiona launched into a monologue about what a pity it was that her daughter and Daisy were no longer close friends. 'Don't you remember they were inseparable last year?' she said. 'I really thought Lara had a friend for life. You must have thought the same, I'm sure. Do you know what happened?' She carried on talking, without waiting for an answer. 'Lara says Daisy's changed, but there must be more to it than that. I told her, you don't give up on friends just because they change, do you? And how much can she have changed anyway? That's what I told Lara, but she just said it was nothing to do with me.' She shrugged. 'You know what these girls are like.'

'Yes,' Christine muttered, forcing a grin and wondering how she could extricate herself from the situation without being rude. 'I don't know what gets into Daisy sometimes.'

'Well, I do. If you ask me, it's boys,' Fiona whispered theatrically. 'I wonder what they fell out about, or should I say *who*? I suppose they both fancied the same boy.' She gave a knowing wink. 'We remember what it was like to be fourteen, don't we? Every little thing seemed so important and nothing was more important than boys. Well, never mind. They'll get over it and hopefully come to their senses and realise that boyfriends come and go but a girlfriend can be a friend for life.'

Before Christine could respond, Fiona hailed another mother who was passing by and Christine seized the opportunity to sidle away. On her way home, she mused about what Fiona had said and wondered whether she was right. Christine had been so ready to blame Peter she might have missed the obvious reason for her daughter's unhappiness. Perhaps, after all, there was nothing more sinister behind Daisy's angst than typical teenage relationship problems.

27

EACH TIME SHE CALLED him her heart seemed to race, but the ringing always stopped before it went to voicemail. After a frustrating day, she was forced to conclude that there was a problem with his phone. Irritated that he hadn't realised there was something wrong and found another way to contact her, she bought a cheap phone from a grubby little shop in a side street and was almost surprised when he picked up straight away.

'Hello?' Hearing his voice made her feel slightly dizzy. 'Hello? Who's there?'

Had she had been at home she would have been sitting down but, too impatient to wait, she had called him from the pavement right outside the phone shop.

'It's me,' she blurted out excitedly.

She waited for him to launch into a stammered apology for his failure to contact her. Obviously he hadn't meant the terrible things he had said, but all the same it was unkind of him to have spoken like that to her, of all people, when he knew she loved him better than anyone else ever could. It was almost as though he didn't *want* to be loved, but she knew that couldn't be true. She tried not to think about the horrible things he had said, but his words kept reverberating in her mind. Apparently she disgusted him, which was an absurd thing to say, given the passionate nature of their affair. Claiming he had never wanted a serious relationship with her was just more nonsense, because they already *were* involved in a serious relationship. The poor boy was so confused it was pitiful. She smiled, thinking how magnanimous she was going to be and how grateful he would be when he understood that she forgave him wholeheartedly for his thoughtless remarks.

The phone cut out.

She dialled his number again and this time the line went dead after only one ring. She was becoming distraught. If she couldn't speak to him, how were they ever going to sort out their misunderstanding? There seemed little point in trying again straight away. Nevertheless, she tried a few more times before resigning herself to waiting until she was home to call his number once more from her new phone. This time, it didn't connect at all. Clearly his phone was still malfunctioning, which meant there was only one thing for it. She was reluctant to follow him, like some weird stalker, but she had no other choice. It might feel humiliating, chasing after him like this, but as long as it meant they would be together again, nothing else mattered. She didn't know where he lived, but he had told her he worked at a hotel in the centre of town. It was simply a question of going into every hotel in York until she found him. It wasn't as if she had anything better to do.

However long it took, she would track him down and then she would show him how ardently she loved him. In the face of such devotion, he was bound to admit his passion and stop trying to hide it. She knew he loved her deeply and was just bowled over by the strength of his feelings. It was perfectly understandable. He was young to be dealing with such a powerful emotion. Once she found him, she knew she would easily persuade him they were destined to be together and then everything would return to how it had been before their stupid falling-out. He couldn't run away from her forever. But before she could persuade him there was nothing to be afraid of, she had to find him.

The staff at the first hotel she tried were no help. No one seemed to have heard of anyone working there called Daniel. She went through the same frustrating rigmarole at the second hotel and the third. She persevered, but she was beginning to lose hope when, at the seventh hotel she tried, she finally received the answer she wanted. This one was a functional hotel in the centre of town, too small to even have a restaurant of its own. Guests, she was told by a receptionist, were given vouchers for breakfast at the restaurant next door. Jeannie looked appraisingly at the receptionist who was probably in her early twenties and undeniably attractive, with a short blonde bob and large blue eyes. Looking at the girl, it struck Jeannie that there could be another reason why she had been unable to contact Daniel. Perhaps the truth was that he had deliberately stopped taking her calls. As soon as the idea occurred to her, she dismissed it with a shudder.

'Actually, I'm not looking for somewhere to stay,' she said, forcing a smile. 'I'm looking for someone.'

The girl looked at her with a puzzled frown.

'He's called Daniel,' Jeannie pressed on with dogged determination, 'and I think he might work here.' She was about to continue, when the girl broke into a smile.

'Oh, Daniel,' she said. 'If you mean Daniel Barker, then yes, he works here. He's not in today. You can leave a message for him, if you like. I'll make sure he gets it.'

Jeannie couldn't decide whether to trust her. If the girl was after Daniel herself, she was bound to try and fob off any potential rival for his attention.

'Are you close to him?' she enquired, studying the girl's reaction carefully.

To be dumped for this attractive airhead would be devastating after everything Jeannie had done to ensure she and Daniel could be together. He belonged with her, not with some young floozy who wouldn't know how to appreciate him. He needed the discernment of an older woman, someone who really understood him. But she couldn't say any of that aloud.

The girl looked puzzled. 'What do you mean?'

'Don't worry about it,' she replied. 'There's no message.'

She hurried out onto the street, breathing fast and reeling with excitement. Daniel might think he could avoid her, but she wasn't going to give up on him so easily. Now she knew where he worked, all she had to do was watch him and find out where he lived. She would soon discover if he was seeing anyone else. The more she thought about everything that had happened, the more likely it seemed that someone was trying to steal Daniel away from her. In fact, there was no longer any doubt about it. There wasn't a fault with Daniel's phone. The reason she hadn't been able to contact him was because he was refusing to talk to her. She hadn't believed him when he had told her it was over between them, but it seemed he had meant it. To the consternation of a young woman who was walking past, without warning Jeannie burst into despairing sobs.

'Oh dear,' the woman said. 'Is something wrong? Is there anything I can do?'

'Oh, mind your own business,' Jeannie snapped, sniffing back her tears. 'What's it got to do with you?'

The stranger looked put out and seemed about to retort, but she evidently thought better of it and stalked away, affronted. Jeannie regained control of herself quickly. There was no time to lose. Glancing around for somewhere to conceal herself, she spotted a café across the street and went in. A table by the window was free and she took a seat and ordered tea. She had a clear view of the hotel over the road and resolved to return there the following day. She checked the hours on the menu and decided to arrive as soon as it opened in case Daniel was on an early shift. Out of sight in the café, she would sit in the window and observe Daniel arrive at work and wait for him to emerge. When he left the hotel, she would slip swiftly out of her hiding place and follow him, taking care that he didn't spot her. Once she had discovered where he lived, it would be simple to ascertain what was going on. And if he was being unfaithful, then she knew what to do. Any rival for Daniel's affections must be eliminated, swiftly and permanently. That prospect didn't bother her. After all, she had done it before. She smiled grimly to herself. As long as she continued to be careful, nothing could go wrong. Far from troubled by what she would need to do, she realised she was looking forward to it. When it came to true love, she now knew that anything was possible.

28

MOST OF DAISY'S TEACHERS seemed happy enough with her progress, or at least were not sufficiently worried to raise any issues. Nevertheless, Christine had a sneaking suspicion that Mrs Proudy might actually have had a point when she raised concerns. She had complained about Daisy's 'belligerence' and suggested something might have happened to 'disturb' her. Shocked by the teacher's forthright comments, Christine had done her best to dismiss the suggestion which felt like an accusation. But however strenuously she attempted to conceal the truth from other people, she couldn't ignore the fact that Daisy's behaviour seemed to be increasingly unstable. Christine missed Peter more than she would have thought possible, because there was no one with whom she could share her anxieties. Other mothers might sympathise and possibly even understand, but they might be indiscreet. She didn't want her problems to become a source of gossip. She certainly wasn't going to share the fact that Peter appeared to have abandoned her. The more she thought about it, the more convinced she became that, while his disappearance might not have been the cause of Daisy's surliness, it certainly wasn't helping. There was no doubt that, since her father had gone, Daisy had become more volatile than ever.

Fiona's theory about Daisy's behaviour was curiously comforting. Boy trouble was relatively easy to understand and it sounded so normal. Christine was determined to learn the truth but was nervous about asking Daisy directly. Instead, she resolved to search her daughter's room while she was at school and see if she could find anything that would help explain Daisy's concerns. She prevaricated for a long time before reaching a decision and bounding up the stairs. Feeling like a criminal, she opened the door to Daisy's room and went in. Expecting to be confronted with a mess, to her surprise, she found clothes hanging in the wardrobe, with T-shirts folded and stacked on the shelf and underwear arranged neatly in the chest of drawers. There were no wrinkles in Daisy's bed cover and her bin was empty. On the surface, there was nothing to indicate any reason for Daisy's distress. But there was something almost impersonal about how tidy the room was, as though Daisy was hiding something manic beneath a façade of order. Yearning to penetrate her daughter's shield of hostility, Christine wept.

Not for the first time, Daisy was late home that evening and Christine waited anxiously for her to return. The time she arrived home from school had become erratic. When challenged, Daisy had retorted that the buses were infrequent and often full. Christine's offer to collect her from school had been dismissed with an unpleasant scowl, as though Christine had wanted to throw her daughter into a cold shower, not give her a lift home to save her waiting for the bus.

'Don't you dare come and pick me up from school,' Daisy had snapped. 'I'm not five years old. God, why are you so determined to embarrass me? Can't you just leave me alone?'

Christine could have pointed out that she hadn't actually done anything that might embarrass her daughter; she had only offered her a lift. It wasn't as if she had turned up at the school gates unexpectedly. But she didn't bother to argue. She had discovered through bitter experience that confronting Daisy only exacerbated her bad moods.

When the bell rang, she hurried to open the door, assuming that Daisy had left her key at home or else couldn't be bothered to rummage for it in her bag. She hoped she hadn't lost it.

Plastering a welcoming smile on her face, she prepared to greet her daughter and was disappointed to see that it wasn't Daisy on the doorstep after all.

'What's happened?' she asked, suppressing a sour feeling of dread. 'Is something wrong?'

'Nothing's wrong,' the detective answered. 'I just wanted to check whether you've thought of anywhere your husband might be.' She paused before asking if they could go inside.

Christine frowned, but she couldn't really refuse. Besides, the police could have come up with some information about where they thought Peter had gone. It might look suspicious if his wife showed no interest in learning of his whereabouts. Without another word she led the way into the living room, muttering that she hoped this wasn't going to take long because she was expecting her daughter home at any moment.

'I don't want her upset any more than she already is,' she added irritably. 'She's naturally worried about her father. I've tried to reassure her that he's probably away with his work, but I don't think she believes me. Seeing you here is only going to get her all worked up again.'

'I'll make this brief,' the inspector replied. 'Your husband opened a bank account recently and we wondered if you could tell us about it.'

'What account? I don't know what you're talking about. Peter didn't open any bank account recently. He would have told me.' Christine hesitated. 'Do you mean you think he was leaving some money for me because you believe he was planning to leave us? That's ridiculous. He would never have abandoned us. Never.'

The inspector shook her head. 'Are you quite sure he didn't tell you about an account he opened recently? It was about a month ago. We're working on tracking down the source. We're confident we'll trace it quite soon but it would be quicker and better for you in the long run, if you told us what these payments were for.'

Christine shook her head. Since Peter had disappeared, she had felt so alone. Life seemed to be spinning into a nightmare scenario where nothing made any sense. Only a week ago everything had been fine, apart from Daisy's adolescent moods which she and Peter had assured each another she would grow out of. She hadn't yet; in fact she had been getting worse. But then he had disappeared and now a police inspector was pestering her with crazy allegations of a bank account she knew nothing about. She insisted that she didn't know what the detective was talking about and eventually the inspector left, after reminding Christine to let the police know if she heard anything from Peter. Christine shut the front door behind her with a sigh of relief and returned to the kitchen to see to the dinner. Soon after the inspector had gone, the front door slammed. Daisy was home. Christine called up to her but she didn't answer. With a sigh that sounded a bit like a sob, Christine put the kettle on. There was no point in trying to talk to Daisy. She would call her when supper was ready and hope she would come downstairs then and eat something.

When her phone rang, she almost didn't answer but there was a faint chance it could be Peter, so she picked it up and checked the screen. Once again she was disappointed, because it wasn't her husband calling, but her friend, Lucy.

'I missed you at the gym today,' Lucy burbled. She sounded curiously excited. 'Is everything okay?'

'Yes, no,' Christine replied. All at once she began pouring out her concerns about Daisy. Lucy listened without interrupting until Christine had finished.

'What about your husband?' Lucy asked at last, when Christine fell silent. 'Doesn't he have something to say about it? He is her father, after all. Your daughter does have two parents.'

'She's not exactly badly behaved,' Christine equivocated, succumbing to an impulse to defend Daisy that was almost involuntary. 'She's just going through an awkward adolescent phase, you know. We have to make allowances.'

'Not if she's being rude, you don't,' Lucy replied tartly. 'That sounds like unacceptable behaviour to me. You know, there's never any excuse for rudeness. It's your job to teach her some manners. If you can't do it yourself, you should get your husband to speak to her. One of you, at least, ought to instil some discipline into her. It's never too late to start.'

Christine knew her friend was only trying to be supportive, but she wished she would stop talking about Peter. Of course, Lucy had no idea that Peter had walked out without a word of explanation, or that he had apparently opened a bank account recently without telling her.

'You need to ask your husband to speak to her,' Lucy persisted, oblivious to Christine's discomfort. 'My husband always dealt with matters of discipline,' she added, and paused as though waiting to hear Christine's response. 'I'm just trying to help,' she added irascibly when Christine didn't answer. 'Teenage girls can be a real trial but it's up to you to set her some boundaries.' When Christine still didn't answer, she went on more gently. 'Try not to be disheartened. It's not your fault she's finding it hard, going through puberty. They do grow out of it. Has your husband spoken to her? I know when my husband stepped in, that was when my daughter really started to take our criticisms on board. Children never listen to their mother.'

Christine dithered. Her friend had no idea Peter was missing. Rather than feeling inclined to talk about him, Christine fervently wished she could forget all about him. Replying shortly that she would think about what Lucy had said, she made the excuse that she had to attend to her cooking and ended the call. She went to the bottom of the stairs and shouted that supper would be ready soon. Daisy didn't reply.

29

DNA EVIDENCE HAD IDENTIFIED the dead man as missing bank manager, John Hodgson. His wife had been reluctant to go to the mortuary to make a formal identification. They had reassured her that it wasn't strictly necessary for her to corroborate the DNA evidence. At first she had seemed relieved, but she changed her mind after a few days and requested permission to see him. Geraldine arranged to meet her outside the hospital, ostensibly to support her and help her to find the way to the mortuary through the back entrance to the hospital. Geraldine's real motive for being there was to observe Jeannie's reaction on seeing her dead husband. Although, as yet, there was no evidence linking Jeannie to the attack on her husband, she remained on the list of suspects. While the manner of his death made it unlikely, it was not impossible that she had been responsible for the fatal stabbing.

Ariadne argued that living with John would have afforded Jeannie more reliable and less strenuous opportunities to kill him. The serious crime team had come across several cases where a victim had been murdered by a spouse. Most of the attacks occurred within the privacy of the victim's home, not out on the street where the killer risked being seen. At the same time, there was no denying that Jeannie had an obvious motive for wanting her husband out of the way. On his death she had inherited his entire estate and was now, if not wealthy, at least very comfortably off, owning a valuable property in addition to her late husband's savings. A few of Geraldine's colleagues doubted she was strong enough to have carried out a violent assault on her husband, but even the most sceptical of them agreed that she could have employed a hitman to do the job for her.

Geraldine arrived at the hospital first. She was beginning to think Jeannie might have changed her mind when she spotted her approaching the entrance, looking fraught. She was shivering as she greeted Geraldine and clutched her arm as though in need of support. Whether or not she was responsible for her husband's untimely death, the prospect of seeing his corpse might be upsetting. Guilt and grief were both powerful emotions and it was impossible to determine which was causing Jeannie to tremble. Having offered a few words of reassurance and condolence, Geraldine led the widow to the visitors' entrance to the mortuary where an attendant greeted them and escorted them to the waiting room. There, the attendant talked to Jeannie and prepared her for what she was about to see. When Jeannie was ready, the attendant took them to see the body. Obliged to stand back, Geraldine wasn't able to see Jeannie's face once they were in the room with the body.

John was lying under a sheet. The attendant gently lifted the top and folded it back to reveal a face which Geraldine had not seen since the post mortem. He had been cleaned up and only by looking in the right place could she discern where his head injury was concealed. Although pale, he looked as though he could be asleep. Jeannie let out a whimper and covered her face in her hands. Geraldine stifled a sigh. Even if she had been staring directly at Jeannie, she wouldn't have been able to see her expression. She wondered if the widow was looking appropriately wretched or maliciously jubilant. Neither, of course, would prove her guilt or innocence. All the same, Geraldine wished she could have observed an involuntary reaction from Jeannie. The widow's shoulders heaved and she began to sob, mumbling incoherently from behind her hands.

Her voice was muffled but after a moment, the words: 'It's him, it's him,' could be heard. Without removing her hands from her face, Jeannie swung around and shuffled towards the door. The mortuary assistant took her by the elbow and guided her from the room. Geraldine followed sombrely. So far, the visit had revealed nothing that might indicate that Jeannie was guilty.

Seated in the visitors' room, Geraldine waited for Jeannie to lower her hands from her face. She had stopped sobbing. After a few minutes, she dropped her hands and reached for the tea the mortuary assistant had fetched from a machine in the corner of the room. The cup shook in her hand. Geraldine smiled sympathetically at her, registering that her eyes were wet with tears. All the same, there was something not completely credible about Jeannie's grief.

'So do you think Jeannie killed her husband?' Ariadne asked when Geraldine shared her suspicions with her friend.

'I was standing directly behind her so I couldn't see her reaction when she first saw the body,' Geraldine admitted. 'And then she covered her face before we left the viewing room.'

'Do you think she did that deliberately?' Ariadne asked. 'I know you said she was crying, because you saw her eyes were wet, but that doesn't mean her tears were genuine. Some women can make themselves cry when they want to. My sister used to do it all the time and my parents always fell for it,' she added with a touch of asperity which Geraldine found slightly surprising in someone who was usually sympathetic towards everyone. 'She might have been genuinely upset or she might have been deliberately trying to pull the wool over your eyes.'

'I have no idea whether her tears were genuine or not,' Geraldine admitted crossly.

'You're not wrong to suspect Jeannie,' Ariadne said. 'I mean, she certainly has a motive, but her situation is no different to any other wife who stands to inherit her husband's estate. It doesn't mean she's implicated in his murder. We don't have any evidence to suggest she's guilty. We can't charge a woman just because she married a man who was subsequently murdered.'

'I thought you suspected her as well.'

Ariadne shrugged. 'Honestly, I don't know what to think.'

'I know what you mean. This is all still just speculation,' Geraldine said, scowling with frustration. 'Whether or not Jeannie is guilty and whether we suspect her or not, what we need is evidence. And that seems to be in short supply.'

'It's hard to believe the killer left no trace at the scene of the attack,' Ariadne said.

'Although that in itself could be a kind of clue, because doesn't it suggest that this was a planned attack and not a random mugging?' Geraldine replied thoughtfully. 'And Jeannie wouldn't be worried about leaving any traces of DNA on the body, because she was with him regularly.'

Everything seemed to come back to Jeannie, but absence of evidence against anyone else was not proof that John's widow was guilty. They needed more than that if they were going to build a case against Jeannie and wherever they looked, evidence seemed to elude them.

'A clever killer, that's all we need,' Ariadne said. 'Or a lucky one.'

'We're just going to have to be cleverer,' Geraldine replied.

'And luckier?'

Geraldine shook her head. 'We can't rely on luck,' she said. 'It's dedicated detective work that's going to help us find this killer.'

She tasked Ariadne with re-examining Jeannie's alibi and Naomi with setting up a team to take a further look at CCTV from the street where John was killed. But she was aware that they were going over old ground and she was worried that their usual approach wouldn't be enough to uncover the truth. So far in her long career, she had always successfully completed murder investigations. She hoped this would not be the first time she led a team to failure.

30

Daisy grabbed a new box of tissues from the bottom of her wardrobe and sat on her bed. Ripping off the perforated oval opening on the top of the box, she set to work shredding one tissue after another. It wasn't as satisfying as cutting herself, but it left her with no residual pain and, more importantly, it was easier to hide than nicks and blood stains. Mrs Proudy had been giving her funny looks and Daisy was convinced the old cow knew what she had been doing. As if it was any of her business, or anyone else's for that matter, what Daisy chose to do with her own body. She had to do something to distract her from the memories that tormented her night and day. Everyone was driving her nuts. All of her teachers were intrusive, but Mrs Proudy was the worst of the lot. It was just Daisy's luck to be saddled with her as a form teacher, having to see her horrible leering face every morning. And then there was her mother who was on at her from the minute she got home until she left the house in the morning, pestering her to eat, to do her homework and to spend time together. Her mother seemed to want to talk endlessly about nothing at all and was constantly on at her to respond to her badgering, however much Daisy insisted she had nothing to say.

She could hardly admit that there was only one thing on her mind and that was something she could never reveal to anyone. If they ever found out what she had done, she didn't know exactly what might follow, but she knew that she would be in the most terrible trouble. She had never meant for it to happen and, in a way, none of it had really been her fault. That was to say, she hadn't intended to harm him, but he had driven her too far. In the end it had been the impulse of a moment to launch herself at him. He hadn't seen her coming and then wham! Her blow had caught him off guard, causing him to fall with a resounding crash. The noise had seemed deafening and she had frozen, paralysed with shock, expecting people to come running to find out what could have caused such a racket.

How could she begin to explain how years of pent-up frustration and loathing had erupted in an uncontrollable outburst of fury? A blood-red filter had seemed to fall over her eyes and she had struck without warning or restraint. The resulting devastation had been astonishing and she had remained rooted to the spot, shaking as a wave of dreadful joy throbbed in her veins. Coming to her senses, she had turned and fled before anyone found her there at the scene of the attack. Having acted without thinking, she nevertheless couldn't deny that she was completely and solely responsible for what had happened, not unless she lied. And that was exactly what she had been doing ever since. The strain of maintaining her deception was wearing and since that glorious and terrible moment she had lived in constant fear of discovery.

She had no idea what might happen to her if she was found out. She would deny the accusation of course and, in the absence of any witnesses, it was possible they wouldn't be able to prove anything against her. But she had no way of knowing whether she would get away with it. She couldn't even hazard a guess. She imagined trying to defend herself. Whatever accusation was levelled at her, she was prepared to lie through her teeth, vigorously refuting the charge. It would be too unfair if she was convicted of a violent assault when he had been the one who had provoked the attack by tormenting her for so long. She imagined they would say she had been wrong to take the law into her own hands instead of reporting him for abusing her. And in any case, she had no way of proving that he had behaved inappropriately towards her. He certainly wasn't going to help her.

Of course, she wouldn't be entirely alone. They would give her a lawyer whose job it would be to defend her, but she didn't know what would happen if the lawyer didn't believe her. Would they still agree to defend her, knowing she was guilty? She didn't have a clue how the legal system worked. What if everyone suspected her and no one was prepared to defend her? She would have to manage on her own. She pictured herself, all alone in a courtroom like the ones she had seen on the television, facing a stern-featured judge and a group of unsympathetic grey-haired jurors. They would probably all be ready to convict her on account of her age alone. Worst of all, everyone she knew would be watching the case unfold. Her mother would be there, staring apprehensively at the judge and jury, or weeping noisily. Perhaps Mrs Proudy and other teachers from her school would be in the courtroom, listening sceptically and muttering to one another that they weren't surprised, each one them claiming they had always known she was a bad lot and would end up getting herself in trouble. But, of course, they would all cover their backs and pretend to be astounded that she had ended up facing criminal charges.

'If only we'd realised how unhinged she was, we would have referred her for psychiatric treatment,' Mrs Proudy would claim. 'But she's a devious creature and she hid her madness from everyone. Her own mother had no idea how sick she was, so how were we supposed to know?'

She had worked her way through half the box of tissues before she burst into tears of self-pity and had to press a hand over her lips to stifle the sound of her sobbing. Eventually her crying fit passed and she flung herself on her pillow, worn out. Miserably, she gazed around her room. She had once been so happy here, but that was before she had started to develop physically, attracting unwanted attention. At first she had found it unsettling but then it had become disturbing. He had caught her unexpectedly in deserted corners, forcing her against the wall, pressing against her with his smelly body. She had wanted to shout at him to get off her and leave her alone, but every time it happened she had been too scared to call out, afraid that no one would believe her. Just the memory of it made her shudder. All of that was over, for good, but now she faced another problem and that was his fault too.

She drew another tissue out of the box and began tearing it into shreds which fluttered down to join a growing pile of white scraps on her bed. From downstairs she could hear her mother calling her for supper but she ignored the plaintive cries. Only when she heard her mother coming upstairs did she hurriedly hide the shredded tissues that formed a mound of white on her bed, ephemeral as a snowman in changeable weather. Grabbing handfuls of fragments of paper, she stuffed them under her pillow, and turned to face the door. Glancing down, she spotted a few stray scraps of tissue that had escaped her scrabbling fingers and floated down to the floor. Swearing, she hurled herself from the bed just as she heard her mother knock at the door.

'What do you want?' she yelled, frantically gathering up the detritus of her flimsy destruction. 'Don't come in!'

'Supper's ready,' her mother called out wistfully; she didn't open the door but waited outside for permission to enter.

'Go away!' Daisy shouted as she shoved the renegade pieces of tissue under her pillow to join the others.

'Aren't you coming down for supper?' her mother's voice reached her, muffled by the door.

'I'm not hungry.'

'Daisy, you have to eat something.'

'Go away and leave me alone.'

'I'll keep your supper warm for you.'

After a moment, Daisy was relieved to hear her mother going back downstairs. She picked up the half-empty box and began methodically tearing up the remaining tissues, but the activity was no longer as comforting as it had been earlier. With an angry sob, she hurled the box across the room. It knocked over a mug of coffee that had been standing on her desk, untouched, for a couple of days. Thankfully, it missed her desktop computer and keyboard; a brown puddle oozed over one side of the desk, staining an art project she had started, and dripped on to the carpet. She wasn't bothered about her school work, nor did she care about the carpet. All the same, she put the tissues which remained intact to good use, mopping up the spilled liquid, sobbing to herself all the while.

31

GERALDINE AND KEY MEMBERS of the investigating team were summoned to an impromptu briefing, which suggested the detective chief inspector had new information that she wanted to discuss with them. Geraldine and Ariadne hurried to the major incident room together, catching a few minutes to chat along the way. There was barely time to establish that neither of them knew what the summons was about, before they arrived and greeted their assembled colleagues. Binita arrived a moment after them. Looking around to check that everyone was there, she nodded at Detective Sergeant Naomi Arnold who had been tasked with looking into Peter's finances. Her colleagues all knew that Naomi had discovered the bank account he had recently opened, of which his wife claimed to be ignorant.

'Are you sure she didn't know about it?' Binita asked Geraldine.

Geraldine shrugged. 'It's impossible to be absolutely sure. She told me she knew nothing about any bank account Peter had opened last month, but she could have been lying. I definitely have a feeling she's keeping something back, but whether it's that or something else is difficult to say.'

'As you know, payments have been made into a new bank account opened in Peter Selby's name,' Naomi said. 'The payments were made a month apart. Each was for five hundred pounds.'

'So that's a thousand pounds so far,' a sergeant muttered fatuously.

167

'Both payments were made by John Hodgson, from his own personal account, the second one just a couple of days before he was killed. We've checked and this has been confirmed by the bank. The payments were made from John's own account.'

There was a brief silence while the assembled officers digested this information.

'So John Hodgson recently began paying money to Peter Selby and a month or so after these payments began, John was killed by an unknown assailant and Peter disappeared. The two men are clearly linked, but how and why?' Binita said. 'That's what we have to find out. So, any thoughts on avenues to pursue?'

'If John was paying Peter, then it looks as though John owed Peter money for something or perhaps Peter was blackmailing him,' Ariadne suggested. 'But if John was paying him, why would Peter have killed him?'

'Unless Peter *was* blackmailing him and John decided to stop paying or report him to us for blackmailing. It is a crime, after all, and possibly whatever secret about John Peter had discovered wasn't that terrible, or at least wouldn't attract a custodial sentence. He might have been having an affair and not wanted his wife to find out.'

There were a number of plausible explanations for monthly payments of five hundred pounds going out of an account in John's name to Peter's account and blackmail was certainly a possibility. Ariadne was instructed to organise a small team of constables to question the staff at John's bank again and see if there was any rumour of misappropriation of funds, or any illicit activity, or perhaps an affair, for which he might have been blackmailed. Christine having denied any knowledge of the payments, Geraldine went to pay a visit to John's wife and see if she could shed any light on the situation. If Jeannie had discovered that John was having an affair, that would give her a powerful motive for murdering him in a crime prompted not by avarice, but passion.

She found Jeannie at home. The house looked exactly the same as Geraldine remembered it, but the garden seemed less neat somehow. Presumably John had been the one to tend it. In little more than a week, a few weeds had begun to sprout between the shrubs. Perhaps they had been there before and Geraldine hadn't noticed them. Having always lived in flats without a garden of her own, she wasn't particularly attuned to garden maintenance, although she and Ian enjoyed visiting parks and public gardens. Jeannie came to the door after a brief delay. Her hair was once again tightly permed and she was dressed in a black skirt that was rather short and a tight dark grey jumper. She evidently liked to show off her figure, but this time her clothes were suitably sombre for a widow. As before, Jeannie reached up to pat her curls and Geraldine recognised this was a habit of hers.

'Inspector,' she greeted Geraldine. 'Well? I hope you've brought me news of my husband's mugger. It's been over a week, you know. I would have thought you could have come up with something by now.'

'We haven't traced his assailant yet, but we're working on several leads.'

'Is that true? Or does that mean you have no idea who's responsible for my husband's death?'

Geraldine hesitated to reply.

'I hope you're not going to abandon your investigation?'

There was something wistful in the glance she gave Geraldine, as though she couldn't bear to think of her husband's killer escaping justice.

'I assure you we won't stop until we find out who killed your husband. I came here to ask you about something else related to our investigation. We want you to tell us everything you know about your husband's financial situation.'

Jeannie let out a curious bark of laughter. 'Oh dear, I'm afraid I can't help you with that. He was a bank manager, you know,' she added with a touch of fatuous pride. 'He dealt with all our money matters. I really don't know anything about it. They could probably help you at the bank?' she added.

'Your husband was making monthly payments of five hundred pounds to a man called Peter Selby,' Geraldine said. 'He's a salesman, so we think your husband might have bought something on hire purchase and was making monthly payments.' That wasn't strictly true, although Peter was a salesman of sorts, but it sounded plausible and not too accusatory.

'I know nothing about that,' Jeannie said. She sounded awkward, as though embarrassed that she was ignorant of her husband's transactions. 'We didn't really talk about things like that at all. Money and so on. I left everything like that to him. He was good like that. He looked after me. I wouldn't put it past him to have started a savings scheme of some kind for me without letting me know. He was always keen to take care of me.'

The problem with that theory was that Peter Selby had opened a new personal bank account into which John Hodgson had been making payments. There was no other activity on the account which appeared to have been opened with the sole purpose of receiving payments from one payee, a man who had been murdered.

Geraldine collected Tom from the childminder and listened responsively to his babbling in the car. He was beginning to form recognisable words, although his meaning was often obscure. But all the time she was driving home and answering Tom's chattering, she was thinking about the relationship between John and Peter. Somehow, if they could only solve that conundrum, she felt fairly sure they would discover who had killed John, if his death had indeed been deliberate murder and not an accidental fatality in the course of a violent mugging. Ian had made dinner and they chatted inconsequentially as they ate, frequently interrupting their conversation to address Tom, who chuckled with delight every time they spoke to him.

'Do you think he understands what we say?' Ian asked.

'Of course he does.' She turned to her son. 'Tom, where's your hand? Show me your hand.'

Tom obediently raised his podgy little fist and waved it in the air, crowing with pleasure when Geraldine clapped her hands and told him what a clever boy he was. Only later, when Tom was asleep, did Geraldine discuss her thoughts on the case with Ian. But he was as bemused by it as she was. They agreed the team needed to investigate further to dig up more information.

'They have you on the team. You've never failed yet.'

'I'm glad you have such faith in me,' Geraldine replied, smiling.

'And you've got Naomi on the case, haven't you?' Ian asked. 'She's good at this kind of online research, isn't she? Between her and the forensic accountants, you'll get to the bottom of it.'

Geraldine sighed. 'I really hope you're right.'

She wished she shared Ian's confidence, but somehow the team seemed to be struggling. She had an exasperating feeling the solution was right in front of her, but she just couldn't see it.

32

IT WAS NEARLY DARK and she still hadn't seen Daniel leave work. The café had been closed for some time but she remained in position, hiding in a shop doorway, her eyes fixed on the front of the hotel. She told herself it didn't matter how long she had to wait. It would be worth it in the end. Her only fear was that he might already have left and she had missed the chance of seeing him. She could always come back the following day and the day after that, returning again and again, but she didn't want to wait that long. In the meantime, she could be lurking in the shadow of a shop window to no purpose while he was happily ensconced at home, wherever that was, with another woman. Thinking about her situation, she cursed herself for her oversight. It was ridiculous that she didn't know where he lived, especially since she hadn't been able to take him home with her, for obvious reasons. Once, she had suggested they go back to his lodgings, but he had refused, saying his place was a mess. When she had assured him she really didn't care how untidy he was or what his rooms were like, he had become defensive. Reluctant to alienate him, she had capitulated immediately and since then they had always met in hotel rooms. The arrangement had seemed to work well. Only now did she appreciate her stupidity, when it was too late. But regrets were futile. She needed to act.

Standing in the shop doorway she started to fret, despite her determination to wait patiently. She regretted not having started her vigil earlier. There could be another way out of the hotel where he worked, a back exit that couldn't be seen from where she was standing, across the street. Knowing he worked irregular hours she hung on, in case he was working late that day. She still wasn't quite sure what he did, although he had explained it to her. His job had something to do with accounts and it sounded deadly dull, although he had told her he enjoyed his work.

'It's just a question of seeing that everything tallies as it should,' he had told her once. 'Imagine a gigantic jigsaw and your job is to make sure every piece is where it should be, in the right column. It can be challenging but it's ultimately very satisfying when it all works out. It's a job, anyway. Of course, without the accounts programmes it would take forever.' He had laughed.

Although she liked to see him laugh, she had frowned and told him she didn't know what he was talking about.

'Before long, AI will be doing everything and I'll be out of a job,' he added, suddenly crestfallen.

'If you're half as good at your job as you are in bed, then they're lucky to have you,' she had replied. 'And I know one activity where AI will never replace you. Now stop talking about work and come here.' She had patted the bed and he had obligingly come over and lain down beside her.

Lost in the memory, she almost missed him when he emerged from the front entrance of the hotel. He strode off, head down, collar up, the skirts of his raincoat flapping around his legs. She loved seeing him in that long coat which she thought made him look like a spy. He had laughed when she told him that and had called her a silly goose. On his lips the insult had sounded like a term of endearment. Shaking off her reverie, she slipped from the sheltered step where she had been hiding and set out in pursuit. He didn't have a car so she was fairly sure she would be able to follow him, but once he set off, she struggled to keep pace with him. If he looked round, she was ready to pretend to be looking in a shop window if she was passing one, or to turn away completely. She was wearing a new black hooded jacket which he had never seen and was confident he wouldn't recognise her from behind. If he did manage to spot her, she would act as though she was astonished at bumping into him. He might suspect she was following him, but she was prepared to deny the accusation with as much indignation as she could muster, or perhaps she would feign amusement. She rehearsed a few possible responses under her breath as she trotted along behind him, doing her best to keep out of sight while not losing sight of him.

'Following you? Why would I want to follow you? I'm just doing some shopping.'

'At this hour?'

She shook her head, dismissing that imaginary exchange as too implausible.

'I'm just on my way home from meeting a friend,' might sound more convincing. She would do her best to carry it off, although the truth would probably be obvious. She debated with herself whether it actually mattered if he saw through her subterfuge. After all, her pursuit of him was testimony of the strength of her feelings, as if he needed any more proof of her love after she had killed her husband for him.

He walked on, unaware of her scurrying frantically after him. She hoped he wouldn't catch a bus, as that would make it tricky to avoid being spotted. He had once mentioned that he lived near the hotel where he worked, but she didn't know how close. Passing a couple of bus stops, he kept going along Walmgate to Lawrence Street and along Millfield Lane. Young and fit, he could certainly walk further than her, as well as considerably faster. After nearly half an hour she was ready to give up. Her legs were aching and she was breathing heavily. He might not even be going home, in which case her arduous excursion was pointless. On the point of accepting that she would have to devise a different plan, she saw him slow down and turn into Tang Hall Lane. She hovered on the corner, watching him walk away, her reluctance to lose sight of him battling with her fear of being discovered. Effectively, she was stalking him. Were he to catch sight of her in the street where he presumably lived, it would be obvious she was spying on him. She could hardly claim to be on an errand in this quiet residential street. Lying about having a friend who lived in Tang Hall Lane might just land her in even more trouble if he decided to challenge her.

But he didn't look around, and she saw him walk up to one of the blocks in the lane. There was nothing more she could do for now, short of loitering on the street corner indefinitely. She turned and hurried away, resolving to return the following evening with her car so she could watch the building unobtrusively. She wasn't sure which flat was his, but if she parked across the road a few doors further on, she would be able keep an eye out and see his approach in her rear view mirror. Sitting in her car every evening, hunched down out of sight behind the steering wheel like a private detective, she would watch his block of flats and follow him whenever he went out. If he met another woman, she would know what to do.

She shivered with anticipation. He might think he could dump her but he was going to discover that he couldn't simply walk away from her, not after everything she had done for him. They were inextricably connected, not only by their enduring devotion, but also by the terrible secret that had removed the only obstacle to their love. Although Daniel knew what she had done, he hadn't reported her to the police, which made him an accessory to the murder. That was how she knew that he loved her as much as she loved him. He would realise the truth soon and then nothing would ever come between them ever again. She smiled, remembering the touch of his lips and the feel of his body, making her feel young and desirable once more. Soon they would be together for the rest of their lives and nothing would ruin their happiness. Humming to herself, she walked back into town, this time setting her own pace.

33

GERALDINE WAS FEELING FRUSTRATED. Not only was the case she was involved in complex, but the team couldn't seem to find a clear path through all the confusing evidence. They had suspected a connection between John and Peter for a while, since one had been killed and the other had disappeared on the same day. The discovery of John's payments to Peter confirmed that the speculation had been justified and there was indeed a link between the two men. What the police hadn't yet been able to find out was how or why the two men knew one another. Jeannie and Christine claimed to know nothing about any financial arrangements between John and Peter. No one else was likely to be aware of the reason for the transactions. Nevertheless, they were keen to ask everyone associated with each of them individually, in case someone had information that might help them to work out what had been going on.

Geraldine was sitting in the canteen with Ariadne, discussing what could have linked the two men, before they set off to try and discover what lay behind John's payments.

'It looks as though he was starting to make regular monthly payments,' Ariadne said. 'If it was blackmail, that would mean he had been doing something he didn't want other people to know about. So far we've not managed to find any evidence that he was helping himself to bank funds, but he was the manager and so presumably he would have known how to cover his tracks if he was stealing.'

Geraldine nodded. 'That all sounds plausible, only it's hard to see how Peter could have discovered any irregularities in John's dealings at the bank. If the payments had been made to one of John's colleagues, then that might make sense. Someone at the bank could conceivably have stumbled on some irregularity. But Peter was an estate agent. How could he have found out about it, if John was misappropriating bank funds?'

'Maybe Peter was blackmailing him about something else. What about Lily Transom, the woman Eileen suspected might have been having an affair with him?'

Geraldine shook her head and assured her friend that had proved to be a dead end. Just to be sure, she had checked out Lily's story and corroborated everything John's former colleague had told her over the phone. After questioning another of his former colleagues, Emma, she had grilled Eileen, who had been the source of the rumour suggesting John had been having an affair. The story had turned out to be groundless speculation. But there remained clear evidence of a connection between John and Peter. The fact that money had changed hands between the two men was enough to convince Geraldine that solving the murder case would lead them to find the missing man, Peter. The most likely explanation was that Peter had killed John and then panicked and fled. They had searched records of trains and buses leaving York without finding any trace of his leaving the city. All the taxi services had likewise drawn a blank. Peter's car was parked on his drive. They were fairly sure he was still in York, but he had gone to ground somewhere and they needed to find him as soon as possible.

'People don't just disappear,' Ariadne said.

'Not without good reason,' Geraldine added.

Geraldine decided to run her concerns past Binita, who listened in grim silence, finally agreeing that they needed to explore the reason for the payments John had made to Peter. If nothing else, the fact that neither Christine nor Jeannie claimed to know about the money changing hands rang alarm bells about the relationship between their husbands, suggesting that the transactions had been kept secret. Geraldine agreed with her senior officer that the payments could be perfectly innocent, but they might turn out to be a lead worth pursuing.

'It could be the key to Peter's disappearance,' Binita agreed. 'And we need to find him urgently so we can question him about John's death. If he doesn't show up soon, we'll do a television appeal and see if anyone in York has sighted him. He's hiding out somewhere and, wherever it is, someone must be helping him.'

Geraldine had a new theory about Peter's whereabouts which she ran past her senior officer. Binita agreed that it was possible. In the meantime, she sent a team to question Eileen and other staff at the bank again, this time focusing on John's payments to Peter. No one there appeared to know anything about it.

'Eileen was pretty sharp with me,' Ariadne said. 'She told me in no uncertain terms that what John chose to do with his own money was no one else's business. According to her, he didn't discuss his finances with her and she didn't pry into his personal circumstances, and she didn't think anyone else should either. I don't think she was hiding anything. I suspect she spoke that way because she believed she was protecting his reputation.'

Geraldine nodded, imagining the peremptory manner in which Eileen had addressed the detective sergeant. While Ariadne was occupied supervising a team at the bank, Geraldine set off to speak to Peter's wife. This time, she had agreed with Binita that she would take a search team with her. Visual identification image detection officers were still trawling through CCTV from trains and buses that had left York over the preceding week, but so far there had been no sighting of Peter leaving the city. Minnie wasn't a particularly reliable witness, but in any case she hadn't been able to say whether she had seen Peter leave Drakes Close. It was possible that Peter had been hiding in his own house for a week, with Christine covering for him.

Christine looked anxious when she saw Geraldine on her doorstep. 'If you haven't come to tell me you've found him, you might as well turn round and leave straight away,' she said. 'You can carry on hounding me until you're blue in the face, but I've told you everything I know, several times. I've no idea where my husband is and that's the truth.'

She sounded sincere, but Geraldine needed proof. 'I've brought a few colleagues with me,' she said quietly. 'We'd like to search the property. We can wait for a search warrant if you insist, but we would like to get this over with.'

Christine shrugged. Watching her closely, Geraldine didn't detect any change in the other woman's worried expression.

'Go ahead. Be my guest. Search as much as you like,' Christine said, sounding resigned. 'I've got nothing to hide. And if Peter's still here, he must have found a secret chamber I don't know about. Perhaps there's a concealed door in the wood-panelled library,' she added with a flash of irritation.

Geraldine summoned the search team and they set to work, checking each of the rooms.

'It's all clear down here,' one of the constables told Geraldine. 'We're just heading upstairs.'

'Please don't go in my daughter's room,' Christine called out, suddenly apprehensive. 'She doesn't let anyone in there.'

'I'm sorry,' Geraldine said, 'but we have to search everywhere.'

'There wouldn't be much point otherwise,' one of the constables pointed out cheerfully. 'Don't worry, madam, we won't disturb anything.'

Christine scowled but there was nothing she could do. Murmuring reassurance, Geraldine went upstairs to oversee the search of Daisy's room herself. At first sight it looked like a typical teenage girl's room with a bed, a built-in wardrobe and a small desk for a computer. The walls were covered with posters of what Geraldine guessed were singers, their faces plastered in black make-up and piercings. What was unusual was the amount of what appeared to be confetti which a constable discovered concealed under the duvet and pillow, and in the bin.

'It's not confetti, it's tissues,' a female constable called out. 'She likes ripping up tissues.'

'What a waste,' her male colleague replied.

'What a weirdo,' the female constable muttered, barely audibly. 'Still, teenagers, what are you going to do?'

They could see there was no one else in the room. Nevertheless, they checked under the bed and in the wardrobe, anywhere a man might be concealing himself from their search. There was no basement, but the team searched in the loft. They found no sign of Peter anywhere in the house. A pair of constables went out into the garden and looked in the shed.

'They're certainly thorough,' Christine admitted, almost admiringly, as she watched the search team through the window. 'I hope they'll be finished soon. Daisy will be back from school in an hour or so and I don't want you lot crawling around the house when she gets home. They'd better not have moved anything in her room.'

She was clearly more concerned about upsetting her daughter than about her house being searched from top to bottom. Geraldine was convinced they wouldn't find Peter there.

'Is that everywhere?' Geraldine asked a constable as she followed Christine downstairs. Her colleague nodded. 'What about the garage?' Geraldine enquired.

The constable shook his head. 'We haven't looked in there yet,' he said.

'Look in there, if you want to,' Christine said. 'There's an internal door to it off the kitchen. The key's hanging on a hook beside the door. But it's just full of junk. If you're going to look in there, please get on with it. Daisy will be home soon. I really hope you're gone by the time she gets back,' she added plaintively.

Geraldine thought of the expression Ariadne used when she teased Geraldine about her pedantic approach to her work. 'No stone unturned,' she murmured under her breath. 'Search the garage,' she instructed the constable. 'And then we'll call it a day and leave Christine in peace before her daughter gets home.' She smiled reassuringly at Christine, who returned her gaze blankly.

34

As the search team went off to look in the garage, Geraldine turned to Christine to repeat her assurance that they should be gone in a few minutes. Geraldine followed Christine back into the bright, spacious living room. As before, she silently admired the fireplace and the view through the bay window. Despite the disruption to the household, it was a peaceful room. Geraldine could picture herself living in a house like this with Ian and Tom. So far she had resisted Ian's wish to move from their flat to a house with a garden which, he insisted, would be better for them as well as for Tom. She understood Ian wanting them to buy a home together. Although they were settled where they were, Geraldine had bought the flat before she entered into a relationship with Ian, using equity on the flat she had previously bought in London with money she had inherited from her mother. She had chosen the flat for herself and in some ways it remained her flat.

It had already become cramped when Ian moved in and now they had all of Tom's accoutrements to accommodate as well as Ian's few belongings. It was surprising how much space one small child took up, with his cot and changing table, along with a little cupboard for his clothes and a variety of brightly coloured containers for his toys. As Tom grew, he was going to need more space. In addition, Ian was keen to get a dog, which meant they would have even more pressing need of a garden. Geraldine had not yet agreed to that.

'One step at a time,' she had said.

'But we're agreed we want to move to somewhere larger,' Ian had replied, and she was unable to raise any credible objections to his proposal.

'Let me just get this case over with and then we'll have more time,' she had told him.

'You've said that before,' he reminded her with a tolerant smile. 'There's always going to be another case. Sooner or later we need to tackle this, Geraldine. We can't stay here forever.'

Sitting in Christine's neat and comfortable living room, Geraldine smiled. A house like this would suit her very well. She gazed through the window at the far end of the dining room which looked out on a well-stocked back garden. The sun was shining and she could picture Tom and Ian kicking a football around on a lawn like that, with a small dog capering around them. She was drawn abruptly back to the present by the sight of a constable emerging from a shed at the far end of the garden.

Christine looked understandably pale and drawn. 'I should check her room, but I wouldn't know if they'd moved anything or not,' she admitted wretchedly. 'I know it sounds daft, but I daren't go in there when she's at school. I'd like to change the sheets more often, but she doesn't want me to go in there. I suppose she's entitled to her privacy.'

Geraldine was tempted to point out that this was Christine's house and she should be able to go wherever she wanted in it, but she said nothing. Not for the first time, she wondered about the dynamics within the Selby family where Daisy's behaviour sounded as though it bordered on coercive control.

Christine looked around helplessly and then, without warning, started to cry. 'I'm so sorry,' she blurted out, sniffing and visibly struggling to recover her self-control. 'I'm sorry. It's just that everything's been so difficult since Peter disappeared. Daisy's been impossible and I'm so worried you'll still be here when she gets home. It's bound to upset her and I know nothing I can say or do will placate her. Everything seems to upset her these days.

She seems to be, I don't know how to explain it – spiralling out of control. I never appreciated it when he was here but I think maybe Peter was acting as a restraint on her, a kind of grounding influence, if you know what I mean. Fathers are supposed to be the figures of authority in a family, aren't they? Although I'm not convinced anyone still subscribes to that old-fashioned theory. But since he left us, Daisy's become more withdrawn than ever and her behaviour has – well, deteriorated, I suppose you could say. If she was sullen and unresponsive a few weeks ago, she's now become quite aggressive. I sometimes think she's like a cornered rat.' She shrugged and looked shamefaced. 'That's not a nice thing for a mother to say, is it? But I'm nervous about approaching her at all these days. Even her school seem to think she's having problems. Her form teacher intimated as much.' She gazed at Geraldine in evident consternation. 'I didn't know what to say to them.'

'Do the school know about her father's disappearance?' Geraldine asked gently. She hoped to keep Christine talking. If she let her guard down, she might let something slip that would help the police to discover Peter's whereabouts.

Christine shook her head. 'It might have been a mistake to keep quiet about what's going on here, but I just can't bear the thought of her form teacher snooping into our family affairs, quizzing Daisy about it and generally poking her nose in where it's got no business to be. I've been wondering if my arguments with Peter upset Daisy.' She broke off, as though realising she had been indiscreet. 'The thing is,' she stammered, 'we've not been getting on too well lately, but that's only because we've been arguing about Daisy.' She stifled a sob. 'And now he's gone and I don't know what to do.'

Geraldine was hopeful she might be able to draw Christine out, but before she could speak again, a constable rushed in, red-faced and panting. Geraldine frowned at the interruption and made a mental note to talk to him later about maintaining a professional approach at all times and being sensitive to what was going on around him.

'There's something you need to see,' he blurted out unapologetically. He drew in a shuddering breath and hesitated, perhaps recalling where he was. When he glanced apprehensively at Christine, Geraldine thought she understood.

'Wait here with Mrs Selby,' she told the constable and he nodded, looking relieved.

'What's going on?' Christine asked, looking from the constable to Geraldine and back again. 'Do you know where my husband is?'

'Wait here,' Geraldine repeated.

With a depressing sense of foreboding, she made her way through the kitchen to the garage. The rest of the search team were standing in a row at the far end of the garage, their expressions sombre.

'He's in there, Ma'am,' one of them said solemnly. 'In the disused freezer.'

Geraldine carefully made her way over to a dilapidated freezer in one corner of the garage. The lid had been flung back allowing her to look inside without stepping right up to the battered appliance. One glance was enough. Accustomed to viewing the dead and already forewarned that he was in there, it was still a shock to find herself staring into the unseeing eyes of a corpse. Until he had been formally identified they couldn't officially name the deceased, but she had seen enough images of the missing man to recognise Peter Selby. The freezer wasn't switched on but it was fairly cold in the garage. Protected from insect activity or exposure to the air, he had scarcely decomposed and it was difficult to judge how long he had been there.

'Call it in straight away,' she snapped, her professional training overriding her reaction to the body. She nodded at the sergeant who was leading the search team. 'Don't let anyone in before the SOCO team get here. I'll go and speak to his widow.'

As she made her way back to the house, she wondered whether Christine would be shocked by the news or if she already knew what had been concealed in the old freezer in her garage. 'I wonder how long he's been there?' she muttered to a constable stationed at the door.

'And who else knew about it,' the constable replied.

'That's what we need to find out,' Geraldine said, but she was smiling grimly because the location of the body narrowed down the list of suspects.

Back in the house, Geraldine watched Christine closely as she asked her to accompany her to the police station to answer a few questions. She decided to make the request sound casual, so as not to alert Christine to what was happening. She wanted to remove her from the house before the pathologist and the SOCO team arrived. Once they turned up, the flurry of activity around the garage would betray the presence of Peter's corpse. On the other hand, if they could catch Christine by surprise in an interview, she might incriminate herself. If she wasn't responsible for her husband's murder, then it might be unkind to keep the discovery of his body from her, but given where Peter had been discovered, Christine was almost the only suspect.

'What? No. I mean, I can't. Daisy will be home soon. She's going to want her supper. You said you'd be gone before she got back,' Christine protested.

'I'm afraid I'm going to have to insist,' Geraldine said. 'Is there anyone else Daisy could go home with? A relative or a neighbour?'

Christine shook her head wildly. 'There's no one,' she replied angrily. 'No family who can help. There's Lucy, I suppose,' she replied uncertainly. 'I could call her and ask her to meet Daisy at the school, if she's free. That way Daisy won't have to come home to the house, if you're still here. At least she's met Lucy, even if only briefly. But do I have to come now, just when Daisy's due back? Can't it wait?'

'I'm afraid not.'

'All right, let me just make a call.'

'You can do that on the way,' Geraldine told her.

'I don't see what the hurry is,' Christine muttered sourly as she picked up her bag and followed Geraldine out to the car.

35

'THAT'S FUNNY,' SUZIE SAID, leaving her post at the window and joining him on the sofa.

'What is?'

Daniel leaned forward to spear an olive. Watching her soft lips remove it delicately from the cocktail stick he was proffering, he smiled, knowing she trusted him not to jolt and prick her skin with the point. He suppressed an urge to throw his arms around her and promise he would never hurt her; he didn't want to scare her off by seeming too keen. She was so adorable; he could hardly believe she was there, in his home. Living alone, he usually left things just lying around and he had spent hours tidying in preparation for her visit. For once, there were no dirty plates or empty beer cans strewn around the place. He wondered whether she had taken particular care over her appearance for their date or if she had come in what she had been wearing all day. Her pale blue floaty kind of skirt looked like something she might wear for going out, but her navy jumper was quite ordinary.

'Oh, it's probably nothing,' she replied. 'It's just that – no, it's too silly. Don't worry about it.' She looked faintly embarrassed so he didn't press her to explain herself, instead asking if she was hungry.

She smiled and admitted that the olives had whetted her appetite. He topped up her glass of expensive Italian red wine and turned towards the kitchen.

'I'll just go and check on the pasta bake,' he said.

'I never thought I'd be lucky enough to meet a man who could cook,' she grinned up at him.

'You haven't tasted it yet,' he warned her.

He didn't tell her that he had been practising making this dish all week. This would be the sixth time in a row he had prepared it and he was thoroughly sick of it, but he had the recipe off pat and he hoped she would be impressed. Barring accidents, he was confident he could pull it off. Leaving Suzie sipping her wine, he went to the kitchen and felt a twinge of culinary pride as he manoeuvred the pasta bake out of the oven. If things went well with Suzie and he cooked for her again, he would practise another dish until he had perfected it to maintain the impression that he could cook. As he was dishing up, his phone rang. He glanced at the screen and swore under his breath. Eventually she would get the message and stop chasing him, but in the meantime the stupid bitch was really grating on his nerves. Quickly he silenced his phone, hoping Suzie hadn't heard it ring, before he carried the plates into the living room that doubled up as a dining area.

'This looks wonderful,' Suzie said, turning away from the window where she had been standing looking out.

Daniel beamed and pulled out a chair for her. She took her seat with a sigh of contentment and smiled at him. Sitting down, he thought the table looked rather dull and kicked himself for not having prepared a bowl of salad to add some colour, or lit a candle to create a romantic atmosphere, but it was too late to make any changes. At least he had spent the previous day tidying and cleaning, and the apartment didn't look too shabby. She had said how nice it looked and had seemed genuinely impressed with it. As long as she didn't look in any of the cupboards which were crammed with random possessions, it would be fine. She picked up her fork and he realised he was holding his breath as she took her first mouthful. He lowered his eyes before she noticed him staring at her. Her cheeks were flushed from the wine and her eyes were bright.

'You look beautiful,' he blurted out almost involuntarily.

'Thank you,' she murmured, adding that the food was excellent.

The conversation flowed easily as they questioned each other about their work and exchanged anecdotes.

'I don't know how you manage to teach so many children, all at once,' he told her. 'I've got a ten-year-old nephew and he's uncontrollable. And there's just one of him.'

The dinner went well and he was very pleased with the result of his efforts.

'I didn't make this,' he admitted, laughing, as he served waffles and ice cream with butterscotch sauce for dessert.

As they returned to the sofa, Suzie paused by the window to look down at the street.

'That's funny,' she said again.

'What is?' Daniel asked.

'There's a car outside.'

'Well, it is a street,' he replied, grinning.

He was completely in control of himself, but drunk enough to feel that he was an irresistible master of witty repartee. He had produced a perfect dinner, he was a charming and debonair host, and if Suzie wasn't already smitten with him, he was convinced she soon would be. She didn't seem to be in any hurry to leave.

'No, I mean, it's the same car,' she said. 'I noticed it parked there over the road when I arrived, and it was there when we sat down to eat, and it's still there now.'

Daniel frowned, unsure where this was heading. 'So someone's parked in the street. What's funny about that?'

'It's just that there's someone in the car. She's been sitting there for hours. Do you think she's all right?'

Daniel felt a flicker of alarm run through him like an electric shock because he realised who it must be. Praying that he was mistaken, he stood up and went over to look outside. Standing to one side of the window so he couldn't be seen from the street, he peered down. He didn't recognise the car, but it occurred to him that she might have hired a car for one specific purpose: to spy on him.

'Do you think we should go and see if she's all right?' Suzie asked.

'No,' he replied, more brusquely than he had intended.

She looked at him, startled.

'That is,' he went on, 'it's a public highway. Whoever's in that car isn't doing anything wrong. They're probably waiting for someone.'

'Daniel, she's been there for hours.'

'It could be an unmarked police vehicle on surveillance. We shouldn't interfere.' He smiled reassuringly. 'In any case, you don't know how long the driver has been sitting there. You haven't been standing at the window all the time, watching, have you? I dare say whoever it is left their car for ages while they went home for dinner and now they're getting ready to go out again. I don't think we need to worry about it.' He pulled at the control and the curtain slid across.

She nodded and smiled. 'I'm sure you're right and there's nothing to worry about.'

He returned her smile, hiding his feelings. Because he was worried. He was so worried that his overwhelming emotion was relief when he succeeded in persuading Suzie to stay the night with him. Suspecting he was being stalked by a woman who was obsessed with him, he was afraid of what might happen to Suzie if she walked out of his front door into the darkness of the night. He almost told her what was on his mind, but held back, not wanting to sound conceited. And, after all, he could be wrong. He was hardly the sort of man to drive women crazy with desire. Suzie would probably find such a claim ridiculous. He resolved to put off mentioning his fears until the morning. If the car they had seen was still there when they woke up, he would tell Suzie about his sinister ex.

After a glass of wine, he gazed at Suzie and thought how beautiful and precious she was. If anything were to happen to her, he would never recover. Impulsively he reached out and cupped her chin in his hand.

Without really meaning to say anything about it, he heard himself warning Suzie about his crazy stalker. He did his best to play it down and gave no hint that he had been in a relationship with her. To admit to being involved with a woman so much older than he was would be mortifying.

'We only met a couple of times,' he lied, 'but she developed this weird crush on me. I know it sounds unlikely, but the point is, you mustn't let her near you.' He paused. 'I think she might be jealous.'

Suzie looked bemused. 'It sounds like de Clérambault's syndrome. You know, where someone becomes freakily fixated on someone they don't really know. I read about it somewhere.'

He nodded, relieved that she believed his story.

'How will I know it's her if I do see her?' she asked.

'Wait here.'

He found a passport sized photo Jeannie had given him and handed it to Suzie, who raised her eyebrows in surprise at the printed picture of a middle-aged woman pouting at the camera. She stared at it for a moment before saying that Jeannie looked old. Daniel laughed to hide his embarrassment.

'Why have you kept her photo?'

He shook his head. 'To begin with, I kept it in case she persisted in pestering me, so I could show it to the police. But it's more important you keep it, so you remember what she looks like and can avoid her. Take it and put it in your bag now.'

'If you insist,' she replied, doing as he asked and slipping the photo in her beaded bag. 'I'll keep the photo of the crazy woman.' She smiled and he thought how adorable she looked.

'Never mind about her,' he said, leaning forward to kiss her.

36

CHRISTINE ARRIVED AT THE police station apparently shocked and close to tears. Her once-flawless make-up looked as though it had been hurriedly applied without the use of a mirror; black smudges under her eyes gave her a slightly clownish appearance and her hair, which had been neatly coiffured, was now dishevelled. A fortnight earlier, she would most likely have been shocked at her own appearance. But what struck Geraldine most forcefully was an air of self-control so subtle it could easily be overlooked. It manifested in a fleeting squint of her eyes and the way her lips were pressed together, as though she was determined to weigh up every word she uttered. It remained to be seen whether her disturbed state was due to learning that her husband's body had been stored in their old freezer for over a week, or to her fear of being accused of murder. Either way, Geraldine doubted they would get much sense out of her for a while.

Asked whether she wanted to call a lawyer, Christine just stared blankly at her interlocutor without answering as though she didn't understand what was being said to her. By the time a duty brief arrived, she had drunk a cup of sweetened tea and seemed to have recovered her composure. Geraldine observed Christine closely across the interview table. For a moment, she was barely conscious of Ariadne's presence at her side and felt as though she was alone with the suspect. Christine was gazing around warily, but there was a curiously calculating expression on her face. Ever since she had been informed that her husband's body had been found, she had maintained a determined silence and Geraldine wondered whether she was as confused as she appeared.

If anything, the lawyer at her side appeared more agitated than the suspect she was there to defend. With a pale complexion and widely spaced, round eyes, she blinked nervously and appeared to be constantly surprised. Added to that, she didn't look old enough to be qualified. Wearing a crimson jacket that was too large for her, she resembled a child dressing up in her mother's clothes. Geraldine thought this was probably the first time she had defended a suspect facing a murder charge. Observing the flustered young lawyer, Geraldine wondered how confident Christine was feeling. Lately, the lawyers Geraldine saw all looked as if they were fresh out of school, but she was aware that they were only getting younger relative to her.

As Geraldine prepared to start the interview, Christine interrupted the routine preamble, breaking her silence for the first time since she had heard about the discovery of the body in her freezer.

'Where's Daisy?' she demanded. 'I won't say another word until I know she's safe.'

Geraldine reassured her that Lucy had met Daisy from school and taken her home.

'And what have you told her about what's going on?' Christine leaned forward in her seat and stared fiercely at Geraldine. 'Does she know what's happened?'

Geraldine explained that apart from Christine so far no one outside the investigating team knew Peter's body had been found. The next day either Christine herself, or else a well-trained family liaison officer, would face the unenviable task of revealing the truth to Daisy. After that, as Geraldine knew but refrained from pointing out, the media would get hold of the story and emblazon headlines like: 'Body in freezer' and 'Shock contents of family freezer' on their home pages. Some might imply Peter's wife was guilty of killing her husband. Journalists were bound to mention that it was the police, not a member of the household, who had made the gruesome discovery. The reports would be merciless and horribly predictable, asking whether it was plausible that a wife could be ignorant of the fact that her husband's body had been stored in a disused freezer in her garage. It was a reasonable question and one which Geraldine needed to put to Christine. For now, she returned to the subject of Daisy, and how much she knew about the discovery of her missing father's body.

'We can't keep it from her indefinitely,' Geraldine said gently.

'I'm not suggesting keeping anything from her,' Christine replied sharply. 'She has a right to know her father is dead,' she added in a curiously distant tone of voice.

For a moment, she seemed to switch off as though she was uninterested in the interview. That was odd, given that her own liberty might shortly be at risk. Geraldine wondered if Christine understood how close she was to facing a murder charge and how damaging even the mere accusation might prove for her. At the same time, she appreciated the suspect might be putting on an act, pretending to be incapable of knowing what she was doing.

'Let's go back to the beginning,' Geraldine suggested, with an encouraging smile. 'When did you last see your husband alive?'

Christine scowled. 'I've only ever seen him alive.'

'When was the last time you saw him?' Geraldine rephrased her question, noting that Christine was more alert than she appeared.

'You probably know the answer to that better than I do, because we've been through this already, more than once. It was on Monday morning, just over a week ago, as I've said repeatedly. Look, this is pointless.' Christine turned to the doe-eyed lawyer sitting beside her. 'How long can they keep me here? I want to get back to my daughter. She needs to be at home with me. This is all going to be disturbing enough for her without her being foisted off on other people.'

'This could drag on for a few hours, maybe overnight,' the lawyer murmured anxiously. 'And then they'll have to release you,' she added quickly, before Christine could respond.

Christine turned back to Geraldine. 'Look, I take it you've brought me here because you think I killed my husband? Well, I didn't. Inspector, I'm not a complete moron. Do you really think I'd be stupid enough to leave his body there, in my own garage, where my daughter could have come across it?'

Geraldine gazed steadily at Christine as she posed her next question. 'Did you keep your garage locked?' she asked quietly.

On the point of answering, Christine suddenly shut her mouth and lowered her eyes. 'No comment,' she muttered almost inaudibly.

After that, Christine refused to answer any further questions and the lawyer insisted on taking a break so she could confer with her client. Geraldine terminated the interview and she and Ariadne went to talk to Binita.

'It seems clear enough,' the detective chief inspector said cheerily. 'Since no one else had access to her garage, there is really only one suspect. It's time to charge Christine Selby with murder.'

Ariadne went to fetch coffees from the canteen before going to discuss the situation back at Geraldine's desk.

'What bothers me is that I can't believe she would have left the body where her daughter might come across it,' Geraldine said.

'She probably never meant to leave it there but just hadn't worked out how she was going to move it. The attack might not have been premeditated and then, once she realised he was dead, she might have panicked and not known what to do. In any case, she seems as though she might be a bit unhinged,' Ariadne suggested. 'She's probably going to pretend she's not responsible for her actions. But it must have been her. There's no one else it could be. Did you see the way she suddenly stopped talking when she realised the game was up? If her brief hadn't insisted on taking a break, she would have confessed then and there. She's that close to caving in. The next time we see her, I think she's going to confess.'

Geraldine shook her head. 'I'm not sure.'

Ariadne shrugged. 'Well, I don't see how you can have any reservations about it. Obviously, she's guilty and once she confesses, that'll be that.' She grinned.

By the time they resumed the interview, Christine appeared to have made a decision.

'I am perfectly calm and in my right mind,' she said, speaking slowly and clearly. 'I killed my husband. I didn't mean to kill him. We'd been arguing and on the spur of the moment I pushed him into the freezer and closed the lid.'

She stared defiantly at Geraldine who gazed back at her in silence, while the lawyer asked to speak to her client in confidence.

'My client is upset—' the lawyer burbled, aghast. 'She doesn't know what she's saying.'

Christine turned to the lawyer. 'Of course I know what I'm saying. I have nothing to add. I've confessed and am ready to face the consequences of my crime.'

The lawyer remonstrated and started fussing about how Christine was temporarily unhinged by her grief at the loss of her husband, but Christine turned on her and snarled at her to be quiet. The lawyer stared at her client in panic but kept silent.

Geraldine frowned. 'How did you do it?'

Christine looked surprised and a little put out that the interrogation was continuing.

'I pushed him into the freezer,' she replied shortly.

'Your husband was a fairly powerful man,' Geraldine went on smoothly. 'He kept himself fit. How tall are you?' She paused.

'We're interested to know you how you managed to overpower a tall, strong man and lift him up over the edge of a chest freezer.'

Christine nodded as though she had been expecting this question and answered promptly. 'It wasn't difficult because he was already leaning over the freezer. I hit him on the head and shoved him inside it and slammed the lid shut before he could escape.'

'Why was he looking inside a disused freezer?' Geraldine asked, doing her best to sound sceptical.

Christine sniffed. 'He was just looking to see if there was anything in there. We were thinking it was time to get rid of it and I asked him to make sure it was empty. As he leaned over, it struck me that this would be the perfect way to get rid of him so I knocked him out and pushed him in.'

'And then you left him to suffocate in there?' Geraldine enquired.

Christine nodded.

'Wasn't that a bit risky?' Geraldine asked. 'What if he'd recovered?'

'There was no chance of that. The lid was airtight. The freezer wasn't working, but the seal on the lid was intact.' She spoke so dispassionately, it was hard to believe she was anything but a cold psychopath.

But Geraldine had to be completely satisfied. 'Where did you hit him?' she asked.

Christine looked baffled. 'I've told you what happened. I've confessed to killing my husband. What more do you need from me?'

'You said you knocked him out when he was leaning over the side of the freezer. Where did you hit him?'

'Oh, on the head.'

'It must have been on the back of his head, as he was leaning over, so he didn't see it coming. And you would have had to hit him right at the top of the spine for the blow to knock him out,'

Geraldine said, nodding as though what they were discussing confirmed what the post mortem had shown.

'Exactly,' Christine confirmed. 'I hit him on the back of his head and pushed him in the freezer.'

'What did you hit him with?'

This time Christine hesitated, as though afraid she had admitted too much. 'I can't remember. I was in a daze. I just grabbed something and hit him and then I pushed him over the edge. It all happened in a blur.' She burst into tears and the lawyer insisted on terminating the interview. 'My client is distressed,' she said. 'She doesn't know what she's saying.'

Geraldine thought Christine knew exactly what she was saying. Whether or not she was telling the truth was another matter.

37

No one else on the team seemed to share Geraldine's reservations about Christine's guilt.

She did her best to ignore her misgivings, but she couldn't dismiss them. Feeling uneasy, she decided to investigate further. With that in mind, she went to speak to the pathologist again. Hurrying past Avril with a muttered apology for being in a rush, she went to find Jonah. He looked up and grinned on seeing her and – after making his usual quip about her not being able to keep away from him – he turned to Peter Selby, lying motionless on his back. His bloodshot eyes were staring straight at the ceiling and his skin was an ugly mottled dark purple.

Leaning towards the grotesquely discoloured face, Jonah spoke cheerfully. 'You find my comments entertaining, don't you? You know, you're free to heckle if you don't appreciate my humour.' He put his head on one side, his ear to the dead man's face for a few seconds, before he straightened up. 'No? See, he's silent as the grave – which is where he's going as soon as we're done with him.'

Geraldine grimaced at Jonah's poor attempt at a pun. She scolded him for his appalling taste in jokes, although she appreciated this was his way of dealing with his horrific work. They exchanged a smile of complicity, both understanding the unspoken game they were playing. Their macabre greetings over, she enquired about Peter's cause of death and Jonah finally cast aside his levity and settled down to work. 'Enough of this banter,' he said, waggling a finger at her with mock severity.

'I know you only come here to flirt with me, but seriously, Geraldine, we have work to do. So let's get on with it.' He inhaled deeply and closed his eyes for an instant, as though refocusing his mind. 'Now, you want to know the cause of death? It's a little tricky to be specific about what actually finished him off, but there are a number of factors you need to consider. First, he was hit on the head and that blow might have knocked him out. At any rate, he would probably have been stunned. He must have been heavy and difficult to shift, but if he was already leaning over the side of the freezer where he was found, it might have been possible for someone to manoeuvre him inside it.'

'Could a woman have done that?' She wanted to add 'or a girl', but held back.

'I'd say it would have taken a huge effort but yes, it's certainly possible.'

Geraldine nodded to show she was following and Jonah continued.

'So, we have him somehow doubled up inside an old freezer, probably unconscious, suffering an epidural hematoma.'

'Caused by the blow to the head?'

'Indeed. While such a condition is not necessarily fatal, without treatment to remove the hematoma it would almost certainly lead to physical weakness and seizures, if not death. And then there's the issue of the airtight container he's trapped inside. Assuming he was unconscious, or too weak to open the lid, it was only going to be a matter of time before he suffocated. And I'm afraid that's exactly what happened.'

'So he was left in there after a knock on the head and suffocated.'

'In short, yes. Death from asphyxiation isn't always a completely clear-cut diagnosis and there were other issues at play here, as I mentioned.' He reached forward and delicately touched a large bruise on the dead man's temple. 'There are signs of visceral congestion from dilation of blood vessels, and petechiae – where veins have been broken by intravascular pressure – still visible in the eyes. But the most obvious sign of the cause of death is the marked discolouration of the skin through cyanosis, which is an indication of asphyxiation.'

Geraldine frowned. 'Show me again where he was hit.'

'Here, right on the side of the head.' Jonah pointed once again to the large contusion on Peter's left temple. 'The skin is so discoloured, it's hard to spot, but you can see the indentation from the blow and the injury to the skull is clear evidence of a heavy blow right here. Whoever hit him nearly had his eye out. They definitely weren't playing nicely.'

'Could the killer have dealt a blow like that if they were standing behind him?'

'No. Unless they had superhuman strength, they must have been standing at his side.'

'But then surely the victim would have seen the weapon coming at him?'

'Not if his assailant was standing slightly behind him and his head was turned slightly away from them.'

Geraldine frowned. What Jonah was telling her seemed to confirm her suspicion that Christine had lied about killing her husband.

'Could he have been hit on the back of the head as well?'

'If he was, it wasn't done with sufficient force to leave any trace of the blow. I can't say for certain that he *wasn't* hit on the back of the head, but there's nothing to show that such a blow *was* dealt.'

Driving back to the police station after logging her report, Geraldine considered what Jonah had told her. Given that Christine seemed obsessed with protecting her daughter, Geraldine was already fairly convinced that Christine was unlikely to have left the body anywhere in the house where Daisy might come across it. As far as she knew, Daisy was the only other person who had access to the garage. Christine must also have realised that. If she believed that Daisy had killed her father, it was plausible that Christine had confessed to the murder in an attempt to protect her daughter. The more Geraldine thought about it, the more convinced she became that this was the most likely explanation for Christine's confession. Her thoughts turned to Tom and she wondered what lengths she might go to in order to protect him. Would she risk life imprisonment – as an ex-police officer – to prevent her son being convicted of murder? Her adult life had been devoted to fighting crime. To give up her own freedom so a murderer could escape justice went against everything she believed in. But she couldn't be sure she wouldn't make the sacrifice she suspected Christine was making. What kind of a police officer did that make her? But what kind of a mother would fail to do everything in her power to protect her child?

38

AFTER CHRISTINE HAD BEEN locked up in a horrible cell for twenty-four hours, the stout custody sergeant opened the door and told her to follow him. Nothing loath to escape her claustrophobic prison, she accompanied him along a grey corridor back to the desk to collect her shoes and bag. After that, another officer escorted her to an interview room where the dark-haired inspector was waiting for her. Slightly puzzled about having her belongings returned to her, Christine steeled herself for the transfer to prison. Now she had confessed to murder, there was no other possible outcome. She couldn't contain her surprise when the dark-eyed inspector told her she was free to go, but was not to leave the city.

'You mean you're letting me go?' she blurted out. 'Aren't you going to charge me? I told you, it was me. I did it. I killed him.'

The inspector appeared to hesitate. 'We can't charge you without evidence which we're still in the process of gathering,' she replied cautiously, before adding, 'but we expect to have this case wrapped up soon. We'll keep you informed. For now, you can go and fetch your daughter and take her home.'

Christine frowned, wondering what to say. Having confessed to killing Peter, she didn't understand what was going on. A wave of exhaustion washed over her. All she could think of was that she was miraculously free to take Daisy home, so that was what she would do. After spending a night in a police cell, where she had struggled to find a comfortable position on the hard bunk and had barely slept, she was suffering from a stiff back and a pounding headache. Ignoring an almost overwhelming desire to just walk out and go home, she was on the point of demanding an explanation, but she was too slow. Before Christine had a chance to work out what she wanted to say, the inspector turned away. With a nod to a constable to escort Christine to the entrance of the police station, the inspector left the room and the opportunity to speak to her was lost.

Dumbly Christine followed the constable along another grey corridor to the entrance to the building. Tomorrow she would return to the police station and find out what was happening, but for now she wanted to focus on her daughter and work out who was going to be responsible for her, now she was effectively on her own in the world. Her father was dead and her mother would soon be incarcerated for years. Christine sighed, aware that her confession had changed everything. Her priority right now was to minimise Daisy's suffering and ensure she received the help she needed. Doing her best to suppress her terror at the prospect of spending years behind bars, she called Daisy and learned that she was at home in Drakes Close. Lucy was with her.

Lucy made a huge fuss of Christine when she arrived and even Daisy grudgingly admitted she was pleased to see her.

Although Christine disliked the thought of Lucy taking over her house, she acknowledged the sense in her bringing Daisy home. Daisy wanted to know what was going on and why her mother had been absent overnight. Christine glanced at Lucy, who was obviously pretending she wasn't listening, and thanked her for meeting Daisy from school and looking after her overnight.

'No problem. I'm more than happy to help. But how are you? Tell us what happened. What did the police say? Why did they keep you overnight?' Lucy's eyes were wide with concern, but Christine wasn't about to launch into an account of her experience while Daisy was in the room. With a pang, she remembered that Daisy didn't yet know that her father was dead.

Christine shook her head. 'I'm sorry. I'm really too knackered to talk to you right now. I'll call you tomorrow, okay?'

'But what do the police think happened?' Lucy pressed her. 'Do they have any idea who did it?'

Concerned that Lucy was going to give away the fact that Peter was dead, Christine repeated firmly that she would call her the following day and hustled Lucy out of the house before she could say any more. When the front door closed on Lucy, she insisted Daisy accompany her to the living room instead of running straight upstairs. With a grunt, Daisy complied. Sprawling on an armchair, she scrutinised her chipped nail varnish and appeared to be ignoring her mother.

'There's something you need to know.' Christine paused and reached out. She managed to touch Daisy's hand before it was snatched away with a mumbled expletive. Christine sat forward and spoke as gently as she could. 'Your father didn't leave us. Not deliberately, that is. There's no easy way to tell you this. Your father... is dead. The police have found his body.'

Daisy didn't look up, but she stopped picking at her chipped nails. 'Where did they find him?'

'In the garage. But you knew that, didn't you?' Christine said softly.

'What do you mean?'

'There's nothing to worry about. I told the police it was me. No one's going to come along and start asking you awkward questions. All you have to do is keep quiet and no one will suspect you. And whatever happens I'm going to make sure you get the help you need.'

'Oh my God!' Daisy cried out, looking stricken. She sat bolt upright. 'You think it was me, don't you?' She paused, frowning. 'But then that means it can't have been you. Why did you confess to something you didn't do? That's mental, Mum.'

'I couldn't let you suffer any more than you have done already,' Christine replied, struggling to keep her voice steady.

'I don't know exactly what he did to you, but you mustn't blame yourself for what happened. I understand you were driven to do it. And I'm sure you never meant to hurt him. You were a victim—'

'No, no!' Daisy leapt to her feet. 'You've got it all wrong. It wasn't me. He never did anything bad, he was my dad. I didn't even know he was dead.' She began to cry. This time, when Christine reached out to hold her hand she didn't recoil. 'You confessed because you thought it was me but it wasn't, it wasn't,' Daisy mumbled through her tears. 'Why did you do that?' But they both knew the answer to her question. 'It wasn't me, it wasn't. You have to believe me.'

'I do believe you,' Christine assured her, but she was afraid Daisy must be lying. Because if she hadn't killed Peter, then who could have done it? 'We'll get through this,' she assured the weeping girl. 'We just have to stay strong and stick to our story.'

'What story?' Daisy asked wretchedly, sniffing back her tears. 'I haven't been telling any stories to anyone. I'm not lying. It wasn't me. You have to go back to the police and tell them it wasn't you or you'll go to prison and dad's killer will never be caught.' She paused, hiccupping, her eyes surrounded by wet smudges of black make-up. 'You confessed to killing him to save me,' she said and burst into tears again.

As Daisy flung her arms around her, Christine was overwhelmed by a combination of relief and horror. She had salvaged her relationship with her daughter, quite dramatically as it turned out, but at what cost? Now convinced that Daisy was innocent, she couldn't believe she had ever suspected her of murdering her father. But that meant she had confessed to the police for nothing and would be spending years in prison locked up for a crime she hadn't committed. Daisy would go into care and the real killer would be free to walk the streets with impunity. Emboldened by their lucky escape, they might decide to kill again and there was nothing Christine could do about it. She hugged Daisy tightly and promised to go to the police and retract her confession. She didn't add that they probably wouldn't believe her, in which case she would face a murder charge. Given her confession, she might not escape a conviction. She felt her legs trembling and was glad she was sitting down.

'Mum,' Daisy said, drawing back from her mother's embrace.

Christine nodded but didn't trust herself to speak. She was afraid she would break down in tears. Reminding herself that she had to stay strong for Daisy's sake, she tried to force her lips to smile.

'Why don't you sit down and I'll make a cup of tea?' Daisy said. 'You must be tired after spending a night at the police station.'

Christine's self-control crumbled and she began to cry. 'That would be lovely,' she managed to mumble through her tears.

39

THE TEAM WERE DISMAYED to learn that Peter Selby's case hadn't been concluded after all.

'I was so sure it was his wife,' Ariadne said to Geraldine who grunted and agreed that it was a reasonable supposition since it was usually the spouse who was responsible when a married person was murdered. 'She seemed like the obvious suspect and she even confessed,' Ariadne went on in an aggrieved tone, as though they had somehow been cheated out of a successful conclusion to the investigation.

Binita went over the evidence several times with the team. Findings from the post mortem contradicted what Christine had claimed in her statement. They realised she had made a false confession even before she had retracted it, claiming grief had temporarily driven her mad. She insisted she hadn't known what she was saying.

'I hope we're going to charge her with wasting our time,' a disgruntled detective constable muttered audibly.

'Not to mention pissing us off with her shenanigans,' another constable added.

'It's still possible she was confused,' Ariadne suggested. 'It would be easy to forget exactly where she had hit her husband in the heat of the moment. The back of the head, the side of the head, she could well have muddled them up. The assault must have been over in a moment.'

'And if she didn't do it, who did?' someone asked.

Binita frowned. 'We'll keep Christine at the top of our list of suspects for now.'

Unless she was crazy, the only plausible explanation for Christine's false confession was that she suspected her daughter had committed the murder. No one was comfortable with the idea of a fourteen-year-old killing her own father, but it was a lead they had to follow up. Geraldine went to Daisy's school to see if she could discover anything that might help them to build a picture of the girl, before they spoke to her in person. Whether or not Daisy was responsible, her father had just been murdered and she was bound to be disturbed, either from grief or guilt, or perhaps a combination of the two. Whatever had happened to Peter, his daughter's interrogation would have to be sensitively handled. In the meantime, Binita was keen to glean as much background information about the girl as possible.

Geraldine found a space in the car park at the school, which was housed in a large concrete block, with several smaller structures and a sports field adjacent to the main building. After a short delay while the school secretary spoke to the deputy head, Geraldine was taken to a classroom to meet Daisy's form tutor. Mrs Proudy was a short, thin woman who glared at Geraldine through black-framed glasses. She had a pointed nose and chin, and a sour expression that was quite off-putting. To a teenager she would probably have come across as humourless and intimidating. Thanks to her witchlike appearance, Geraldine thought she had a fairly shrewd idea of what her pupils might call her behind her back. When she explained the reason for her visit to the school, the teacher sniffed disapprovingly, as though Geraldine had brought a foul smell into the classroom.

'You're here to enquire about Daisy Selby?' Mrs Proudy repeated. 'Very well, I'll do my best to help you. What, exactly, do you want to know?'

'Just your impression of her would be very helpful.'

'You know, of course, that father was recently murdered,' Mrs Proudy began. 'So she's not been in school for a few days.'

Geraldine inclined her head but didn't point out that she was involved in the investigation into the murder, which she assumed must be obvious. 'I'm really interested in Daisy's conduct before that tragedy occurred. Was she a happy girl, would you say?'

'Hardly. As I told her mother, Daisy's a belligerent girl who courts controversy.' Mrs Proudy stopped talking suddenly, almost as though she had just remembered being warned not to speak to the police.

'Has she always been so aggressive?'

'No, not according to her reports. This kind of behaviour seems to have emerged only this year. But teenagers often change as they grow up and rarely for the better. I did enquire whether there had been any problems in the family that might have caused a shift in her attitude towards any form of authority, but her mother was adamant that she's fine at home. Clearly that's not true, at least objectively speaking, but parents are often the last to see when there's an issue or acknowledge when their child is experiencing problems. A child's state of mind can be tricky to diagnose. It's not a hard science. But Daisy's clearly a troubled girl by any criteria and I don't suppose what's happened recently is going to help her to settle down.' She sighed. 'I'd say this was the last thing she needed. If she wasn't so surly and unapproachable, I'd feel quite sorry for her.'

'What about her relationship with her parents? Was there any animosity there, do you think?'

'Doubtless some teenage rebelliousness, but that's not uncommon. Beyond that, I can't really say. Her mother was very defensive about her and flatly refused to admit there were any issues at home. Her father didn't come to parents evening,' she added, a hint of disapproval in her tone. 'They don't always. Really, you wonder why some people have children; they seem

SILENT TIES

to bother so little with them when they reach the awkward teenage years.'

'I think he didn't come to parents evening earlier on this week because he was dead,' Geraldine remarked acidly.

Mrs Proudy didn't react to the implied censure, merely repeating that Daisy was a difficult girl.

'You mentioned Daisy had aggressive tendencies,' Geraldine prompted her.

'I used the word belligerent,' Mrs Proudy pointed out. 'Aggressive was your word.'

'What made you say she was belligerent?' Geraldine continued, feeling she was being corrected as though she was a child.

'She attacked one of the boys here,' Mrs Proudy said.

Taken aback by this information, Geraldine felt a pang of unease as she asked the teacher to elaborate on what had happened. If she confirmed that Daisy had violently assaulted a boy, then that might sway the view of the police and a jury.

Mrs Proudy shook her head. 'As it turned out, she wasn't entirely to blame. We discovered this particular boy had been targeting her for months, harassing her and allegedly assaulting her.'

'Assaulting her?'

'She alleged he pushed her up against a wall and groped her. Daisy was questioned after she attacked him and she told us everything. The boy didn't try to deny her accusation. It's a great pity she didn't come to us sooner, but he's now been dealt with very severely, I can assure you. We have a zero tolerance policy here towards bullying of any kind and this sort of sexual harassment is most definitely unacceptable. But she ought to have spoken to a member of staff sooner and not taken it upon herself to react with a violent outburst.' She shook her head. 'Most of our pupils are well behaved and sensible, but there are always the occasional bad apples.'

It wasn't clear whether she was referring to Daisy or to the boy who had been pestering her.

'She must have been traumatised by the experience,' Geraldine said, wondering if her harassment at school had caused Daisy to turn on her father and completely lose her self-control. 'I'm surprised the boy wasn't removed from the school altogether. Was this reported to the police?'

'I assure you he was punished very severely. But as he's only fourteen, the head didn't feel it was necessary to involve the police. We're hoping he's learnt his lesson.' She paused. 'He's not the brightest of our pupils and I assure you he's being dealt with appropriately. As for Daisy, she's been offered counselling. We planned to discuss it with her mother only then the murder happened and it didn't seem the right time. But the school counsellor is aware and will be following up as soon as Daisy returns to school.'

Feeling apprehensive, Geraldine took her leave. A troubled teenager who had been sexually harassed by a male classmate seemed like a credible suspect. Perhaps Christine's initial instinct had been right after all and Daisy had attacked Peter in the heat of the moment. She wasn't sure what she had been expecting to find, but it certainly wasn't this. With a sigh, she set off back to the police station to report her findings.

40

CHRISTINE NEEDED TO SORT out who was going to take care of Daisy, as it was looking unlikely that they would be able to stay at home together. At fourteen, she would be taken into care, unless her absent grandmother decided to step in and look after her. Christine wasn't sure which would be worse. Everything in her life was degenerating into such a mess. She bitterly regretted her confession, but she couldn't turn the clock back. She would just have to keep on retracting her statement and hope the police would believe her. She had a horrible feeling they would go ahead and charge her with murder. And there was still the risk that if they believed her protestations of innocence, they might turn their attention to Daisy. Christine wasn't confident her daughter would be able to cope with the pressure of being interrogated. Even if the police eventually let her go, the psychological damage might prove devastating.

Not until Peter's killer was caught and behind bars would she and Daisy feel safe, and be free to mourn their loss. However things played out, Christine wasn't ready to give up without trying everything she could think of to assist the police in tracking down the real killer. So far, she had been so distracted by the police investigation, she had hardly had time to process the fact that Peter was dead. Even now, she couldn't allow herself to give way to emotion until she had discovered who had killed him. She resolved to start by searching through all of her husband's possessions to look for any trace of an enemy who might have wanted him murdered. She couldn't think why anyone would have hated him that much, but there had to be a clue somewhere in his belongings, some paperwork that would solve the mystery. She cursed the police for taking away his phone and his laptop, because there might have been an email or text that would have helped her, but in the meantime all she could do was look through whatever papers they had left behind. Without his electronic devices, she realised it wouldn't leave her much to go on, but she had to do something. She would start by searching his desk. If the killer proved too elusive to track down, she would stand by her own confession and do whatever she could to ensure Daisy was settled where she at least had a chance of being happy.

Daisy was shut away upstairs in her room when Christine opened the first drawer in Peter's desk. Obviously the police had searched it, but she went through everything in there, hoping against the odds that she would stumble on something the police had overlooked. The chances were negligible, but she pressed on, driven by a determination that was almost manic. She found an envelope right at the back of the drawer. Wondering if the police could have missed it, she scanned through the flimsy scraps of paper it contained. They were receipts for purchases of clothes, some of which he had bought for her. The memory made her eyes water and she returned the papers to the envelope, her hopes fading, just as the doorbell rang. Expecting the police had changed their minds and had come to take her back into custody, Christine hesitated before deciding not to put her shoes on. She wasn't in any hurry to return to a police cell.

Relieved to discover it wasn't the police after all, she wasn't surprised to see Lucy standing on the doorstep. She really didn't want to talk to her just then, but she couldn't give Lucy the brush-off after she had been kind enough to look after Daisy.

'I know it's early,' Lucy said. She sounded slightly breathless, as though she had been running. 'I wanted to see you in person to ask if there's anything I can do. Is Daisy all right?'

Thanking her, Christine was already regretting having opened the door, but she did her best to hide her impatience.

'What did the police want with you?' Lucy asked, her face twisted with worry.

Christine shrugged and stood aside to let her friend in.

'Christine, what's going on?'

With a sigh, Christine admitted that the police had found Peter's body.

Lucy was shocked. 'What?' she blurted out. 'I don't believe it. They found his body? You mean he's dead? Oh my God, Christine, I'm so sorry. Does Daisy know? Where did they find him? Are they sure it's Peter?'

Christine nodded. She wished Lucy would go away, but at the same time she was pleased that she was no longer alone with her thoughts.

'I'm just so worried about what's going to happen to Daisy if they lock me up,' she admitted, relieved to have someone in whom she could confide. 'I mean, the police seem to suspect I killed him, although it's odd because they took me in for questioning and then they let me go.' She shrugged. 'I keep thinking they'll come for me and then Daisy will be all on her own.'

'Why would they suspect you?'

Christine admitted that she had confessed to killing Peter in the mistaken belief that her daughter was guilty. Now that she was convinced of Daisy's innocence, she explained that she had retracted her statement and hoped the police would believe her. Lucy frowned, but she didn't say anything.

'You don't think they'll believe me, do you? I can tell from your expression. You look so worried. But listen, this isn't your problem.'

'It's not that.' Lucy paused, her expression thoughtful. 'They wouldn't suspect Daisy, would they? I mean, if you deny it was you? I'm just saying, you should think this through carefully before you keep insisting that it wasn't you after all. I mean, obviously it wasn't you.' She gave an awkward laugh. 'I'm not accusing you of anything. I'm just saying they're bound to think you confessed to protect Daisy and then thought better of it.'

'Like I said, it's not your problem. But if you want to know, what I'm thinking is, someone killed Peter and it wasn't me or Daisy. So I'm going to do whatever it takes to find out who it was.'

Lucy abruptly changed the subject, asking where the body had been found.

'It was in the garage. I can show you, if you like?'

She led her friend to the garage. Lucy looked around and frowned.

'I suppose the police took the freezer away?' she asked.

Christine felt a sudden stab of alarm. 'How do you know there was a freezer in here?' she asked.

Lucy didn't falter for an instant as she replied that Christine had brought her in there once to show her all the clutter. Christine shook her head. She was positive that had never happened. She would have been too embarrassed to show anyone the mess in the garage.

'Oh, it must have been Daisy then,' Lucy answered when Christine denied having brought her there. 'What does it matter?'

Realisation struck Christine like a blow to her guts. 'It was you,' she hissed, before she could pause to think about what she was saying. 'You've been in here before and that's how you knew about the freezer. You killed him. Why? Were you having an affair with Peter?'

A strange expression contorted Lucy's features. 'What are you talking about?' she snapped, but they both understood she knew exactly what Christine meant. Without warning, Lucy lunged forward and reached for Christine's throat. Christine felt hands curling around her neck, gripping with an almost mechanical power. Frantically, she tried to hit her assailant but Lucy pushed her against the wall and kept pressing on her windpipe until she could scarcely breathe. She kicked out and Lucy yelped as Christine's shoe caught her on the shin.

Lucy's voice seemed to reach her from a long way away. 'Everyone will think you took your own life after killing your husband. I'll tell the police you were feeling overwhelmed with guilt. It's for the best, because this way Daisy will be safe. That's what you want, isn't it?'

'Why?' Christine managed to croak.

'Why did I kill him? I had to,' Lucy replied calmly.

There was a rushing sound in Christine's ears and she could hardly hear what Lucy was saying.

'He was blackmailing me, you see. I couldn't let him get away with that.'

Christine struggled to remain conscious. She had a vague memory of the police inspector asking her about payments that had been made to Peter, but Lucy's voice was reaching her from somewhere far away and her words made no sense. Her last thought was to hope Daisy would not believe the false narrative that her mother had killed her father.

After that, she was only dimly aware of falling to the floor before she blacked out.

41

As usual, her decision log took Geraldine considerably longer to complete than she had anticipated.

'If only we didn't have to account for all our actions in such detail, we'd have more time to actually get on with the job,' she grumbled aloud.

Ariadne, sitting opposite her, overheard her muttering and smiled. 'You know it's for your own protection,' she called out. 'Most of us would never remember why we do half of the things we do if we didn't write them down at the time, giving reasons for everything we say and do.'

'Of course you would.'

'Do you remember your reasons for everything you did a week ago? Or two weeks ago? Or three? Seriously?' Ariadne sighed. 'Yes, I suppose you remember everything, but we're not all blessed with such infallible memories.'

'If I couldn't remember, I could at least make a reasonable guess,' Geraldine replied. 'Which is all I do anyway when I'm writing up my decision log. I mean, do you really know why you do what you do? We're not allowed to say we did something because it just felt right, even though that gut reaction is often all we have to go on. Everything has to be explained and justified, just in case we ever have to defend ourselves if a complaint is made.'

'Exactly,' Ariadne countered. 'It's for our own protection.'

'We all know it's a waste of valuable time when we could be out and about doing actual detective work,' Geraldine insisted.

'There's probably something we should be investigating right now, but we're both stuck at our desks writing up our logs for people who spend all their time ticking boxes. They ought to get off their backsides and help us out, instead of reading our reports and asking us to be more specific. Seriously, you know I'm right.'

Ariadne smiled. 'You sound as though you could do with a drink.'

Geraldine hesitated. She was feeling disheartened by the way the investigation was going and concerned that they might end up having to accuse a troubled teenager of committing a horrendous crime. More than anything, she wanted to continue investigating, hopefully discovering new evidence that would shed a different light on the case. The time she was obliged to waste in unproductive work didn't help to lift her spirits. The demands of her paperwork seemed to be growing exponentially and she couldn't wait to finish.

'This is all so pointless,' she muttered. 'Seriously, how is this helping us identify John's assailant or Peter's killer? We still don't even know if it was the same killer.'

Ian had suggested she was getting bogged down in the minutiae of the case and he was right. Somehow she was struggling to take a step back and get any sense of perspective on what had happened, which made the idea of going for a drink with her friend tempting.

'I've got to pick Tom up in half an hour—' she began.

'Great! That gives us half an hour,' Ariadne replied promptly.

'And I was thinking of dropping in to see Christine on my way to the childminder,' Geraldine added. Her voice sounded tentative even to her own ears. She wasn't sure why she felt a curious compulsion to go and talk to Christine again. She suspected she was subconsciously searching for a reason to charge Christine in order to exonerate Daisy, even though the girl was hardly likely to thrive with her mother in prison.

'That can wait until the morning, surely,' Ariadne said. 'She's not going anywhere. She can hardly make a run for it with her details so widely circulated.'

Geraldine smiled and closed her tablet with a decisive click. 'Come on, then,' she said. 'One swift half and then I really do need to go and fetch Tom. I don't want to be late, even though my childminder is very understanding.'

'And presumably she's on the clock?' Ariadne asked, smiling.

'Yes, but that's not the point. I don't like to take liberties unless I have to.'

They set off together. The sun was shining and, for a few minutes, Geraldine felt as though a weight had lifted from her shoulders. She and Ariadne could have been any two friends popping to the pub for a quick drink on their way home at the end of the day, breezily leaving their work behind them until the morning. But as they sat down at a slightly sticky table in the pub, she was conscious that her job was different to most people's and she was fooling herself if she thought she could dismiss her concerns and responsibilities so readily.

'Cheer up,' Ariadne said, looking anxious. 'You seem really fed up. Is everything okay with you?'

Geraldine nodded and confessed that the case was getting her down. She didn't admit that she didn't relish the idea that they might have to charge a teenager with murder. She had the impression that life was hard enough for young people and Daisy had struck her as a vulnerable young woman desperately in need of support rather than someone who could handle any more stress. But the investigation had to proceed, regardless of Geraldine's personal feelings.

'Everything's fine,' she replied. 'Honestly, it's just this case. I feel as though we're going round in circles with it.'

'It's always like this, though. What is there about this case that's affecting you? I mean, it's not like you to be so pessimistic.'

Geraldine sighed. 'I feel sorry for Daisy,' she confessed, aware that she was making a mistake allowing herself to give way to an emotional reaction to a suspect. She hoped it wasn't a blunder to admit her weakness to a colleague, even if Ariadne was a friend. She knew she ought to have kept her thoughts to herself or shared them with Ian. She trusted Ariadne, but she wasn't sure she could trust herself to be objective. If her response was coloured by knowing that Christine and Daisy were mother and daughter, her own maternal instincts might be interfering with her ability to remain detached. And as well as all the misgivings she was able to articulate, she had an uneasy feeling that she had overlooked something vital, only she didn't know what it was.

'I feel so confused,' she added.

'You're probably just tired,' Ariadne suggested, 'and that's why you're not thinking clearly. Is Tom waking you up at night?'

Geraldine shook her head. She couldn't explain it, but she knew that her feelings about Daisy were somehow tied up with her feelings towards Tom and that didn't bode well for her career or her responsibilities as a mother.

'I'm just confused,' she repeated. 'But I'll get over it. It's okay. I'm fine.' She laughed, knowing that Ariadne wasn't fooled by her claim. 'Now, how are things with you?'

They chatted inconsequentially for a quarter of an hour and then Geraldine gulped down the remainder of her half-pint and stood up, scraping her chair legs on the floor.

'See you tomorrow.'

'I hope you get a good night's sleep,' Ariadne called out.

Geraldine left, feeling drained. She hoped Ariadne's wish would come true. She really needed to sleep well and wake up feeling more positive and ready to throw herself into the investigation. As she drove to the childminder's, she was again troubled by a feeling that she was missing something important. If she could only work out what she had overlooked, she might uncover the truth. But however frantically she wracked her brains, the relevant information eluded her.

42

SHE HAD PLANNED HER surveillance in meticulous detail. It was time-consuming, but she told herself it would be worth it in the long run and, anyway, it wasn't as if she had anything better to do. She was actually rather proud of herself for being so thorough in her preparations. One way or another, she was confident she would successfully resurrect her relationship with Daniel. Whether he recognised it or not, they belonged together and she was determined to win him back, whatever it took. But first things first, before anything else she needed to gather as much information as she could. The more she knew about her rival, the easier it would be to track her down and neutralise the threat.

So far all she knew about the other woman was that she was young and blonde, and she had lured Daniel into thinking he was interested in her. The longer this nascent relationship was allowed to continue, the more dangerous it became. Somehow, it had to be stopped, whatever the cost. But she needed more information. Her initial tactic was to watch Daniel's flat to find out more about the woman who was visiting him. It was possible she was just a friend or a relative, but Daniel had apparently ditched his one true love around the time this other woman had entered his life. For the first time it crossed her mind that he could have been cheating on both her and the other woman at the same time, but she dismissed that idea straight away. She refused to entertain the possibility that he had been unfaithful to her while they were together. They had been too happy and too much in love for that to be true. In any case, when he had first embarked on a relationship with the other woman was irrelevant. The upshot of all this speculation was that she had to go and in order to get rid of her once and for all, Jeannie needed to find out more about her. So she would continue with her surveillance operation until she was ready to strike. And when the time came, she would not falter.

Concerned that the same car parked in the street night after night might attract unwanted attention, she considered using different cars hired for a day at a time. On the other hand, if Daniel were to see the same car he might quite reasonably assume that it belonged to one of his neighbours. She didn't think he was familiar enough with any of them to know whether or not they had changed their car. In any event, it seemed a negligible risk. Her own appearance was a different matter. If Daniel were to spot her, then she would be forced to abandon her surveillance which meant she might never succeed. Having bought half a dozen pairs of sunglasses, all distinctive but none ostentatious, she spent a morning scouring charity shops for different jackets with hoods. Armed with these disguises, she was confident she could escape his notice. Obviously she couldn't spy on him indefinitely, but all she had to do was hold her nerve and act promptly, and she should be able to remove her rival very soon.

So far, she didn't think Daniel's relationship with the other woman could be more than a casual fling. She had to be eliminated before it went any further. She was already spending the night with him. The thought of another woman in his bed made Jeannie grip the steering wheel until her fingers hurt, while her jaw ached from being clenched. To avoid any questions from other residents in the street, she decided not to park outside the same house twice in a row. Despite all her precautions, she remained worried that Daniel might spot her and she was afraid she could only get away with her surveillance for a few more days. But she had to keep going. She and Daniel had come too far to give up on their love affair now. He was a fool not to acknowledge the unbreakable bond between them, but he was clearly frightened by the strength of his love. She understood; she knew only too well how overwhelming such feelings were. Once her rival was out of the picture, she would make him realise that it was fine to feel such a powerful love for another person.

In the back of her mind, she heard an echo of her mother's voice telling her she was crazy to think she could coerce other people into doing what she wanted.

'People have their own ideas about what's right for them,' her mother had told her. 'You can't expect everyone around you to fall in with your plans. You can't control the world, you can only control your own response when your wishes are thwarted. You have to grow up and accept the fact that life is full of disappointments and you're powerless to change that. Life isn't perfect. If you can't accept that, then you're going to end up very unhappy.'

Naturally, she hadn't listened to her mother's warnings and had refused to accept that disappointment was inevitable in life. Of course, if you expected to be defeated, you lost the struggle before you'd even started, which was stupid. And she wasn't stupid. Far from it. If success hadn't always fallen in her lap, the answer had always been simple. She had done whatever was necessary to get what she wanted. When fortune hadn't seemed inclined to favour her, she had created her own fortune in a way that didn't seem to occur to most people. She had worked hard to remove the obstacles to her marriage to a prosperous husband with independent means and now it was time to force the issue again. This time, it wasn't money she was after but love. Nevertheless, the principle remained the same. She would do whatever was necessary to get what she wanted. With enough determination and cunning, she could not fail.

She saw Daniel arrive home from work at his usual time, followed around an hour later by the young woman she had observed visit him the previous night. Jeannie watched the building all evening and late into the night, but Daniel's visitor didn't emerge from his front door. Scowling, she settled down to spend another hour in her car. Not until she was convinced that the girl was going to stay the whole night with Daniel did she drive off, shaking with rage. By now she had to acknowledge that he had replaced her with some young tart. That the bitch didn't deserve him was obvious, as was the fact that she had to be removed from his life. Once that was done, Jeannie was confident she could persuade Daniel to come to his senses and return to her. And this time, they wouldn't be furtively scurrying in and out of hotel rooms. With her being so recently widowed, they would allow a short time to pass to avoid arousing suspicion, after which they would marry and Daniel would move in with her. It was all so simple. All she had to do was get rid of this one hindrance. Once that part of the plan had been executed, everything else would follow like clockwork.

There was no point in sitting in her car all night. She was cold and stiff and needed the toilet. She would need to return early enough to see the woman leaving the premises, so she could follow her. There had to be a way to reach her, even if it meant breaking into her rival's home. Of course, she was reluctant to do that, knowing it would be difficult to avoid leaving traces of her own DNA behind. It would be far better to kill her out in the open air, where she could have minimal contact with her victim. But before she could plan what to do, she needed to know where the woman lived, where she worked and her route between the two. It might take a few days to gather the necessary information, but at the first opportunity she would strike and she would not fail. It wasn't as if she was a novice. She smiled to herself as she drove home, imagining Daniel's surprise when she turned up at his flat and how happy he would be to see her again. With the blonde bitch out of the way, he would be eager to fall into her arms once again.

43

ON SATURDAY MORNING, GERALDINE woke up early after a disturbed night. She could hear Tom chattering in the nursery as she lay in bed wondering whether to stay there or get up and start her day. Ian was still asleep but he woke up as she was getting dressed. He watched her drowsily for a moment before asking why she was already up. When she explained where she was going, he fell back on his pillow with a groan.

'At this time in the morning?' he protested feebly. 'It's the weekend. You're not even supposed to be working today.'

'I want to catch her before she goes out. I won't be long. Tom's awake—'

'Don't worry,' Ian replied, yawning. 'I'll see to him.'

As he spoke, Tom called out and they exchanged a smile. Although Tom's yelling had occasionally been inconvenient when they were out, both of them had confessed to being pleased to have a robust infant with sturdy limbs and powerful lungs.

Stopping only to grab a quick breakfast of toast and tea, and log her movements, Geraldine drove to Drakes Close. On the way, she concentrated on slowing her breathing in an attempt to quell an irrational sense of urgency about speaking to Christine again. There was no answer when she rang the bell. She tried again, but there was still no response, nor any evidence of movement inside the house. Doubtful that Christine and Daisy would have gone out so early on a Saturday morning, she concluded that they must both still be asleep. Now that she was there, she was no longer sure why she was calling on Christine at such an hour or why she had felt compelled to go there. Having resisted the urge to speak to Christine the previous day, she guessed she subconsciously felt guilty about choosing to go for a drink with Ariadne instead of following her instinct.

In spite of the hours Christine had spent at the police station, there were still unanswered questions. Why hadn't she reported her husband missing when he had first disappeared? How could she not have known about the bank account he had recently opened? And what kind of relationship had he had with his daughter? Even though Geraldine was there early, no one came to the door when she rang the bell. As she turned to leave, she thought she heard a tapping noise coming from the garage. She walked over to the up-and-over door and pressed the side of her head against it but was met by silence. The metal of the door was uncomfortably cold against her ear and she drew back, scolding herself for imagining things. An experienced detective, she was trained to deal in facts, not fancies. But as she walked away, she heard the sound again. This time, when she listened with her ear against the door, she was sure she heard a faint groan accompanied by a scratching sound. She almost dismissed it as central heating pipes creaking, but she couldn't ignore the possibility that something – or someone – was trapped in the garage.

She tried to open the door but it was locked. She shook it and heard a muffled groan, apparently in response to the clatter she was making. There was no longer any doubt that someone was in the garage and they were trying to attract attention when the door rattled. She ran to the front door, summoning back-up to help her gain access to the garage. This time, when she rang the bell she banged on the front door as loudly as she could and yelled for someone to let her in. After a few moments, the front door opened and she saw Daisy blinking at her in confusion.

'Didn't you hear the bell?' Geraldine blurted out, exasperated.

'Sorry,' Daisy replied in a tone that made it clear she was not apologising. 'I was listening to music.'

'I need to get into the garage,' Geraldine said. 'Where's your mother?'

Daisy shrugged. 'In bed, I suppose. What's going on?'

'Don't worry,' Geraldine hastened to reassure her. 'I think your mother's locked herself in the garage.'

It was possibly an animal trapped in there, but Geraldine didn't waste time speculating. If Christine was in the garage and unable to call out, time might be pressing. She called for an ambulance.

Daisy stared at her. 'What?'

'There's an internal door to the garage, isn't there?'

'Yes, it's off the kitchen, but—'

'Wait in the hall and let the paramedics in as soon as they ring the bell.'

With that hurried instruction, Geraldine ran to the kitchen and flung open the door to the garage, noting that it wasn't locked. Daisy shuffled at her heels, ignoring Geraldine's instruction to wait in the hall.

Christine was lying on the floor, her wrists and ankles bound, and her mouth gagged. There was a small pool of blood beside her head. She wasn't moving. Yelling at Daisy to stay back, Geraldine ran forward and was reassured to find a pulse in the prone woman's neck.

'She's alive,' she called out. 'Daisy, she's alive. Run and fetch some scissors.' She pulled out her phone and summoned an ambulance before starting to fumble with the string securing Christine's hands and feet. A long time seemed to elapse before Daisy returned with a pair of nail scissors.

'These are all I could find,' she sobbed. 'There should be a big pair in the kitchen but I couldn't find them.'

'These are perfect,' Geraldine reassured her.

'Mum, Mum, what happened?'

Before Christine could respond, they heard a siren in the distance.

'Mum, are you all right?' Daisy wailed. 'Is she going to be all right?'

Carefully Geraldine slipped one thin blade under the gag, and released Christine who groaned. A few moments later there was a loud knocking at the front door. Geraldine looked up.

'That must be the ambulance,' she told Daisy. 'Go and let them in. Go! Your mother needs them.'

Daisy ran off and returned with a couple of paramedics who examined the injured woman before carrying her on a stretcher to the waiting ambulance. Geraldine drove Daisy to the hospital. On the way, she questioned her very gently, interspersing her enquiries with reassurances that Christine was going to be fine. She hoped that was true.

'Was anyone else at your house yesterday?'

'Only Lucy.'

'Lucy? Who's Lucy?'

'She's mum's friend. She picked me up from school one day when mum wasn't around.'

'What can you tell me about her?'

'Nothing. She's mum's friend. That's all I know. But I don't really like her. She's weird.'

'Weird how?'

'I don't know. Just weird. Are you sure mum's going to be okay?'

Daisy burst into tears and Geraldine wasn't able to question her any further. Within a few minutes they arrived at the hospital where a nurse took responsibility for looking after the distressed girl. To Geraldine's relief, she was told that Christine was conscious and was able to answer a few questions. Lucky to escape with her life, she had been badly bruised before being trussed up and left alone in the garage. She was dehydrated and suffering from shock, with her neck bruised from being strangled. Like her husband, Christine had been alive when the killer had left her to die. Presumably her attacker had intended to return at some point to dispose of the body, but before they could return, she had been discovered alive.

'You can't stay long,' a nurse warned Geraldine. 'She needs to rest. She insisted on speaking to you straight away, but she's been sedated so you're unlikely to get any sense out of her. This way.'

The nurse led Geraldine to a small side ward where Christine lay with her eyes closed.

Eschewing any preamble, Geraldine went straight to her questions. 'Did you see who attacked you?'

With an almost imperceptible movement of her head, Christine nodded and muttered inaudibly.

Geraldine leaned forward until she was almost touching Christine's face. 'Who was it?' she demanded urgently.

Christine's eyes flickered open for an instant. 'Lucy,' she croaked.

'Who is Lucy?'

'Lucy,' Christine rasped hoarsely. 'Lucy. Keep away from Daisy.'

'Where does Lucy live?'

Christine did not respond but lay immobile with her eyes closed.

'Where does she live?'

There was no response.

'Christine, where does Lucy live?' Geraldine repeated.

Christine gave a slight shake of her head. Without opening her eyes, she murmured her daughter's name. 'Daisy,' she moaned. 'Daisy.'

'What is Lucy's surname?'

'Lucy,' Christine murmured and sighed.

A nurse arrived and Geraldine was peremptorily asked to leave.

'I just need a few more minutes with her,' she said, but the nurse was insistent. 'One more minute,' Geraldine begged desperately, but she could see there was no point.

Christine had fallen asleep and the police would not be able to wake her to question her again for a while.

'Is she likely to make a full recovery?'

The nurse gave an optimistic reply, before hustling Geraldine from the room. Christine knew the identity of her assailant and Geraldine was fairly sure it was the same person who had attacked Peter and left him to suffocate in the disused freezer. But all Christine had been able to tell Geraldine about the culprit so far was her first name, Lucy. Daisy was the only other person they knew had met her mother's friend. Geraldine hoped that she would know Lucy's full name and remember her address. Feeling uneasy, Geraldine went to an interview room to talk to the girl. With Christine sedated, they would have only the account of a confused teenager to help them track down a serial killer who might, even now, be planning her next murder.

44

WITH CHRISTINE IN HOSPITAL under observation, Daisy had been placed in the care of social services. She was accompanied to the police station by a fussy woman who assured Geraldine that she would halt the interview at the first sign her charge was becoming distressed. Although she was small, the social worker gave the impression that she was formidable. Her eyes glittered shrewdly above a thin smile as she addressed Geraldine and Ariadne, who were preparing to question Daisy. The subject of their discussion was staring fixedly at the table and fiddling with the frayed cuffs of her jumper, seemingly oblivious to the conversation around her. Seated at her side, the social worker watched the young girl closely, occasionally turning to glance at Geraldine. She seemed an unsympathetic woman to be supporting a troubled young teenager but, to be fair, her job was to make sure no one made Daisy uncomfortable and she was probably very effective in her role as guardian.

Geraldine wasted no time in reaching the point. 'Daisy, this is very important, so please listen carefully,' she began.

Daisy didn't look up. Her chaperone folded her arms.

'Daisy, we need you to tell us about Lucy.'

'She's my mum's friend,' Daisy muttered without looking up. 'That's all I know.'

'Is she nice?'

'Ask my mum.'

Geraldine enquired what Lucy looked like and Daisy mumbled a generic description of a woman with brown hair. She didn't know Lucy's second name and had no idea how old she was. All she was able to tell them was that Lucy looked like a witch.

'You're doing well,' Geraldine encouraged her.

Daisy glanced up, squinted furiously at Geraldine and snapped that she didn't appreciate being patronised.

Geraldine pressed on. 'Daisy, we need you to tell us where Lucy lives.'

'How should I know? I told you she's not *my* friend.'

'Don't worry,' Geraldine said, with a quick glance at the social worker. 'Just do your best to tell us everything you know. Can you remember the name of the road where she took you?' She paused but there was no response. 'How did you get there?' Daisy stayed silent. 'Was it far from your school?'

When Daisy spoke again, her response was not what Geraldine had been hoping to hear. 'I don't know where she lives. I've never been to her house. I don't know anything about her and I don't want to know.'

Geraldine took a deep breath, hiding her impatience. 'We know you stayed with her while your mother was at the police station,' she said gently.

'Yes, but I never went to her house. She took me to a hotel for a night and then she took me home.'

Encouraged that she had finally succeeded in persuading the girl to at least talk to her, Geraldine pressed on without missing a beat. All Daisy could remember was that the hotel was somewhere in the city and she hadn't liked it very much.

'In the city? That's very helpful,' Geraldine encouraged her. 'Was there anything in particular you didn't like about it?'

Daisy shook her head and muttered that it had been boring.

'Now, think carefully. Can you remember the name of the hotel?'

Daisy shook her head again. Geraldine asked her to close her eyes and describe the hotel where she had stayed.

'I can't remember,' Daisy said sullenly. 'I can't remember anything about it.'

'What about the room where you stayed? What can you tell us about that? Was it noisy there?'

'It was a room, a room with a bed and there was a bathroom. I don't know what else you want me to say.' Without any warning, she burst into tears.

Predictably enough, the social worker sprang to her feet and announced that the interview was over. She turned to scowl at Geraldine and Ariadne as she hustled Daisy from the room.

'That woman's a liability,' Geraldine grumbled as she and Ariadne left the room. 'We should charge her with obstruction. I know she's just doing her job,' she added wearily, 'but someone needs to tell her that we're not the bad guys.'

No sooner had they sat down than they were summoned to a briefing to review what had been learned so far about the woman whom Christine had accused of assaulting her. Until Christine regained consciousness, her daughter was the only link they had to Lucy, and Daisy was proving useless as a witness.

'You can't blame her. She's only fourteen,' a middle-aged constable said. 'And she must be feeling distraught over the death of her father and her mother being in hospital. It's a wonder she can remember anything at all of the events of the last few days.'

As a matter of urgency, a team was set up to check all the hotels in the city to try to find out where Lucy had taken Daisy. They only had Lucy's first name and a very approximate description of her, but they did have an image of Daisy to assist with the search. They soon ascertained that no one with a first name 'Lucy', or a first initial L had stayed at a hotel in York on the night when Christine had been detained at the police station. Evidently Lucy had checked in under a different name. There wasn't even a record of a woman accompanied by a girl of Daisy's age checking in anywhere that night.

'Why would she check into a hotel under a false name?' Ariadne wondered aloud.

'Why stay at a hotel at all?' Binita asked.

'We don't even know that Lucy is her real name,' Geraldine pointed out. 'But if she did attack Christine – and possibly Peter – and left them to die, then she'll be doing everything she can to cover her tracks.'

'She must realise we're on to her,' Ariadne agreed. 'Thank goodness she let Daisy go,' she added with a shudder.

It was hopefully only a matter of time before Christine regained consciousness and was able to tell them where they could find Lucy. Until Christine's assailant had been apprehended, measures were in place to ensure Daisy was kept safe. In the meantime, the search for the woman named Lucy continued. All the local hotels were contacted again in the hope that further questioning would jog someone's memory. But hotels in York were busy, and no one recalled a middle-aged woman with brown hair and a face 'like a witch' checking in with a young companion on the night of Christine's detention. They were going to have to rely on the memory of a traumatised woman recovering from shock, assuming she recovered with her memory intact. The doctor had been optimistic. They could only hope his positivity would prove justified. Without help from Christine they might never trace her erstwhile friend.

In addition to problems with the ongoing investigation, it would be cruel for Daisy to lose both her parents to violent assailants within the space of a few weeks. The poor girl was troubled enough, without having that additional burden of grief. Thinking about Daisy, and what she had already suffered, Geraldine was more determined than ever to find out who had assaulted Christine and murdered Peter. It was looking increasingly likely that one person had been responsible for both of those attacks, but even that was no more than speculation. Without any evidence to point them in the direction of the killer, or killers, they were stumbling around in a fog.

45

NICKI TRIPPED OVER THE strap of her rucksack and swore out loud. She only ever mislaid her keys when she was going to be late for work. After scrabbling frantically through her coat pockets, she finally found them in the bottom of a bag which she had already searched a couple of times, missing them in her agitation. While she was pulling her shoes on she breathed deeply, trying to calm herself down. It didn't help. She knew she was in trouble. She had already been late for work three times in the past fortnight, and she had only been in the job for a few months. Just the previous week her boss had intimated that he wasn't going to put up with what he described as her 'slapdash attitude' for much longer. Incensed by the accusation, she had protested, insisting that she worked really hard. It was true. She usually served more customers than anybody else.

It wasn't simply a matter of professional pride. She liked to keep busy and she enjoyed chatting with people. The main attraction of the job, apart from the regular wage, was talking to customers and keeping them happy. As far as she was concerned, she was doing an excellent job, but her boss clearly didn't share her opinion. Somehow he couldn't get it through his thick skull that, far from being a liability, she was an asset to the bar. Obsessed with punctuality, he didn't appreciate her diligence. It was a complete travesty. She had been tempted to him ask if he would prefer her to turn up on time and doss about, like some other staff she could name. But, of course, she had held back from confronting him. When all was said and done, he was the boss and she was just a bartender who didn't want to lose her job.

The sun was setting by the time she left home, but if she ran to the bus stop and didn't have to wait too long, she might not be late. A fine rain was falling and she pulled up her hood without slowing her pace. Attempting to do up her jacket as she scurried along the street, she cursed as the zip caught. Distracted by fiddling with it, she tripped and nearly fell over something. Glancing down, she was taken aback to see a woman sprawled at her feet on the wet pavement. Nicki couldn't stop if she was to have any chance of getting to work on time, but curiosity compelled her to pause and look more closely. The woman was lying on her back, staring up at the sky, seemingly oblivious to the rain. At first Nicki assumed she was drunk or stoned, but something about the woman's position didn't look right. Having collapsed and passed out in the street, she could be in need of urgent medical assistance. She might even die if she was left here, exposed to the chilly night air. As though seeking to exacerbate Nicki's concern, the rain became heavier.

The woman appeared to be dressed to go out for the evening in a thin jacket over a flimsy skirt. She was wearing one high-heeled sandal. The other, having fallen off, lay a few inches away beside a beaded handbag. Presumably her evening's entertainment had started early and she had taken one too many pills before leaving home. Nicki vacillated. This really wasn't her problem, but she couldn't just leave the woman lying there, unconscious, in the gathering dusk and rain. 'Might as well be hung for a sheep as a lamb,' she muttered; she was going to be late for work anyway. Resigned to missing the bus, she crouched down and waved her hand in front of the woman's eyes. The woman was so out of it, she didn't even blink.

'Hey,' Nicki called to her, growing increasingly concerned. 'Are you okay? Can you speak to me?'

Wobbling, she put her hand down to steady herself and felt something sticky on the pavement. With a grimace, she clambered awkwardly to her feet, and saw in the light of a street lamp that her fingers were stained dark red. A disturbing thought struck her like a blow and she recoiled. Resisting an urge to shake the woman to make her wake up, she stared in horror. The woman still hadn't stirred. She hadn't even blinked. If the woman had been the victim of a violent attack, anyone who touched her could be in serious trouble. It was probably too late for Nicki to avoid leaving her DNA all over the scene. She had left a bloody hand print on the pavement in her struggle to stand up. Even as she was wondering whether the rain would wash it away, she knew there was really only one course of action open to her.

Frantically she wiped her wet fingers on the dead woman's coat before taking her phone out of her bag, taking care not to touch it with her soiled hand. Having called the emergency services and reported her finding, she turned away from the body. Her voice was shaking by the time she called her boss.

'Where are you?' he demanded. 'You know this is one of our busiest nights.'

The magnitude of what she had just seen had finally hit her and she was shivering. Gabbling in her shock, she told him what had transpired when she was on her way to work.

'A body?' he repeated sarcastically. 'You've found a dead body? If this is another excuse—'

'I'm not making this up,' she stammered, stumbling over her words. 'The police will be here any minute. They'll tell you. Or perhaps you'd like me to take a photo of the body and send it to you,' she snapped. If she hadn't exactly expected sympathy from her boss, she certainly hadn't been prepared to be greeted with blatant disbelief. She tossed a final barbed comment at him. 'Maybe she topped herself because she had a horrible boss at work.' Without waiting for him to respond, she hung up.

A few seconds later, she heard the shrill wail of an approaching siren and a police car pulled into the kerb. Two uniformed officers jumped out and ran over to her. She was stupidly relieved to see that one was a woman. Catching sight of the body, the policeman squatted down to check for any signs of life before stepping back and nodding to his companion. Then he was on his phone, talking rapidly while the policewoman turned to Nicki.

'Are you Nicki Sullivan?' she asked.

As Nicki was about to answer, her phone rang. Checking the screen, she saw her boss was calling her.

The policewoman paused. 'Do you want to take that?' she asked kindly. Her tone made Nicki relax slightly. She reminded herself she had done nothing wrong.

She shook her head. 'It doesn't matter,' she muttered. 'It's no one important.'

The policewoman questioned her about what had happened, but Nicki had very little to tell her. She had never seen the dead woman before and so had no idea who she was or how she had died. Having reported everything she could remember, which was very little, Nicki felt slightly reassured. Out of the corner of her eye, she watched the policeman checking the contents of the dead woman's bag and asked who the woman was and whether she had collapsed and died from an overdose or been attacked on the street. The policewoman replied that she was unable to share any information; the police would be investigating and no information could yet be made public. As she was speaking, several other vehicles arrived, including another police car. The policewoman noted down Nicki's contact details and told her she was free to go. It sounded like an order.

'Can I stay here and watch what happens?' she asked.

'I'm afraid I need to ask you to leave the area,' the policewoman replied, not unsympathetically. 'We have to set up a cordon around the scene.'

Nicki nodded, understanding this was now a crime scene. And she had been there right from the start. The dead woman hadn't looked any older than Nicki herself, a hideous reminder of the fragility of life. Thoughtfully, she walked away, wondering whether she wanted to return to her job or whether she might do something more positive with her life.

46

THE BRIEFING WAS OVER, the team had dispersed to pursue various tasks and Geraldine was packing up at the end of another frustrating day. She was just about to go home when they received the disturbing news that another body had been found on the streets of York. This time the scene was New Walk Terrace off Fishergate, where a woman had apparently been attacked in the street. There was nothing to suggest this was related to the case Geraldine was currently working on, but since the crime scene was on her way home and Ian was collecting Tom from the childminder, she decided to stop and see how her colleagues were getting on. There was unlikely to be anything she could do to assist them, but she was happy to offer to help. If she was honest, she was fascinated by crime scenes and liked to visit them when she could. She told herself there was nothing ghoulish in her interest; this was purely professional and there was always something new to learn.

Intending to stop only for a moment, she turned off Fishergate into New Walk Terrace where she saw a forensic tent. A SOCO team were already in place, busily scavenging for evidence. A uniformed constable informed her the doctor had been and gone, having confirmed death and made a preliminary assessment at the scene. More would be known after the post mortem but, for now, no one seemed to doubt that the woman lying in the forensic tent had been murdered. Even though the body was out of sight, a few onlookers had gathered and were waiting to see what happened next. With a stifled groan, Geraldine thought she recognised a local journalist among them. The deaths of John and Peter had so far not proved particularly newsworthy, but the addition of another murder might change that. The fact that the third victim was a young woman would almost certainly attract attention from local reporters. So far the disposal of Peter in a freezer seemed to have escaped attention, but Geraldine was aware that it couldn't remain concealed for long. She hoped this latest victim would not be the catalyst that exposed the other two murders to public scrutiny.

'What do we know about her?' Geraldine enquired, nodding towards the tent.

A young policeman standing inside the cordon shook his head. 'Not much as yet. They found her bag. Everything seems to be there: bank card, credit card, phone, house keys, make-up and mirror, and even cash. There's other bits and pieces. A biro and some tissues.'

'Any defence wounds?'

He shrugged and muttered that she would have to wait for the post mortem to tell them that. He was just there to help protect the site. He seemed unsure of himself. Clearly young and inexperienced, it was understandable he would be nervous. This was probably the first serious crime scene he had attended. She thanked him and walked towards the tent, thinking this sounded chillingly like the attack on John Hodgson.

'Her name was Suzie Phillips,' a SOCO told her. 'The medic thought she might be in her late twenties, but we'll soon know more.'

Pulling on gloves, Geraldine asked to see the girl's bag. An officer handed her an exquisitely decorated beaded bag which somehow made the death seem even more poignant. A girl who had appreciated beautiful possessions could no longer enjoy anything. With a sigh, Geraldine looked through the contents. Rarely taken aback by anything she found at a crime scene, she let out a gasp of surprise on finding a small photograph.

'I know this woman,' she said. 'What did she have to do with Suzie Phillips?'

The SOCO shook his head. 'Search me,' he replied and turned back to his work, scrutinising the cordoned-off area of pavement outside the tent.

Geraldine took a screen shot of the photo on her phone and logged it before returning the picture to the beaded bag. Then she set off back to her car, giving the young constable a nod on her way. The discovery of Jeannie's picture in this latest victim's bag suggested the two attacks on the street were linked and she decided it was time to bring Jeannie to the police station for further questioning. Jeannie presumably had no idea that her picture had been discovered in a bag belonging to a woman who had just been killed. Nor could she know that Suzie had been murdered — unless she was responsible for killing her. If that proved to be the case, then it increased the likelihood that she had killed her husband in the same way. Having messaged Binita, Geraldine drove to Park Street, a side road off the A1036 where Jeannie lived. There was no one in. Returning to the police station, she went straight into a briefing that Binita was holding.

'So we now have a third murder that appears to be connected to our case,' Binita was saying. 'Ah, Geraldine, you've just come from there. Fill us in on your discovery.'

Briefly, Geraldine explained how she had come across a photo of Jeannie Hodgson in the victim's bag. Ignoring a slight buzz of muttered comments from her colleagues, Geraldine continued. 'It wasn't signed or anything but it was definitely Jeannie Hodgson.'

One of the team wondered aloud whether the photo could have been given to a man who was involved with both of them. Other members of the team voiced their doubts about that, pointing out that Jeannie was old enough to be Suzie's mother. Some of them thought she might actually be her mother, which would explain what the picture had been doing in Suzie's bag.

'Why would she carry around a picture of her mother?' someone asked.

But there could be no doubt in anyone's mind that Jeannie had somehow been involved with Suzie. Another theory was that John and Suzie had been having an affair, which Jeannie had discovered. In a fit of passion, she had then attacked her husband, after which she had pursued Suzie and killed her in an act of revenge against the woman who had stolen her husband's affections. It sounded crazy, and didn't really account for the picture in the victim's bag, but it was plausible that John might have abandoned his wife for a younger woman.

Whatever the truth about the relationship between Jeannie and Suzie, the police had to find Jeannie as a matter of urgency. So they were now searching for two missing women, both of whom were suspected of foul play. Jeannie was the main suspect in her husband's murder, as well as Suzie's. In a macabre kind of mirroring, unless Christine was lying, Lucy had attacked her, and possibly killed Peter. In that instance, the hypothesis seemed to be that Peter had been having an affair with Lucy but had decided to stay with his wife. Lucy had killed him and had then gone on to attack his wife. They were looking for two women, both of whom they believed had killed, or had attempted murder, more than once. Finding both of those women was now a priority.

'Unless—' Geraldine began and stopped, aware that what she was thinking was probably preposterous. 'It does seem coincidental that both these women have disappeared at the same time,' she murmured.

'Do you think they were working together?' Ariadne asked Geraldine.

Geraldine shook her head. 'I don't know. But something feels a bit odd about it all. Something isn't right.'

Ariadne shrugged. 'Three dead bodies. You can say that again.'

They still didn't have a clear description of Lucy, but they did have several images of Jeannie which would be circulated to every transport route out of the city. Jeannie didn't own a car, but John's had gone missing so his registration number was added to the search list. With luck, if Jeannie attempted to drive anywhere, she would be stopped and brought in for questioning. They couldn't yet confirm her guilt, but the evidence against her seemed compelling.

'Why else would she have gone into hiding if she wasn't guilty?' Geraldine asked, and no one came up with any reason to defend Jeannie.

Convinced Jeannie was guilty of at least one murder and probably two, they had to find her. At the same time, they didn't want to lose sight of the need to track down Christine's elusive friend, Lucy. In hunting for the two missing women, they were going to have their work cut out. Jeannie seemed to have vanished without trace, while they hadn't even managed to get hold of Lucy in the first place. Geraldine and Ariadne drove straight to Jeannie's house but, once again, no one came to the door.

47

THE FOLLOWING MORNING A receptionist in a local hotel called to say that two guests possibly answering to the description of Lucy and Daisy had stayed at her hotel on the previous Thursday night, when Christine had been detained at the police station. Trying to control a flutter of excitement, Geraldine went to the hotel to question the receptionist in person. This was too important an exchange to carry out through an online or phone conversation. Observing the receptionist's reactions to questions, as well as hearing her answers, could potentially be revealing.

The hotel was part of a large chain, clean, modern and impersonal. A young woman in a crisp uniform was standing behind the reception desk. She confirmed that she had contacted the police that morning to report that she might have seen the woman the police were looking for.

'Why didn't you come forward before now?' Geraldine asked. 'The description was circulated twenty-four hours ago.'

In her eagerness to find out more, Geraldine realised she must have failed to conceal her frustration because the receptionist bristled.

'As soon as I saw the message, I called you. I told your colleague, when I phoned the police station, that I wasn't working yesterday. We had a new girl covering reception and she isn't familiar with all our systems yet. I don't think she realised what was going on. She probably didn't even spot your message. In any case, she wasn't working on Thursday evening so she wouldn't have known anything about it.'

Seeing that the receptionist appeared slightly affronted, Geraldine hastened to thank her for being so efficient and calling the police as soon as she returned to work. Mollified, the receptionist showed Geraldine the electronic entry, where a guest had signed in at five twenty on the previous Thursday afternoon, under the name A Smith. That had probably been a false name, but the hotel hadn't asked for identification. This woman, allegedly called Smith, had booked a room with twin beds, one for herself and the other for a young person who had accompanied her. Geraldine showed her a photo of Daisy and the receptionist nodded.

'Yes, that could be her,' she said cautiously. 'I mean, I can't say for sure it's not her. I didn't really get a close look at her. I only spoke to the woman and the girl was kind of hovering in the background. I think it was a girl but it might not have been. I'm not sure she even looked at me and I didn't really look at her.' She paused. 'I think she was wearing a hood. Yes, I'm sure she was.' She frowned, evidently trying to remember and then shook her head.

'What about your security cameras? Could they have captured an image of these two guests?'

The receptionist shook her head again. 'I'm sorry. The film's deleted on Friday night. I'm sure your people could recover it if they wanted to. I mean, everything is saved somewhere, isn't it? But honestly, I wouldn't have thought it was worth it. The film isn't very clear at the best of times. It's more of a deterrent than anything else. The theory is that guests are less likely to run off without paying if they think we've captured them on film.'

Hiding her impatience, Geraldine asked how the woman had paid for the room. Expecting to hear the bill had been paid in cash, she was pleased to learn that it had been paid for with a credit card bearing the name A Smith. If that was an alias, as seemed likely, then the woman had clearly gone to a lot of trouble to cover her tracks. Geraldine sent the details to her colleagues at the police station so they could start trying to trace the owner at once. It being a Sunday, they informed her that was likely to take a little longer than it might have done during the week. However urgently the information was needed, they had to wait for it to be tracked down and that involved some collaboration with the credit card company.

'It shouldn't take more than a day,' the technical support officer assured Geraldine, sensing her disappointment.

'That's a day too long,' she replied tersely. 'I need that information right now.'

But there was nothing she could do to expedite the process. And in the meantime, Christine's former friend remained out of reach. They were all more relieved than ever that Daisy was safe, before Lucy knew the police were hunting for her. No one mentioned that the girl would have been an ideal bargaining chip if Lucy had panicked and decided to kidnap her. Daisy was warned not to have any contact with Lucy and to call for help if she spotted her, and an officer was posted in the corridor outside Christine's hospital room. At the same time, the social worker assigned to her care was instructed to stay with Daisy at all times unless she was in school, where her teachers were informed how vulnerable she was, as the only person able to identify a suspected killer.

'It's that or police protection,' Geraldine told the social worker when she remonstrated that Daisy would feel uncomfortable being chaperoned to and from school. 'It's just until her mother is strong enough to accompany her. In the meantime, we're doing everything we can to apprehend the suspect. She can't stay hidden for much longer.'

Geraldine hoped she was right and they would track down the elusive Lucy soon. There was nothing else to be done so Geraldine went home and did her best to focus on Tom, who was gratifyingly excited to see her. When she admitted to feeling guilty at having abandoned him over the weekend, Ian scolded her for being daft. He insisted that he loved spending time taking care of Tom while Geraldine was preoccupied with her case, and it was good for the baby to spend time with both his parents. In any event, he added, she had only been gone for a few hours and Tom had been asleep for most of the afternoon. She didn't admit that she felt ashamed more because she had forgotten all about her baby than because she had been away from home working. That evening, she resolved to make Tom laugh as much as she could and he chuckled delightedly at her games. But, for once, he was unable to distract her from her work.

The next morning she dropped Tom off at the childminder promptly and hurried to the police station. The technology team were hard at work tracing the identity of the person paying the bills for the credit card opened in the name of A Smith.

'We'll have an answer for you soon,' they assured Geraldine. 'Give us an hour or two and you should hear from us. We'll keep working on it.'

Before the hour was up, they had come up with the name of the person who had paid the credit card bill: Jeannie Hodgson. Geraldine drove straight to the hospital and hurried to the ward where Christine was being looked after. Nodding at the police officer sitting in the corridor, she went in and was pleased to see that Christine was awake.

'What is it now?' she asked wearily. 'You know I'm not fit enough to answer your questions yet.' As if to emphasise her words, she closed her eyes.

Geraldine took a picture of Jeannie from her pocket and held it out for Christine to examine.

'We have reason to believe this woman was in contact with Lucy,' she began.

Before she had a chance to explain that Jeannie had paid Lucy's hotel bill and ask whether Christine had ever seen Jeannie with Lucy, Christine interrupted her.

'That's Lucy!' she cried out, suddenly animated. 'She's a maniac.'

'Are you sure this is your friend Lucy? Are you absolutely sure?'

But Geraldine already knew the answer to her question. She took a deep breath and tried not to react. Her suspicions had been confirmed. Jeannie and Lucy were two names being used by the same woman.

'Christine, I want you to think very carefully. We need to know why this woman befriended you and then turned on you. There must be a reason. Think, Christine. What's going on?'

But Christine shook her head. 'I thought she was my friend,' she repeated plaintively.

Not only was Jeannie no friend to Christine, but she was a killer, and the police had no idea where she had gone.

48

ENGROSSED IN THE MURDER investigation, Geraldine had been feeling guilty about not giving Tom her undivided attention. Even when she had been at home playing with him, she had been preoccupied with the case. That morning, when she dropped him with his childminder, Lisa, she made a point of stopping to check how he was getting on. She had a feeling that was something a devoted mother would do every day, even though Lisa discouraged her charges' mothers from lingering on the doorstep for long, insisting her focus was on the children she was looking after, not their parents. But Lisa seemed happy when Geraldine stopped for a brief chat that morning.

'The little girl I look after is at home with a cough, so it's just me and Tom today,' she explained, smiling. 'There are always coughs and colds around at this time of year, but it's nothing to worry about.'

'How's Tom getting on?' Geraldine asked, not quite sure how to phrase her enquiry, and wondering why this was so much more difficult than questioning a witness.

Lisa reassured her that Tom was making excellent progress.

'That's good to know. You're the expert. I don't have any experience with babies, so it's hard for me to judge.'

The childminder smiled again as she held out her arms to take him. 'You do realise Tom isn't a baby any more. He toddles everywhere and he'll soon be running around.' She laughed. 'I can't take my eyes off him for a second. You're a little bundle of mischief, aren't you?' she added to Tom who tried to grab her nose.

Walking away from them, Geraldine thought how Tom was no longer a baby before she was even used to the fact that she had a baby at all. Her sister, Celia, had warned her that the time would fly by, but she hadn't appreciated just how rapidly her son would develop. She recalled Christine bemoaning how quickly Daisy had changed from a cheerful child into a sullen teenager and she trembled at the future, knowing she couldn't protect Tom for long. In a few years he too would outgrow his parents' control, just like Daisy had done.

The moment she arrived at her desk, she learned that the family of the latest victim had been contacted and her sister had spoken to the police. She had told them that Suzie had recently started a relationship with a new boyfriend. That immediately rang alarm bells but before they could start to draw any conclusions, they had to question the boyfriend in person. The only information they had been given about him so far was that his name was Daniel, and Suzie's sister believed he worked in a hotel in York. She didn't know anything else about him, other than that Suzie had been excited about her new relationship. The sister didn't live locally and hadn't met Daniel herself, but she thought Suzie hadn't known him for long. She had first mentioned him a couple of weeks earlier, since when she hadn't stopped talking about him. Suzie's phone number was being traced and that was likely to give them more information about Daniel. Hopefully he would use his phone and enable them to pinpoint his location soon. Spurred on by this new information, Geraldine settled down to work, all thoughts of Tom and his childminder forgotten.

The connection between Suzie and Jeannie meant that this latest fatality was now part of their ongoing investigation and more officers had been urgently drafted in to help with the increased workload. Even so, the team was seriously understaffed and everyone was going to need to work full time until the case was resolved.

'So much for my being able to focus more on Tom,' Geraldine grumbled to Ian when she met him in the canteen for a quick lunch. 'It looks like I won't be able to pick him up from Lisa today after all.'

Ian smiled at her. 'Don't look so anxious. I'm around and unless I'm forced to join your team, I'll be available for Tom for now. We can't both work long hours, seven days a week. Hopefully the investigation will only take a few weeks, but—' He broke off with a helpless shrug. 'You just focus on your work and get this case cracked as quickly as you can, and in the meantime don't worry about Tom.'

Geraldine muttered that she wasn't feeling worried, she was feeling guilty, but Ian brushed her qualms aside, telling her Tom was perfectly content to be looked after by Lisa and by him.

'So I'm superfluous when it comes to taking care of my own child?' she retorted ungraciously.

'Our child,' he chided her gently.

Before Geraldine could respond, she was summoned to a briefing. Binita wanted to discuss what they knew about Suzie so far. Given the number of bodies that had been associated with the case, a post mortem was being conducted urgently and Geraldine was happy to go and see what the pathologist could tell them. When she arrived, she was disappointed to find that Jonah was not on duty. This was the first time she had met the pathologist who was working that day. He looked as though he had only just left school. She sighed. Lately more and more of her colleagues looked implausibly young to be working in serious crime. The pathologist greeted her sombrely. While his gravity was appropriate for the situation, she missed Jonah's façade of frivolity that helped to make the grisly setting less depressing. She introduced herself and the pathologist nodded without smiling. He seemed nervous, and it occurred to Geraldine that she had probably attended more post mortems than him, even though he was the one carrying out the examination. This might even be the first time he had opened up a cadaver, apart from those he had encountered during his training.

'What can you tell us about her?' she prompted him, adding that any detail, however seemingly insignificant, could be of interest to the investigation. 'We want to know everything you can tell us about her lifestyle and the circumstances of her death.'

The pathologist nodded again. Taking a deep breath, which made him cough slightly, he began.

'The woman was in her early to mid-twenties, possibly a little older.'

'She was twenty-seven,' Geraldine confirmed, resisting an impulse to tell him he was doing well. He might look like a teenager, but he was a qualified professional and, like Daisy, he might not appreciate being patronised.

'She was healthy,' he continued, after acknowledging her interruption. 'I have found no signs of any physical problems. She appears to have had a good diet and she had good muscle tone. She took care of herself.' At this point he paused uncertainly.

'How was she killed?' Geraldine prompted him.

The pathologist appeared to relax slightly – a man more comfortable dealing with the dead than the living.

'She was stabbed forcefully in the back with a long razor-sharp blade. The blow was dealt with such force it penetrated her liver causing a fatal bleed. In addition to that, she hit her head, probably when she fell after being stabbed. Shock combined with the blow to her head knocked her out leaving her bleeding to death.'

'Do you think immediate medical attention could have saved her, if an ambulance had been summoned straight away, for example?'

He nodded. 'I would have thought so, yes. Quite possibly, although there's no knowing for sure.'

'But whoever attacked her effectively left her there to die, when her life could perhaps have been saved by prompt intervention.'

The pathologist raised his eyes from the body. Looking straight at Geraldine, he nodded, understanding the question that lay behind Geraldine's comment.

'Yes,' he said solemnly. 'If you want my opinion, I'd say you should be investigating this as a murder.'

Geraldine gazed at the cadaver and sighed. Although she had anticipated the pathologist's conclusion, it was still sad to acknowledge the violent end of a young life.

'Twenty-seven,' she murmured.

There seemed to be nothing else to say.

49

NOW THEY HAD RETRIEVED Daniel's mobile number from the dead girl's phone, it didn't take the police long to trace him. As Suzie's sister had told them, he worked in a hotel near the city centre. Geraldine called and was told that he was not at work that day. He wasn't answering his mobile and the phone company was reluctant to share his address. It was going to take a little while to access it, so a couple of uniformed constables went to the hotel. When they had disclosed the reason for their visit, the manager gave them Daniel's address without any fuss and they drove straight to Tang Hall Lane to bring him to the police station for questioning. So far there was no evidence to incriminate Daniel in Suzie's murder but he was, at the very least, a person of interest, if not yet an actual suspect. With so many people associated with this case disappearing, everyone was pleased when they learned that Daniel had been brought to the police station. According to the officers who had brought him in, he had accompanied them without demur.

Geraldine made her way thoughtfully to the interview room, accompanied by Ariadne. They were both aware that they were about to speak to a potential suspect in multiple murders.

'We have to get this right,' Geraldine muttered to Ariadne.

Daniel was staring wretchedly at the floor when they entered. He expressed surprise when informed he was entitled to have a lawyer present.

'A lawyer?' he repeated, looking up and sounding bewildered.

'What do I need a lawyer for? I'm not suspected of committing a crime, am I?' He gave a strained laugh. 'What's happened? I don't understand what's going on.' His voice shook and he fell silent and lowered his eyes again. 'I can't tell you anything. I don't know anything.'

Geraldine leaned forward. 'We know you were seeing Suzie.'

Daniel looked up, startled. 'Suzie?' he repeated, seeming shocked. 'Suzie? Oh my God. Not Suzie. Please not Suzie. Tell me she's safe.'

'Suzie's dead. What happened, Daniel?'

He didn't answer.

'Daniel,' Geraldine urged him gently. 'Who killed Suzie? If you know who did it, you must tell us. Was it you?'

Daniel shook his head. 'I can't be sure. That is, I can't believe it. No, it can't be true. Not Suzie. No, no.'

'Daniel, tell us what you know.'

He looked up and frowned. 'What if I'm wrong? But no, not Suzie. It can't be. I warned her. I—' He broke down in tears again. 'It can't be true. Not Suzie.'

'Daniel, you have to tell us what you know.'

He sighed. 'I was seeing someone before I met Suzie,' he admitted reluctantly.

'Who?'

'Someone. An older woman. Older than Suzie that is. Older than me,' he added with a rueful smile. 'But it was over. I finished with her when I met Suzie and told her I wouldn't see her again. She wasn't happy about it. She – she threatened to kill Suzie, but—'

'But you never believed her capable of killing anyone?' Ariadne completed his sentence, with a sympathetic smile, nodding to encourage him to continue with his account.

'Oh no. I knew she was capable of murder. That was never in doubt.'

Geraldine and Ariadne exchanged a fleeting glance.

'What do you mean?' Geraldine asked. 'How could you know that?'

All at once, Daniel clammed up, shaking his head furiously and muttering that it couldn't be true. Geraldine and Ariadne continued questioning him, but he refused to say any more. Shaking his head, he muttered that it was his fault Suzie was dead.

'I should have protected her,' he said with an air of desperation. 'I should have protected her. I knew she was in danger. I tried to warn her, but I was afraid it would frighten her off.'

'Daniel, we need to know the name of the woman you suspect. If there's any chance she's guilty, we need to speak to her. Just tell us her name and we'll do the rest.'

Daniel shook his head. 'What's the point?' he asked dully. 'It's over. Everything's over. It's too late to save her. It's my fault. It's all my fault she's dead.'

'Daniel, we understand you're grieving and in shock, but listen to me,' Geraldine implored him. 'It's not too late to prevent Suzie's murderer from getting away with this. If you know the identity of her killer, you have to help us find her and stop her. If we don't stop her, she could kill someone else.'

'She already has.'

'What's her name, Daniel?'

They threatened to arrest him for withholding information and obstructing the police in the course of a murder investigation, but neither their pleas nor their threats had any effect on him. He just repeated that he didn't care about anything any more. When he repeated that he was guilty of Suzie's death, Geraldine instructed a constable to take him to a cell.

'Yes,' he murmured, looking up with bloodshot eyes. 'Lock me up. I'm guilty as sin. I might as well have killed her myself. I knew what might happen and I failed to protect her. Her death is on me. I wish we still had the death penalty. I don't deserve to survive her. I don't deserve to live.'

Once Daniel had been taken away, Ariadne turned to Geraldine wanting to know why she hadn't charged him with murder.

'He said he was guilty,' Ariadne said. 'We have him on tape admitting it's his fault she's dead. What are we waiting for?'

Geraldine frowned and said she wasn't convinced Daniel had committed the murder, but he knew who had killed Suzie. She wanted to question him again before rushing to charge him. Binita agreed with Ariadne and was impatient to see Daniel charged, but she agreed to wait another day after which they would have to charge him or release him. Geraldine waited an hour before she went to talk to Daniel again. He was lying on the bunk in his cell, his eyes closed. He opened them as soon as Geraldine called his name, but he didn't answer. He remained lying down when she asked him to sit up.

'Daniel,' she said quietly. 'Tell me about the woman you were seeing before you met Suzie.'

Hearing Suzie's name, Daniel let out a low moan. He sat up and began rocking backwards and forwards.

'Who was she?'

But despite her best efforts, she couldn't persuade Daniel to answer her questions. Baffled, she left the cell. He had mentioned a woman he had been seeing before he met Suzie, but all he had divulged was that she was older than him, which didn't narrow the search down much. A team was set up to question anyone who had worked with Daniel, his family and all of his contacts on social media, but no one was able to reveal the identity of his former girlfriend. So now they knew two things about her. She was older than Daniel and they had taken pains to keep their relationship a secret.

'Perhaps he was seeing a married woman?' Binita suggested when Geraldine ran details of the case past her colleagues at a briefing, telling them everything Daniel had said.

'That could have been Jeannie Hodgson,' Geraldine said.

'Suzie had her photo in her bag. What if Jeannie was threatening to attack Suzie and Daniel gave Suzie the photo and warned her to look out for Jeannie? If Jeannie was rejected by Daniel, that could explain why she might attack Suzie.'

Binita nodded. 'For revenge or to get Suzie out of the way so Jeannie could win him back for herself. But why would she kill Peter and attack Christine? What's her connection with them?'

Geraldine shrugged. 'Christine seems as clueless as we are about what motivated Jeannie to attack her family, or why she assumed a false name when they met. I know Christine was confused after her operation, but she seemed adamant she didn't know why Lucy – or Jeannie – would want to harm her family. I think she was genuinely baffled.'

'The only thing that is clear is that we have to find Jeannie Hodgson urgently,' Binita said.

Geraldine went to speak to Daniel again. This time, she took the photograph from Suzie's bag with her. As soon as she held it up, Daniel's shocked expression confirmed her suspicion.

50

A PATROL CAR WAS sent to Jeannie's address but no one answered when two uniformed constables knocked on her front door, nor was there any sign of John's car on the drive or parked on the street nearby. The car could have been in the garage, but that wasn't possible to confirm without breaking into the premises. The officers were instructed to knock on the doors of the adjacent houses and enquire whether anyone had seen Jeannie returning home. There was no answer at the first house they tried. On the other side, the front door was opened by a wizened elderly man who peered inquisitively at the two police officers standing on his doorstep.

'Yes?' he enquired, his bright eyes flicking over their uniforms. 'You'll have to speak up,' he replied, when they asked him about Jeannie. 'I'm a little hard of hearing.'

'Your next-door neighbour,' one of the constables shouted. 'When did you last see her?'

'Wait here,' the old man said, nodding his head and smiling. 'I'll go and put my hearing aids in.' Assuring them that he wouldn't be a minute, the old man shuffled off.

The officers waited but, despite their patience and the old man's willingness to assist them, they learned nothing. They tried asking at other houses nearby. Only one woman was in and she didn't have anything helpful to say.

'They kept themselves to themselves,' was all she was able to tell them. 'I read all about them. He was mugged, wasn't he? Well, I hope you've arrested whoever did it, arrested him and locked him up. We want to be able to walk around the city streets without fearing for our lives. What's going on? That's what I want to know. Everything's going to pot and you lot are doing bugger all about it. And it's not just me saying that. Ask anyone.'

Hands on hips, she glared angrily at the constables who offered her as much reassurance as they could, without being able to confirm that the killer had been caught.

It was possible Jeannie was using her husband's car, so officers were instructed to keep a lookout for it. That paid off when the registration number was recognised by a sharp-eyed policeman in a patrol car. He only caught a glimpse of the driver, but thought it could be a woman. Doing his best to remain inconspicuous by not going near to the vehicle he was tailing, he lost sight of it at a crossroads when a van stopped right in front of him; a bus coming the other way prevented him from overtaking the van. He reported the sighting and two unmarked police cars set out to join the pursuit. Informed that a colleague had caught a glimpse of John Hodgson's car travelling in the direction of the A1036, Geraldine suspected Jeannie might be going home, oblivious to the attention she had attracted.

As she was not far from the junction where the car had been spotted, Geraldine drove straight to Jeannie's house. She arrived before the other police vehicles which were still on their way, negotiating the city traffic. Pulling into the curb, she saw John's car – now Jeannie's – parked on the drive outside the house. There was no sign of the driver. Having confirmed that her colleagues were only a few minutes away, she climbed out of her car and hurried through the metal gate which swung shut behind her with a faint clang. Passing a row of slightly woebegone orange dahlias, she made her way up the short path to the front door and rang the bell. For a moment nothing happened. As she reached to ring again, the door was flung open to reveal Jeannie, looking scrawny and unwashed, and older than Geraldine remembered. Heavy make-up gave her an almost clownish appearance. Geraldine had never understood why some children were afraid of clowns, but she couldn't help feeling there was something sinister about the woman standing in front of her. Ugly, smudged black rings around her eyes seemed to accentuate the malicious intensity of her gaze.

Jeannie scowled. 'It's you again, turning up where you're not wanted. What are you doing here this time?'

'We'd like to ask you a few more questions,' Geraldine said.

With an angry grunt, Jeannie made a move to slam the door but Geraldine put out her foot to prevent it closing. Bracing herself against an attempt to push her away, Geraldine was caught off guard when instead of barging into her, Jeannie lunged forward to grab her arm and yank her into the house. As Geraldine pulled out her phone, she noticed there was a message from Lisa. Alarmed, she clicked on the screen to check why the childminder was contacting her while she was at work. She wasn't paying attention to where she was going and almost tripped. Struggling to keep her balance, she failed to react promptly enough when Jeannie launched herself forwards and threw her to the floor. As Geraldine fell, she hit her head on the wall. Momentarily stunned by the impact, she felt the room spin around her. Her last thought before she slumped to the floor was that Lisa had tried to contact her. If anything happened to Tom and she wasn't there to take care of him, she would never forgive herself.

Opening her eyes, she saw Jeannie leering at her in the dim light coming through the fanlight above the front door, her face a mask of grotesque triumph.

'I'm glad you've come to visit me,' Jeannie hissed. 'You're going to be my ticket out of here. It's lucky for me you were stupid enough to come alone.' Hoarse laughter gurgled in her throat. 'Not so lucky for you. If you ever get out of here alive, I don't suppose your career will be going anywhere after this. Serves you right, you stupid bitch.' She spat.

Geraldine moved her head to glance down at a globule of saliva on her jacket, barely visible in the poor light. With the movement, she became aware of something sharp pricking the skin beneath her ear and realised that Jeannie was holding a knife to her neck. At the periphery of her vision, she saw her phone lying on the floor, out of reach. Grinning, Jeannie slid the tip of the blade around until it was pressing against Geraldine's throat.

'I wouldn't make any sudden movements if I were you,' Jeannie hissed, seeing Geraldine's eyes flicking around. 'You don't want my hand to slip, do you?'

All her training kicked in and Geraldine felt an eerie sense of calm as she answered. 'You won't kill me. You'd lose your bargaining chip.'

Despite years of experience dealing with violent criminals, she was surprised at how steady her voice was. As long as she could stop herself imagining what might happen, she was confident she could maintain her composure in the face of immediate danger. Jeannie was manifestly insane, meaning her behaviour was unpredictable, and Geraldine knew she had killed at least once. Jeannie might decide to plunge the knife in at any moment. Geraldine tried to calculate her chances if she suddenly hit out at the arm holding the weapon. She would most likely be cut, but the knife would be propelled sideways across her throat, not thrust forwards, and so the injury was unlikely to be deep enough to be fatal. But it would be risky. Even a superficial slash across her throat was potentially lethal, but that might be the best outcome she could hope to achieve.

Before she had Tom, she might possibly have attempted a physical response to her situation, but she hesitated to take that risk. There had to be another way. Her safest option might be to hold her nerve until the rescue team arrived; she forced herself to remain optimistic they would save her life. Telling herself that an armed response team were probably already silently positioning themselves around the house, she stared at the floor and kept perfectly still. The last thing she wanted to do was provoke her captor. She knew her colleagues were on their way. When she didn't answer her phone, that would alert them to the fact that she was in trouble. Once they spotted her car outside in the street, they would realise what was happening.

In the meantime, she needed to convince Jeannie that it would be rash to kill her. She wasn't sure if there was any point in appealing to Jeannie's reason, but she had to try.

'You don't want to be charged with the murder of a police officer,' she said in a low, calm tone. 'You'd be locked up for the rest of your life. Is that what you want? Listen to me. I can offer you a safe escape,' she lied, desperate to keep herself alive until help arrived.

'Shut up,' Jeannie snapped. 'Just shut up. I'm thinking.'

'Let me help you.'

'You? Help me?' Jeannie let out a bark of laughter. 'I'm not a complete fool. You're fighting to save your skin, but it's over for you. We both know that, so you might as well save your breath. Your last breath,' she added maliciously.

'If you kill me, you'll have no way of saving yourself. As long as I'm alive, you can negotiate for your release. They'll let you go to save me and you'll be free. Isn't that better than going to prison for the rest of your life?'

For a moment, it looked as though Jeannie was listening to her, speculating. Then Geraldine's phone rang and Jeannie spat again and barked at her to stop talking. At the same time, the knife pressed harder against Geraldine's throat and she felt a sharp sting as the point pierced her skin.

'As long as they think you're alive, they'll do what I ask. That doesn't mean you have to still be alive, they just have to believe it.'

'They're not stupid. They'll need evidence—' Geraldine began, but the knife moved across her throat and the pain intensified, making her gasp.

'I told you to shut up,' Jeannie muttered. 'One more word and you're dead. You're no use to me anyway. You're a nuisance. And you know what happens to people who get in my way, don't you?' A macabre grin stretched her scarlet lips. 'I know what you're thinking. You think I'm crazy, don't you?'

Geraldine started to remonstrate but Jeannie jabbed the knife and she whimpered and fell silent, biting her lip.

'That's what *he* thought,' she went on. 'But he was wrong too, because I'm not crazy, far from it. I'm cleverer than the lot of you. I know how to get what I want and no one is going to stand in my way.'

51

AWARE THAT EVERYONE ELSE would have heard about her father's murder and the attack on her mother, Daisy was nervous about returning to school. She was afraid the other pupils would treat her with open contempt now they had a clear-cut reason to view her as a victim. The taunts previously whispered behind her back would be spoken out loud, and she wouldn't be able to walk along a corridor without running the gauntlet of undisguised sniggering. She wasn't sure which she dreaded more: being ignored or mocked by her classmates. Even those who didn't jeer at her might press her with intrusive questions about why the police had treated her mother as a suspect and she wasn't sure she could cope with that. Not that she was weak, far from it. She had been bullied before, targeted by one of the boys who had taken a fancy to her and pestered her until she had retaliated. Only the teachers knew why she had assaulted him, because Daisy had insisted the other pupils not be told. Not that she was ashamed or regretted what she had done. That oaf had deserved to be thumped. Her only regret was that she hadn't caused him any lasting damage. But she couldn't defend herself against the whole school, nor could she physically attack every pupil who sneered at her.

To her relief, the head teacher had been very understanding about the incident, even though it had resulted in a trip to hospital for the boy Daisy had assaulted. Despite his complaints, he had been fortunate to suffer nothing worse than a black eye and a nasty bruise where he had hit his shoulder against the wall as he fell. What had really surprised Daisy was that instead of punishing her, the head teacher had suspended the boy. If he hadn't been stupid enough to admit what he had done to provoke her, she might not have been treated so leniently. Fortunately for Daisy, he had broken down and confessed that he had been pursuing her. His claims that she had led him on had been quite rightly dismissed once she had shown the head teacher the texts he had sent her. Daisy had been let off on the proviso that she agreed to speak to a counsellor. But after all that, her abuser had been allowed back in school and Daisy suspected he was already busy spreading nasty rumours about her. She could hardly believe she had actually agreed to come back, knowing it was going to be even more horrible than before. Telling herself she could always leave and never return, she walked through the school gates, keeping her eyes fixed firmly on the ground.

She had never exactly been popular and she trudged reluctantly into class steeling herself to face a hostile reception. The room was packed with chattering pupils gathered in noisy cliques, none of which Daisy had ever been invited to join. She told herself she had no wish to be part of one of the gaggles of girls who seemed to spend all their time gossiping, flirting with boys and falling out with each other. Secretly she envied them their friendship groups. She was used to being treated with derision by other pupils, but if anyone said a word about the suspicion that had been directed against her mother, she was afraid she might lash out. She would have to avoid engaging any of the other pupils in conversation; it might not end well. She reminded herself to be careful as she walked in. An awkward hush descended on the chattering students when they saw her. The teacher had not arrived and Daisy felt a flutter of alarm, realising she ought to have checked the teacher was there before she entered. Glancing around, she was relieved to see that the boy she had assaulted was not in the room. The head teacher had assured Daisy that he would be moved to another class and she had kept her word. Daisy was cautiously relieved. With that hurdle hopefully overcome, Daisy still couldn't relax. She still had to face the rest of the class.

Everyone seemed to be staring at her and she lowered her eyes, embarrassed and intimidated. She wished they would all just ignore her, like they used to do. If they started to quiz her about her parents, she might freak out. She wondered whether to turn around and leave, but was reluctant to run away and leave them to talk about her behind her back. As she was vacillating, one of the girls approached her, muttering condolences.

'Yeah, sorry about your dad,' another girl chimed in.

Daisy blinked frantically, but she couldn't stop her tears. Mortified, she covered her face with her hands and tried to suppress her sobs. To her surprise she felt arms around her and was aware of a hubbub of gentle murmurs.

'What a shit thing to happen.'

'I'm so sorry.'

'It must be really difficult for you.'

'I can't imagine what you're going through.'

A sudden silence and a withdrawal of the arms embracing her signalled Mrs Proudy's arrival.

'Now, girls, places please,' she barked.

'She's such a bitch,' the girl who had been hugging Daisy whispered under her breath. She winked at Daisy who gave her a feeble smile. Wiping her eyes, she went to her place, struggling to control her emotions.

It turned out the other girls in her class weren't as unfriendly as Daisy had previously believed. Once she started to talk to them, she discovered they were actually quite nice. Far from shunning her, they seemed to be vying with one another for her attention. Bizarrely, she had become some kind of celebrity at school. She didn't expect her sudden burst of popularity to last long, aware that most of the girls were inquisitive rather than genuinely friendly. In the meantime, she resolved to make the most of her newfound status. Maybe she would even be able to make some real friends. She liked some of her classmates more than others. A few of them actually listened to her with genuine interest and seemed willing to confide their own fears and insecurities with her. It was like a revelation to her to discover how much she had in common with other girls her own age.

When she was small, she had liked playing with other children, but then adolescence had come along and changed everything. Now she began to wonder if it was her own paranoia that had made her view the other girls as her enemies. But her life had moved on, and she saw no point in trying to examine the past. If she had been to blame for her own social isolation, she was also responsible for the new relationships she was resolved to nurture. In any case, she didn't want to analyse her own faults. She just wanted to live a normal life, if that was possible given what had happened to her father. One day she would be ready to mourn his death, but not yet.

52

JEANNIE FELL SILENT, FROWNING thoughtfully. She looked away for an instant, but it wasn't long enough for Geraldine to react. The next second, Geraldine's phone rang and there was a faint clatter as Jeannie stamped on it, jolting the tip of the blade against Geraldine's throat. Abruptly the phone stopped ringing. Growing desperate, Geraldine tensed, preparing to strike Jeannie's arm and force her knife away from her throat. As she clenched her fist to punch, she heard a siren and saw Jeannie stiffen. The point of the knife pricked her flesh, making any movement difficult, but she forced herself to speak.

'My colleagues are outside,' she muttered through clenched teeth, trying not to move her jaw. 'You won't be able to get away by yourself. I can help you.'

'Shut up.'

'Listen to me. We both want to get out of here alive.'

Before she could continue, a man's voice interrupted them, ringing out clearly over a tannoy.

'Jeannie. I know you can hear me. Your house is surrounded. Come out quietly and we can talk. We can't help you while you're in there.' There was a pause, and then the negotiator resumed. 'Trust me, Jeannie. We all want to resolve this. Work with us and let us help you.'

'Sure, sure. Everyone wants to help me,' Jeannie scoffed.

'You can't stay in here forever,' Geraldine whispered. In desperation, she added, 'Don't you want to see Daniel again?'

Jeannie winced as though stung, inadvertently jabbing Geraldine with the knife.

'Give me my phone and I'll tell them you want to speak to him,' Geraldine managed to croak.

Jeannie narrowed her eyes and kept the knife pressed against Geraldine's throat.

'Tell them,' she said, glaring wildly. 'Tell them I want to see him. If they let us leave together, I'll let you go. If not—' She glared at Geraldine. 'You're dead.'

'Jeannie,' the voice reached them over the loudspeaker. 'We have someone here who says he knows you. We found him and he wants to see you. He wants to help you.'

After some crackling, another voice came over the loudspeaker.

'Jeannie, I need to talk to you.'

The words sounded forced, as though the speaker was struggling not to break down.

Jeannie's eyes widened. 'It's him,' she whispered. 'He's here. I knew he'd come. Where is he? Why can't I see him?'

Without releasing her grip on the knife, she looked eagerly towards the window. She only turned away for a fraction of a second, but it was enough. Hoping this would happen, Geraldine had been poised to move. Swiftly she punched at the arm wielding the knife and the weapon clattered to the floor. Jeannie lunged for it but she was too slow. Geraldine grabbed her arm and twisted it savagely behind her back

'Get off! You're breaking my arm.'

Geraldine shoved her erstwhile captor to the floor and slapped handcuffs on her, taking no care to avoid hurting her. Jeannie yelped and protested about police brutality.

'Brutality?' Geraldine repeated furiously.

For an instant she struggled to control an impulse to kick the woman who had threatened to kill her and deprive her child of his mother.

'You're lucky I don't smash your head in,' she snarled, her voice shaking with rage.

A voice over the tannoy recalled Geraldine to her senses. Immediately she regretted her violent impulse. Hauling Jeannie to her feet, she grabbed her mobile and was relieved to see that although the screen was cracked, the phone appeared otherwise undamaged. Guessing that Ariadne would be outside with the rescue team, she called her to tell her she had Jeannie in handcuffs. While she fiddled with the screen, Jeannie spat at her and kicked her.

'Ariadne? Ariadne?'

The line crackled but no one answered. She hit Ian's number with the same result. The phone was dead. Abandoning her efforts to use her phone, she grabbed Jeannie by both arms and tried to propel her towards the front door. Jeannie refused to co-operate. Geraldine wondered whether to abandon her captive and go and open the front door, but she was reluctant to let go of Jeannie's arms. Even though she was handcuffed, she was deranged and desperate, and Geraldine didn't trust her.

'Come on,' she said, hiding her annoyance. 'There's no point in being obstructive.' She tightened her grip on Jeannie's arms while endeavouring to keep her legs out of reach of Jeannie's feet. Finally she gave up trying to push Jeannie to the front door and forced her down on the floor instead. Lying on her front, with her head twisted to one side, Jeannie writhed and kicked until Geraldine sat on her.

'Get off!' Jeannie yelled. 'You're breaking my legs.'

The crash when the front door was broken open resounded through the house. Somewhere, a door slammed shut in a gust of wind that blew in as two hefty uniformed constables burst into the hall. Geraldine rolled off Jeannie and watched with grim satisfaction as the demented woman was dragged away, shrieking about police brutality and vandalism.

'You'll pay for that door!' Geraldine heard her yell. 'Let me go! Let me go! You're breaking my arm!'

Geraldine was clambering to her feet when Ariadne rushed in through the open door. 'Are you all right?'

'I'm fine,' Geraldine replied, struggling against tears that were threatening to overwhelm her. 'Is Tom all right?'

'Tom?'

Geraldine explained that the childminder had called her and she didn't know why.

'Don't worry. Tom's fine. She called Ian when she couldn't get hold of you. That's when we suspected something was wrong. Once your car was spotted, we realised you were in here with that maniac and called the negotiator and the rapid response team to get you out.'

'Is Tom all right? What's happened?'

'He's fine. She called you at lunchtime to tell you he climbed into his stroller by himself.'

Shaking with relief, Geraldine dropped her head in her hands. 'Give me a minute,' she said.

'I'm not sure that's going to be possible,' Ariadne murmured urgently. 'The DCI's here and she wants to see you straight away.'

Geraldine anticipated a reprimand and she wasn't wrong. Stepping outside into the light, she was overwhelmed by the array of personnel and vehicles packed into the road outside Jeannie's house. Virtually everyone she could see was wearing uniform. Those who weren't identifiable as armed response officers were wearing stab vests. The absence of civilians made it obvious Geraldine's colleagues had been working silently outside the house for longer than she had realised, because the entire street must have been evacuated. Binita stepped forward and told Ariadne to take Geraldine for a medical check-up.

'There's no need,' Geraldine said. 'I'm not injured.' As she spoke, she remembered that she had received a knock on the head when Jeannie had first attacked her.

'There's blood on your neck,' Binita snapped. 'Take her to the hospital at once.'

'Come on,' Ariadne urged Geraldine. 'It's just as well to get yourself checked out and you need to get that cut properly cleaned up as soon as possible.'

Accepting the sense of what her colleagues were saying, Geraldine nodded and followed Ariadne submissively to her car. Now that her adrenaline was ebbing, she became aware that her neck was smarting and her head was aching. Seated and belted, she closed her eyes, overwhelmed by a sudden onslaught of pain.

'Stay with me,' Ariadne said, anxiety evident in her voice.

Geraldine smiled. 'Don't worry, I'm not going to pass out. I'm just exhausted.'

'Binita's going to give you a roasting next time she sees you,' Ariadne said. 'She was furious at you for going in there alone.'

Geraldine shrugged and winced when the movement sent a stabbing pain across the back of her neck. She was too tired to explain that she hadn't exactly walked into the house voluntarily but had been dragged inside before she could resist. Whatever excuse she made, the fact was that she had put herself in danger and Binita was bound to berate her. As for Ian, she didn't dare think about what he was going to say about what had happened.

After a thorough check-up, including a scan to rule out any possible head injuries, a doctor confirmed that the laceration to her neck was superficial. Once it had been dressed she was discharged. Ian was waiting for her outside the hospital with Tom in the back of the car. Geraldine managed to control herself until they were nearly home before she broke down in tears.

'I thought I might never see Tom again,' she admitted. 'When I saw Lisa had called and I didn't know why, I was afraid something terrible had happened.'

'Something terrible nearly did happen,' Ian replied, frowning. 'You do realise you could have been killed? Think about the impact it would have on Tom and me if anything were to happen to you. You've got to start behaving more responsibly now we have a baby to consider.'

'He's not a baby any more,' she replied, still sobbing. 'Lisa said he's not a baby.'

'He's a baby as far as I'm concerned,' Ian replied. 'What's more, he's *our* baby and our responsibility. I wouldn't care if a hundred killers got away with murder, as long as we still have you.'

'You don't mean that,' Geraldine whispered.

'Let someone else risk their life next time,' Ian said. 'Not you.'

'I didn't risk my life,' she protested.

'Have you seen the state you're in? Geraldine, you put yourself at the mercy of a serial killer.'

'Ian, please, can we talk about this tomorrow?'

He glanced at her and nodded. 'Of course. But we are going to talk about it.'

Geraldine understood he was only speaking so severely because he had been scared, but she wondered if he was right to challenge her dedication to her work. Being a mother had changed so much in her life; she knew she would prioritise Tom's happiness over anything, even if it meant allowing multiple killers to escape justice. She felt as if her world was spinning out of control.

'Ian, I don't know if I can do this any longer,' she blurted out. 'The job, I mean. I don't know if I can carry on.'

He shook his head, his eyes on the road ahead. 'You just need a good night's sleep. You've been through a terrible ordeal but you'll get over it soon enough. We all lose our nerve from time to time, even the best of us. The thing is, we pick ourselves up and carry on.'

'That's not it,' she said. 'I mean, I haven't lost my nerve.'

'What is it then?'

He drew up in the underground car park of their flat and turned to face her but she looked away.

'I don't know,' she muttered. 'I think you're right. I just need a good night's sleep.'

But she had an uneasy feeling that she was going to feel as confused in the morning as she did in that moment. Her sister had warned her that being a mother wasn't easy. She just hadn't appreciated how hard it was going to be. But Ian was right. She would pick herself up and carry on. What else was there to do?

'Life was so much easier before Tom came along,' she murmured.

'Well, we can't send him back,' Ian joked, but behind his show of joviality she could tell he was troubled.

53

JEANNIE SAT IMMOBILE AS Geraldine opened the interview by repeating the charges. Her face remained impassive when she was accused of murdering her husband and Peter Selby. She didn't even stir as the chubby lawyer at her side assured her in an undertone that the police had no evidence they could use to secure a conviction against her; all she had to do was sit quietly and leave everything to him. Not by so much as a flicker of her eyelids did she reveal that she had heard him. Apparently unfazed by his unresponsive client, he fell silent. Only when Geraldine reached the third accusation, concerning Suzie, did Jeannie's face betray any emotion. She lowered her head too late to conceal the involuntary curl of her lips. Geraldine shuddered on catching sight of her smirk.

Jeannie recovered herself almost at once, sitting bolt upright and readjusting her features. She cleared her throat but as soon as she began to speak, her lawyer cut in, his chins wobbling as he remonstrated with her in a low voice. She hushed him, waving her hand in dismissal, and he subsided, grumbling about not being allowed to do his job.

'I'm here to defend you,' he muttered crossly.

'Thank you, but that won't be necessary,' Jeannie said primly before she turned to Geraldine. 'First of all, I can confirm I never killed my husband,' she said, speaking very slowly as though she was addressing a child. 'It's stupid to suggest that I, of all people, would want to harm him. You seem to have forgotten that we were married for seventeen years. You must realise that what you're suggesting is impossible. I'm sorry to have to point out your blunder, but you've got this all wrong. You should be feeling pretty stupid. I hope you're not going to embarrass yourselves any further.' She smiled thinly.

'We don't think so,' Ariadne said.

'You're clutching at straws here, throwing out allegations without a shred of evidence. Wasting everyone's time, that's what it is,' Jeannie continued. 'If you think you can browbeat me with your insulting accusations—'

'My client has nothing further to say to you,' the lawyer butted in with a faint air of desperation.

Geraldine sat silently waiting to hear what else Jeannie might say.

'As for this other man,' Jeannie went on, raising her voice and ignoring the interruption, 'I'm sorry, but I don't know anyone called Peter, so tell me, why would I kill someone I've never even met?'

Having said that, Jeannie sat back with a satisfied air.

'We're talking about Peter Selby, the husband of your friend, Christine,' Geraldine replied.

'Christine? She was never my friend,' Jeannie scoffed. 'I'm not denying that I met her once or twice, but we've never been anything more than acquaintances. You really need to get your facts straight, Inspector, instead of telling stupid lies. You seem happy enough to accuse me of killing my husband for no reason, so I wonder why you don't accuse Christine of killing *her* husband? I really don't see what someone else's husband has got to do with me.'

She folded her arms decisively as if to indicate that the conversation was over.

Geraldine glanced at the morose lawyer before saying softly that the police had been talking to Daniel.

For the first time, Jeannie's composure was shaken. 'Daniel?' she murmured, looking startled. 'What about Daniel?' But her expression told Geraldine everything she wanted to know.

'Daniel Barker,' Geraldine said quietly. 'We're talking about the man you were having an affair with until recently.'

The lawyer looked helplessly from Geraldine to Jeannie and back again. 'I'd like a private word with my client,' he said, shifting in his seat which creaked under his bulk. 'This interview needs to stop right now.'

Paying no attention to the bleating of her lawyer, Jeannie sat forward and glared at Geraldine. 'Until two weeks ago I was a happily married woman and now I'm a widow, in mourning for my dear husband. Tell me, when was I supposed to be seeing another man? It's a vile accusation.' She turned to the lawyer. 'It's slander. I want her prosecuted.'

'I'm talking about Daniel, the young man you were sleeping with.' Geraldine paused for a second to gauge the suspect's response, but Jeannie's expression reverted to her earlier blank stare. All the same, Geraldine was sure she was listening intently. 'That is,' she resumed, 'he *was* your lover, until he replaced you with a younger woman. That must have been painful for you. In fact, you must have been frantic with jealousy. It's understandable. No one likes being rejected, but to be dumped like that for a younger and more attractive woman must have been really painful for you. Because you were good to Daniel, weren't you? All those nights he spent with you in smart hotels, all paid for by you. You were really generous. You must have thought a lot of him. Did he tell you he was going to stay with you? I don't suppose you expected him to dump you so soon, anyway, not after everything you did for him.'

Jeannie's features twisted with suppressed emotion. 'You have no idea,' she muttered.

'That's enough,' the lawyer said, making a feeble attempt to seize control of the situation. 'My client has no further comment to make at this time.'

'After everything you did for him,' Geraldine repeated. 'I'm surprised you let him turn his back on you like that.'

'He never meant to leave me,' Jeannie blurted out.

'But he did.'

'That was just an aberration, a mistake.'

'Of course it was,' Geraldine agreed. 'You knew all the time it was you he loved.'

'Yes, yes, you're right. It was always me,' Jeannie cried out, in a sudden frenzy. 'I know he loves me. He was never serious about that tart.'

'Stop this, you are not to say another word,' the lawyer blustered ineffectually.

'What I don't understand is how he could betray you like that,' Geraldine continued.

'He never meant to. You have to understand. He didn't know what he was doing. He was frightened by the strength of our passion.'

'You saw a way to bring him back to you, because he'd lost sight of your relationship,' Geraldine suggested softly. 'You knew you could make him see what really mattered.'

Jeannie's eyes were fixed on Geraldine, while the lawyer stared at his client in consternation as she answered. 'I had to make him see the truth of his feelings for me.'

Geraldine nodded. 'With your husband out of the way, there was just one impediment to your happiness with Daniel and that was the woman who was stealing him away from you. Once she had gone Daniel would come to his senses and remember how much you meant to him.'

Jeannie nodded, her eyes shining with frantic animation.

'When Daniel knows what you did for his sake, he won't be able to deny his love any longer. But will he believe what you did so you could be together? If he refuses to believe it, you will have done all that for nothing and that would be a pity. Why won't you let me help you?'

Jeannie shook her head, looking puzzled. 'Why would you want to help me? This is a trick.'

Geraldine gazed at her sadly, hoping the lawyer would keep his mouth shut.

'Jeannie, I know what you did and I understand, and I can help you to make sure Daniel understands too.'

'You think you understand,' Jeannie said, staring into Geraldine's eyes as though trying to read her mind. 'But you have no idea what it means to love unreservedly. No one does.'

Geraldine thought of Tom and nodded. 'I do,' she replied.

'Then you know why I did it.'

'What *I* think isn't important. What matters is making sure Daniel understands. I want to help you. Tell me what you did and I can help you to make this right.'

Jeannie hesitated. She seemed to have forgotten that only the previous day she had been threatening to kill Geraldine. 'All right, but turn that thing off.' She gestured at the tape machine. 'And I can tell him myself, thank you very much.'

Geraldine nodded at Ariadne, who complied with the request. Clearly Jeannie didn't consider how difficult it would be to retract a confession freely given in the presence of two police officers and a lawyer. The lawyer was staring at Jeannie as though transfixed.

'Very well,' Jeannie said, sitting back and patting her untidy hair. 'When can I see him?'

54

'FIRST YOU NEED TO tell me what happened,' Geraldine repeated quietly. 'You know I understand.'

'Don't say another word. If you don't stop talking, I won't be able to help you,' the lawyer warned Jeannie. He wiped his brow, where a faint sheen of sweat glistened.

'I don't need *your* help. How could *you* help me anyway?' she snapped. 'You don't understand what it is to truly love someone. Very few people do.' She glared haughtily around the table. 'We wanted to be free to live together openly. We were growing impatient at having to hide our love, meeting secretly in hotels, never being able to go out together properly. He wanted to take me to nice restaurants where we could have romantic meals together. You have no idea how frustrating it was, always having to meet in private, where no one could see us.'

'With John dead, you and Daniel would finally be together.'

Jeannie nodded.

'Did you really think you would be able to live happily ever after?' Geraldine murmured.

'Why not?' Jeannie protested. 'We're in love. We've waited long enough.'

'And there's the additional benefit that your husband's death left you financially well off,' Ariadne pointed out. 'That must have been an incentive.'

Jeannie shrugged, murmuring that they were going to be comfortable. 'This was never about the money but yes, why

285

wouldn't we have what was legally mine? We're in love. We deserve to be happy.'

'Only sadly for you, your happy ever after never worked out the way you had planned it, because Daniel fell for someone else,' Geraldine said. She shook her head and sighed. 'Clearly he wasn't as in love with you as you thought.'

Jeannie scowled and her cheeks and neck flushed red. 'He's young, and impetuous, and easily influenced,' she replied. 'That little tart seduced him behind my back. She thought she could get away with it, but she was a fool.'

'So she was someone else you had to get rid of,' Geraldine said.

'Me?' Jeannie looked genuinely surprised. 'I never killed anyone.'

'They're just fishing,' the lawyer said.

'I know what they're doing,' Jeannie agreed. She turned to Geraldine, a sly glint in her eyes. 'You can't prove anything against me.'

'You thought you were too clever to be caught, didn't you? And there's no question that you were clever. You were very clever. You planned everything carefully, covering your tracks very neatly. So, first your husband was killed, then your rival and now nothing stands in your way.' She paused but Jeannie didn't respond, so Geraldine changed tack. 'It wasn't all plain sailing though, was it? You had to pay Peter Selby when he started blackmailing you.' That final accusation was conjecture, but Jeannie looked apprehensive.

'That was something you hadn't bargained on,' Ariadne chimed in, following up on Geraldine's guess. 'Fortunately you could access your husband's bank account, but you had to put an end to the payments before John found out. And you didn't want to lose too much of the money you had worked so hard to get your hands on. Peter's greed led to his death and you managed to avoid being caught. Until now.'

'You were clever, but not clever enough to avoid attracting suspicion,' Geraldine added.

Jeannie's flushed face had turned pale, but she vehemently denied any knowledge of money being paid out from John's account and insisted she had no access to it.

'In any case,' she asked, wide-eyed, 'if I was able to get to my husband's account – which I wasn't – why would I have been sending money to someone I didn't know and had never even met?' She tapped the side of her head with a resurgence of her former confidence. 'Really, Inspector, is that the best you can come up with?' She turned to her lawyer. 'How much longer do we have to sit here and listen to this drivel?'

Geraldine went on in a low voice. 'We know it was you, Jeannie. We may only suspect you killed Peter, but we know you killed John and Suzie, so you might as well tell us the truth, because your killing spree is over and so is any relationship you thought you had with Daniel. He doesn't want to have anything to do with you. It's time you surrendered to the inevitable and confessed.'

'I have nothing to confess but my love,' Jeannie declaimed, her eyes shining. 'Nothing can come between me and Daniel. I know you're lying because he would never abandon me.'

'He already left you for a younger woman,' Geraldine pointed out. 'There's no way he's standing by you. On the contrary, you disgust him.'

'Lies, lies, all lies,' Jeannie replied, shaking her head. 'Why are we listening to these filthy lies?' she asked the lawyer before she turned back to Geraldine. 'Don't think I can't see what you're doing. You want to lock me up so you can have Daniel to yourself. But he'll never leave me, never. Not now I've proved my love for him.'

'You can't deny that you attacked a police officer,' Ariadne began, but at that point the lawyer stepped in.

'My client was under the perfectly understandable impression that the inspector was an intruder. My client had no intention of causing her harm but when the inspector attempted to restrain her, my client used reasonable force to defend herself.'

At this point, the lawyer finally got his way and the interview was terminated.

Geraldine and Ariadne left the room feeling frustrated and went to the canteen for a break. After all their efforts, they still had no definite evidence linking Jeannie to the crime scenes and she seemed unlikely to crumble.

'All we've managed to establish is that she's completely round the bend,' Ariadne asserted as they reached their seats.

'Or she knows she's caught and she's trying to convince us she's unhinged.'

They discussed the possibilities, but the one conclusion they agreed on was that Jeannie was guilty and somehow they had to press her to tell them what she had done. Without proof, their case remained precarious, but Geraldine had another approach to try. She outlined her plan to Ariadne who nodded in approval. If this failed, they could only wait and hope that some forensic evidence would emerge to substantiate their suspicions.

'We know you killed John,' Geraldine repeated when they were all seated in an interview room once more, this time with the tape running. 'We have a witness who told us you killed your husband.'

'What are you talking about?' Jeannie waved a hand in the air. 'This is more fantasising. How can you have a witness when there was no one else there?'

'How do you know there was no one else there when he was killed?' Ariadne asked.

But Jeannie was sharp. 'Because it's obvious. If anyone had seen what happened, they would have come forward by now. And if you had a witness, you wouldn't be trying to catch me out like this, pretending you want to help me. So I don't believe for one minute that you have a witness. I'm not an idiot. I know you're lying.'

'Not exactly,' Geraldine replied. 'Daniel told us you confessed to him that you killed your husband. He said you told him you thought he'd be pleased, but he wasn't. He was horrified by what you did.'

'That's another lie!' Jeannie retorted, but her voice rose in agitation. 'Daniel loves me. He wouldn't betray me like that. You can't be expected to understand, but Daniel knows I did it for him. For us.'

'What did you do? Help me to understand. Because if Daniel was lying to us, then how do you know he wasn't lying to you when he said he loved you?'

Jeannie trembled. 'He loves me. He would never lie about that. I know he loves me.'

'I still don't understand. Daniel told us you killed John. He must have really been keen to get rid of you if he deliberately made that up, knowing you would be arrested and charged with murder. Was Daniel really that desperate to get rid of you, enough to want to see you locked up for a crime you hadn't committed?'

'No, no, he doesn't want to be rid of me. He never said anything like that about me. I don't believe it. This is another lie.'

'Well, he said it in the presence of two police officers. We have it on tape. And we have a signed statement from him, all confirming that you told him you killed John.'

Jeannie shook her head furiously.

'He wasn't lying when he told us you killed your husband, was he?' Geraldine pressed on.

Jeannie remained silent, frowning. Geraldine waited without saying another word. The fat lawyer stirred in his seat.

'He wasn't lying,' Jeannie finally mumbled. 'He wouldn't make up something like that, not about me. He couldn't. He loves me. He wouldn't lie.'

'So he was telling the truth when he said you told him you killed John?'

Jeannie suddenly let out a noisy breath, as though she wanted to expel all the air from her lungs, and leaned forward on her elbows.

'I did it for him,' she burst out. 'Everything was for him.'

'You killed John so you could be with Daniel. When Daniel rejected you for someone else, you killed her too, thinking that Daniel would return to you.'

'He didn't need persuading,' Jeannie protested. 'He wanted to be with me, but that tramp had bamboozled him and he wasn't thinking clearly. As soon as I had him back with me, he would have realised how stupid he had been to think anyone else could take my place in his heart.' She slapped her hand dramatically on her chest as she spoke.

'And Peter?' Geraldine urged her gently. 'You killed him too, didn't you?'

'Oh, he was asking for it,' Jeannie said irritably. 'He was a snake, just out for making as much money as he could. He had no heart. A man like that could never understand the bond between Daniel and me. He threatened to tell everyone about us, so I silenced him the only way I could.' She gazed around defiantly. 'What else could I do? He left me no choice.'

'I'd like to have a word with my client,' the lawyer said wearily. 'She is clearly not in her right mind and has committed a crime of passion—'

'Your client has killed three people. Were these murders all crimes of passion?' Geraldine asked him.

'She is not in her right mind,' the lawyer repeated.

'He still loves me, you'll see, he loves me,' Jeannie called out as she was led away. 'You told me you understood but you're just like the rest of them.'

55

WHEN CHRISTINE WAS PHYSICALLY able to take care of herself, with outpatient support to dress her wound, she was discharged from hospital. She was still exhausted and wasn't sure that she was mentally ready to face her daughter. Daisy had visited her in hospital. Although she hadn't appeared sullen, she had been taciturn and Christine had the impression she was being secretive. She had given monosyllabic responses to Christine's questions.

'How are you?' Christine had asked, even though she herself was the patient being treated in hospital.

'Fine,' Daisy had replied, without meeting her mother's eye.

'How's school?'

'Fine.'

When Christine had enquired whether social services were taking good care of her, Daisy had responded with a noncommittal grunt.

'Tell me if you're not happy about the arrangements they've made for you,' Christine had urged her, to which Daisy had muttered that everything was fine. She had never stayed long at the hospital, as though Christine's questions made her uncomfortable.

Christine could only hope that her daughter hadn't become more disturbed than ever by everything that had happened since her father had disappeared. She wondered whether Daisy appreciated how close she had come to being orphaned. Lying in her hospital bed, where time seemed to crawl by, she bitterly regretted her estrangement from her own mother. They had fallen out over something that, on reflection, now seemed trivial, although it had kept them apart for seven years.

Their conflict had arisen over the ownership of a diamond and pearl necklace belonging to Christine's grandmother. Both Christine and her mother remembered she had promised to leave it to them when she died. In the event, there had been no mention of the necklace in the will, with the result that both Christine and her mother had claimed it. The necklace had remained in the custodianship of her mother and Christine hadn't spoken to her since.

'Do you really want to turn your back on your own grandchild?' Christine had snapped at her mother the last time they had spoken.

'I can't believe you would use Daisy to try and pressurise me into giving you what you want,' her mother had replied. 'But my mother gave me that necklace. It's a family heirloom and it's always been passed down from mother to daughter, so it will come to you when I die and not before.'

Nervous about how Daisy would react to her homecoming, Christine clambered into the ambulance and was driven home. Increasingly anxious, she allowed a paramedic to help her to her own front door. She hated feeling so dependent on a stranger.

'I'll be all right now,' she assured them. 'You can go. There must be other people waiting for you.'

'We can't leave you until we've seen you safely inside.'

Christine nodded. 'My daughter will be home from school soon and she'll be keeping an eye on things until I'm a hundred per cent again.' She hoped Daisy wasn't going to make life more difficult for her than it already was.

A paramedic rang the bell.

'She won't be back yet,' Christine said, fumbling in her bag for her key. 'So there's no point in your—'

As she was speaking, the front door opened. To her astonishment she saw her mother smiling cautiously at her.

'Mum!' she blurted out. 'What on earth are you doing here?'

Her mother drew in a breath. She looked nervous. 'Social services contacted me. Daisy wanted me to come,' she added defensively. 'You were too out of it to make any decisions so Daisy and I agreed that I would come here and look after things until you were home. Although, if I'm honest, Daisy's the one who's been taking care of me.' She laughed awkwardly. 'She wanted to be here when you got home, but we weren't expecting you for another couple of hours. Now come on in and sit down. You shouldn't be standing out there.' She looked at the paramedic hovering on the doorstep. 'I'll take it from here. If you want me to stay, that is?' she added, turning back to Christine.

'Of course I want you to stay,' Christine replied without thinking.

'We'll be fine,' her mother said, grinning at the paramedic. 'Come on, Christine, let's get you comfortable with your feet up and I'll put the kettle on. We've got a lot to say to each other, but not right now.'

Her mother fussed around but Christine didn't mind. Her life had taken on an air of unreality and she half believed she must be dreaming. Not until they were both seated with cups of tea and biscuits, did her mother take a box out of her bag. Christine held her breath, thinking she recognised it.

'This is for you,' her mother said. 'Not because I think you have a claim to it – yet – but because I want you to have it.' She sighed. 'I've had a lot of time to think about things and I think grandma promised it to each of us separately. Poor grandma, she did get a bit confused towards the end. But it will be yours anyway when I'm gone, so what's the point in falling out over it? I wish I'd let you take it right away and I want you to have it now.'

'No,' Christine replied. 'I've had time to think about what happened as well – too much time – and it was your mother's. You should have it. No,' she added, when her mother thrust the box at her, 'I refuse to take it. Please, keep it. I'm sorry we ever fell out over it. And thank you for being here for Daisy and me.' She started to cry.

'Stop snivelling and drink your tea before it gets cold,' her mother said, not unkindly. 'Now, how are you feeling, really?'

Christine wiped her eyes and blew her nose before admitting that she was worried about Daisy. 'She's not been herself for a while.'

'Oh, I wouldn't worry about Daisy,' her mother replied breezily. 'If you ask me, she's sensible and well adjusted, and far more level-headed than you ever were at her age.'

Christine shook her head and murmured that her mother didn't know Daisy.

'Well, I've been living here with her for nearly a week and I've had a chance to spend some time with her, and she's – well, she's delightful. Really good company. I taught her how to darn the cuffs of her school cardy and she picked it up really quickly. I don't know how you could have sent her to school looking so scruffy.'

Christine was crying too much to reply but she nodded her head, overwhelmed by a grief she had been holding in for weeks. 'I miss him so much, Mum,' she wailed when she was able to speak. 'I don't know how I'm going to manage without him. I feel like I've been going to pieces.'

'You'll manage because you have to,' her mother replied firmly. 'Now pull yourself together, because Daisy will be home soon. Once you're ready, I suggest you go for bereavement counselling, both of you. It's not good to bottle feelings up.' Her mother sighed. 'I don't think I ever fully acknowledged my grief at losing your father. And then, when grandma died so soon after, I'm afraid I rather took my feelings out on you. We've wasted so much time and I blame myself for that. I wish I could have visited you and built a relationship with Daisy when she was younger. The time I spent with her over the past few days has been far more precious to me than any necklace could ever be.'

Christine sighed. 'Well, you've obviously got through to Daisy. I have to say, I've found her behaviour challenging, to put it mildly.'

'You've both been through a lot, with Peter,' her mother said gently. 'I can stay for a while, if that helps, just until you're feeling strong again.'

'If you're sure?'

'There's nothing I'd like better.'

'Thanks, Mum. I'd like that too. More than anything.'

They heard the front door slam and a moment later Daisy came in. She smiled at Christine.

'Hi,' she greeted her grandmother, before going over to Christine and giving her a kiss on the cheek. 'I'm glad you're home, Mum. I've missed you.'

Christine smiled with relief. No doubt she would argue with her daughter again, perhaps many times, but she knew their relationship was strong enough to survive any disagreements.

56

ONCE HER INITIAL RELIEF at having found the killer was over, Geraldine was disturbed by a familiar sense of dissatisfaction, accompanied by guilt at acknowledging that she was going to miss the excitement of working on a murder investigation. She tried to explain how she was feeling to Ian who, of all people, might be expected to empathise with deflation. She wasn't sure if he was being deliberately obtuse when he professed to have no idea what she was talking about.

'Aren't you pleased that you can spend more time with Tom?' he wanted to know. 'Surely being a mother is enough of a challenge, even for you.'

He probably wasn't deliberately accusing her of being a useless mother, but that was how it felt to her.

'It's not as though I'm never here,' she protested, her guilt switching to anger. 'I've never claimed to be a perfect mother but I do my best. I'd always put Tom first, but I do have a job to do.'

'Hey, hey, calm down,' Ian said, putting his arms around her. 'No one's criticising your parenting skills. I just thought you might be more pleased at having stopped that maniac from carrying on with her killing spree. She probably would have turned on the lover who rejected her next and, if not, then the life of any woman he had anything to do with would definitely have been in danger. You did a brilliant job, that's all I'm saying. You've taken a serial killer off the streets and you should be proud of your success. I'm proud of you.'

'That's not what you said,' Geraldine muttered, slightly mollified.

Ian was right, the case was over and she could relax and enjoy spending time with her family. The sun was shining and they agreed to take Tom to the park. Now he was able to walk, albeit unsteadily, he loved being outside. Apart from all the activity of the wind and birds and people walking by, grass was a safer surface for him to toddle around on than the pavement, where he could hurt himself if he fell. Besides all of that, in a couple of months it would turn wintry and they wanted to take advantage of the mild weather while they could. Ian carried the bag with all the baby paraphernalia and Geraldine took Tom down to the car in his stroller. Eventually they reached the park and Tom squealed with delight when Geraldine placed him gently upright on the ground where he promptly sat down and began tearing up tiny handfuls of grass. For a few moments, he watched them float down to the ground when he released them, before he turned a puzzled face to the blades which remained stuck to his hands. Geraldine and Ian laughed.

'We brought you here so you can run around,' Geraldine said, smiling at her little son.

She jumped up as he clambered to his feet and began waddling towards a small dog that was frolicking nearby. She swept Tom up in her arms and covered his upturned face with noisy kisses as Ian joined them with the stroller.

'Shall we go and see the dog?' Geraldine asked Tom. 'Do you want to see the dog?'

'Gog gog,' Tom replied eagerly.

Geraldine laughed. 'You know,' she said to Ian, 'I could get used to this.'

Yet as she turned to gaze around at people wandering around on the grass, she couldn't help noticing a young woman trailing behind a man, her head lowered submissively; a teenager berating another teenager who was listening in silence, his fists clenched; and an elderly man leaning on the arm of a woman whose eyes narrowed whenever she glanced at her companion shuffling at her side. Looking down at Tom, nestling in her arms, she felt a rush of emotion. Observing the people around them, her love for her son was tinged with anxiety.

'We have to teach him to be cautious about trusting people,' she murmured.

Ian looked at her, catching her serious tone. 'He may have to work that one out for himself,' he said.

She nodded and leaned down to kiss the top of Tom's head. 'But not yet.'

Acknowledgments

I am indebted to Jamie Hodder-Williams and Laura Fletcher for their continuing faith in Geraldine Steel. It is a privilege to work with them and the expert team at No Exit Press, Bedford Square Publishers. My thanks go to Anastasia Boama-Aboagye and Claudia Bullmore for their enthusiastic support with marketing and publicity, Polly Halsey for her invaluable help in production, Jem Butcher for his brilliant covers, Jayne Lewis for her highly skilled copy editing and Maureen Cox for her eagle-eyed proofreading.

My editor, Keshini Naidoo, has been with me from the beginning of the series and I am grateful for her unerring judgement, and her tact in pointing out my oversights.

My thanks go to all the bloggers and interviewers who have supported Geraldine Steel, and to everyone who has been kind enough to review my books. Your support is sincerely appreciated.

I am grateful to my many readers around the world and hope you continue to enjoy reading about Geraldine's investigations.

My final word of thanks goes to Michael, who is always with me.

A LETTER FROM LEIGH

Dear Reader,

I hope you enjoyed reading this book in my Geraldine Steel series. Readers are the key to the writing process, so I'm thrilled that you've joined me on my writing journey.

You might not want to meet some of my characters on a dark night – I know I wouldn't! – but hopefully you want to read about Geraldine's other investigations. Her work is always her priority because she cares deeply about justice, but she also has her own life. Many readers care about what happens to her. I hope you join them, and become a fan of Geraldine Steel, and her colleague Ian Peterson.

If you follow me on Facebook or Twitter, you'll know that I love to hear from readers. I always respond to comments from fans, and hope you will follow me on **@LeighRussell** and **fb.me/leigh.russell.50** or drop me an email via my website **leighrussell.co.uk**.

That way you can be sure to get news of the latest offers on my books. You might also like to sign up for my newsletter on **leighrussell.co.uk/news** to make sure you're one of the first to know when a new book is coming out. We'll be running competitions, and I'll also notify you of any events where I'll be appearing.

Finally, if you enjoyed this story, I'd be really grateful if you would post a brief review on Amazon or Goodreads. A few sentences to say you enjoyed the book would be wonderful. And of course it would be brilliant if you would consider recommending my books to anyone who is a fan of crime fiction.

I hope to meet you at a literary festival or a book signing soon!

Thank you again for choosing to read my book.

With very best wishes,

Leigh Russell

noexit.co.uk/leighrussell

About the Author

Leigh Russell is the author of the internationally bestselling Geraldine Steel series, which has sold over a million copies worldwide. Her books have been #1 on Amazon Kindle and iTunes with *Stop Dead* and *Murder Ring* selected as finalists for The People's Book Prize.

www.leighrussell.co.uk

@LeighRussell

NO EXIT PRESS
More than just the usual suspects

CWA DAGGER AWARDED BEST CRIME & MYSTERY PUBLISHER

'A very smart, independent publisher delivering the finest literary crime fiction' **Big Issue**

MEET NO EXIT PRESS, an award-winning crime imprint bringing you the best in crime and suspense fiction. From classic detective novels, to page-turning spy thrillers and literary writing that grabs the attention. Our books are carefully crafted by some of the world's finest writers and delivered to you by a small, but passionate, team.

In over 30 years of business, we have published award-winning fiction and non-fiction including the work of a Pulitzer Prize winner, the British Crime Book of the Year, numerous CWA Dagger Awards, a British million-copy bestselling author, the winner of the Canadian Governor General's Award for Fiction and the Scotiabank Giller Prize, to name but a few. We are the home of many crime and noir legends from the USA whose work includes iconic film adaptations and TV sensations. We pride ourselves in uncovering the most exciting new or undiscovered talents. New and not so new – you know who you are!

We are a proactive team committed to delivering the very best, both for our authors and our readers.

Want to join the conversation and find out more about what we do?

Catch us on social media or sign up to our newsletter for all the latest news from No Exit Press.

f fb.me/noexitpress 𝕏 @noexitpress

noexit.co.uk